Deadly Pursuit

C. M. Sutter

AUTHOR'S NOTE

This book is a work of fiction by C. M. Sutter. Names, characters, places, and incidents are products of the author's imagination or are used solely for entertainment. Any resemblance to actual events or persons, living or dead, is entirely coincidental.

ABOUT THE AUTHOR

C. M. Sutter is a crime fiction writer who resides in Florida, although she is originally from California.

She is a member of numerous writers' organizations, including Fiction for All, Fiction Factor, and Writers etc.

In addition to writing, she enjoys spending time with her friends and family. She is an art enthusiast and loves to create gourd birdhouses, pebble art, and handmade soaps. Hiking, bicycling, fishing, and traveling are a few of her favorite pastimes.

C.M. Sutter

http://cmsutter.com/

Contact C. M. Sutter - http://cmsutter.com/contact/

Deadly Pursuit: A Detective Jesse McCord Police Thriller, Book 3

A sadistic scene unlike any that Homicide Detective Jesse McCord has ever witnessed unfolds on a park bench in front of him. Jesse knows this isn't just another Chicago murder.

Rage-filled killers are sending a disturbing message, and when a second and third body are discovered with the same vicious signature, police realize the victims aren't random. Instead, each man is carefully chosen for a reason known only to the murderers. It doesn't take long for the killers to raise the ante and add a cop to their list—and one in particular is on their radar. Once their plan is in motion, Jesse McCord is chosen, and they intend for him to be the next person to die.

See all of C. M. Sutter's books at:
http://cmsutter.com/available-books/

Find C. M. Sutter on Facebook at:
https://www.facebook.com/cmsutterauthor/

Don't want to miss C. M. Sutter's next release?
Sign up for the VIP e-mail list at:
http://cmsutter.com/newsletter/

Chapter 1

The wheels protested as Gail turned another corner. The wagon carrying the dead body was heavy—much heavier than she'd expected. They'd already walked a good distance, zigzagging through dark alleys in an effort to err on the side of caution. She was exhausted, but they were almost at their destination and had only one more block to go. They needed to be long gone before the sun broke the horizon and people began their morning routines.

"Come on, Mom, you're moving way too slow!" Gail looked over her shoulder, snarled out a whisper, and grumbled. "This whole shock-value idea was yours, and I really don't want to live out the rest of my life in a six-by-eight-foot prison cell. Now step up your pace! I have to be at work in three hours."

Janet Fremont followed a good fifteen feet behind her daughter and cursed. "I'm twenty years older than you, damn it. Have a little sympathy or maybe just slow down. Either way, stop yelling at me."

Gail pulled off the sidewalk and made sure she and the wagon were tucked under the cover of darkness and the convenient low-hanging branches of a willow tree.

Janet's sneakers squeaked on the concrete until she stopped inches from her daughter's side and sucked in a few exhausted breaths.

"Mom, seriously? You need to keep up since it'll take both of us to put Mr. Smith on the bench. I can't do this alone."

Janet eyed the wagon with a huff as she placed the man's dangling and already discolored arm back under the blanket. "Okay, okay, I'll try to keep up. I guess somebody has to make sure he doesn't fall out of that damn wagon before we get to the park."

Chapter 2

Our commander stormed into the bull pen and air jabbed his finger at each of us. "You four need to get out to Bixler Park right away. Jesse, take the lead and report back to me in an hour. I have a meeting with the chief that I can't get out of."

I pushed back my chair, happy to get away from the mounting paperwork on my desk that morning and be outside working a case instead. "What's going on?" I buckled my shoulder holster, threw on my sport jacket, then grabbed my cell phone and tucked it in my pocket. I looked at Mills, Johnson, and Potter, and they mirrored my movements.

"Nothing good, that's for damn sure. A mother took her toddler to the park a half hour ago with intentions of spending time at the playground but found a dead man sitting on a bench instead."

I shrugged. "So why us? Maybe the guy had a heart attack."

"Not likely. The man's fingers were removed and his teeth were crushed according to the patrol units that arrived fifteen minutes ago."

Henry rubbed his brow. "Shit. Isn't that park-and-play lot only a few miles from here?"

I crossed the bull pen to the door. "Yep, and I know the way. Let's go."

Lutz yelled out as we took to the stairs. "Don and the forensic boys are heading there in a few minutes, and don't forget to call me with updates."

We arrived at the park five minutes later, Frank and I in one cruiser, and Henry and Shawn in the other. The entrances to the park were already blocked with yellow tape, and officers patrolled the sidewalk to keep looky-loos at bay. After Frank snugged the cruiser against the curb, I grabbed two pairs of gloves and jammed them in my pocket as I pushed open the passenger door. To our right, Tillson and Jefferson were talking to the woman who I assumed made the 911 call. She appeared distraught as she bounced a little girl in her arms. Frank and I headed their way while Shawn and Henry took the opposite side of the park and spoke to the officers at that entrance. As we walked, I glimpsed a figure on a nearby bench, covered with a standard-issue blanket kept in the trunks of most of our patrol cars. That had to be our vic. I jerked my chin in his direction, and Frank nodded.

I stuck out my hand as we approached Tillson and Jefferson. "What have we got, guys?"

Tillson took the lead. "This is Caroline Davis, the woman who discovered the body."

"Ma'am." I pushed aside my jacket and exposed the badge attached to my waistband. Mills did the same. "We're Detectives McCord and Mills. Can you walk us through the course of events from this morning?"

She looked at her squirming toddler. "Lilly is getting restless."

"Sorry, but it's necessary, Mrs. Davis. Would you prefer talking over at the swing set? Maybe Lilly will be happier there."

"Okay, let's try that." A look of relief spread across her face as she placed the child in the stroller and headed toward the playground. "Thanks for understanding."

I asked for a second to speak with the officers. "You guys got a statement already? Her full name, address, phone number?"

Tillson patted the notepad that peeked out from the top of his chest pocket. "We did, but she was pretty rattled."

Frank spoke up. "And rightfully so." He looked down the street. "Don and Forensics should be rolling up any minute, so keep your eyes peeled for them." He pointed toward Henry and Shawn. "If you guys need anything before we get back, talk to Johnson and Potter. We won't be long."

We headed over to the playground, where Mrs. Davis had already placed Lilly in a child-secured swing. She gently pushed her back and forth, and the toddler seemed content. The interview could go forward.

I led with the questions, and Frank took notes. "I realize these questions will seem repetitive to you, but as the detectives assigned to this case, we need more details than what the officers asked. Please bear with us."

"Okay." She took her eyes off Lilly for a second while she addressed me. "Go ahead."

"What time did you arrive at the park, and from which direction did you come?"

She pointed at the entrance where Henry and Shawn

stood with the officers. "I live over there."

"And the time?"

"I always leave my house at eight o'clock. By that time, my husband has left for work, Lilly has been fed, and then we come to the playground for an hour before I put her down for a morning nap."

"Was anyone else here when you arrived?"

She furrowed her brows. "Other than the dead man, I didn't see anyone in the immediate area, but a guy did jog by on the sidewalk. It seems that most moms show up around eight thirty." She shrugged. "Maybe it's because my house is only a block and a half away. That was one of the reasons we bought in this neighborhood—plenty of parks."

"Understood." I glanced at the bench, where the body still sat covered. "What path did you walk once you arrived?"

"Well, I came in over there and usually walk directly to the playground. I noticed my sneaker was untied, so I pushed the stroller toward that bench." She grimaced, and her eyes welled up with tears. "I mean, I saw an older gentleman sitting there, but I didn't feel threatened or anything. As I got closer, I saw something was terribly wrong." She coughed, and her voice caught in her throat, then she let out a grief-stricken sob. It was one I recognized from years of interviewing witnesses of horrific crimes, and it often took an hour or longer before the gravity of what they had seen actually hit them.

"Take your time, Mrs. Davis."

She cleared her throat and shook her head as if trying to erase the image. "His hands were folded in his lap, but a blood pool was beneath him. I could see where the blood had stained his pants. I didn't know if I should approach him or scream for help, but in that moment, I wasn't sure he was dead until I moved closer. That's when I noticed his mouth was bloody and his skin was a whitish gray. I pushed the stroller out to the sidewalk and called 911. I'll admit, I was nearly hysterical. It was far from what I imagined a man asleep or dead from natural causes would look like on a park bench."

"And then what did you do after calling 911?"

"I remained on the phone with the operator and stayed where I was until the officers arrived."

"Did anybody come into the park while you waited, or did you see anyone watching from a distance?"

"I don't know. I was terrified, especially for Lilly. I just wanted to go home."

I pulled a tissue from the supply I always kept in my pocket.

She reached out and took it. "Thank you, Detective McCord." She looked over at her daughter's bobbing head. "Can we leave now? Lilly is falling asleep."

I handed her my card. "Yes, go ahead, and please call if you think of anything else. I'll have an officer escort you home if you like."

The right side of her mouth lifted with signs of a slight smile. "Thank you. I'd really appreciate that."

"Not a problem." I called out to Tillson, who jogged over.

"What can I help you with, Detective McCord?"

"Escort Mrs. Davis and her daughter home. It's less than two blocks away."

"Sure thing. Are you ready, ma'am?"

"Yes." With Lilly in the stroller, they exited the park and turned left.

I let out a long sigh. "That couldn't have been easy to see." I jerked my chin toward the bench, where Jefferson had taken over the watch, then I turned to Frank. "Okay, partner, let's take a look."

Chapter 3

Frank and I stood to each side of the covered man, making sure our feet weren't near the blood that had dripped between the slats and pooled beneath him. I tipped my head at Jefferson.

"Go ahead and remove the blanket."

With the blanket taken away, Frank and I moved in closer to inspect the deceased man. His skin was a sickly gray color, and he had stiffened in place, as if he were sitting there on his own accord. Leaning forward, I looked at his mouth, which was halfway open. Blood, now dried, had covered his lips and followed a path down to his chin. I pulled my pen light from my pocket and shined it into his mouth. Ragged remnants of what once were teeth—deliberately bashed to make checking dental records impossible—were all that remained.

"Damn." I slipped on some gloves and handed Frank a pair to put on. I was about to look closer at what remained of the man's hands when Don, Mike, and Danny approached us.

"Better to leave this to them." I backed away as we briefly explained to Don Lawry, our medical examiner, what Mrs.

Davis had discovered an hour earlier.

Don tipped his head toward Mike. "Go ahead and get some shots before I start my examination. I'll be moving in my rolling stool and don't want it to be in your way."

"Yep, got it."

Mike snapped a dozen photographs of the deceased. On his hands and knees, he took more pictures of the underside of the bench and also the blood pool. He zoomed in on the man's mouth and clicked off three more shots. Careful not to disturb the way the man's hands were folded, he caught images of them—minus the tips after the last knuckle of each finger. "Go ahead, Don. We'll take the bench back to the lab with us after everything else is complete."

Danny added that they would scour the bushes for anything that could be considered evidence. Frank and I took spots against a large oak tree as Don moved in to do his field exam. I called out to Henry and Shawn. "See all those older apartments?" I pointed at every street that had buildings facing the park. "Have Patrol start the knock and talks at those apartments. Somebody may have seen something suspicious out their window. We'll pitch in when we're done here and make sure the officers keep track of everyone they talk to. I don't want to re-interview people they've already spoken with."

"Got it." Henry and Shawn gathered every available officer except the ones at the entrances. They continued their foot patrol while keeping people away.

I looked at Don. "Whatcha think?"

"He's definitely in rigor. Can't straighten out his legs, and

I'm not going to try forcing them. No visible signs of what caused his death, though. Snipped fingertips and broken teeth, although extremely painful, wouldn't kill him. There's more here than meets the eye, meaning a tox screen is in order."

"How long do you think he's been out here?" Frank asked.

"Two to three hours, I'd say. Probably before daybreak and before the rigor began stiffening his joints. He was definitely killed somewhere else and then positioned this way just before rigor kicked in. A deliberate act so his body would stiffen in that upright position as if he was an ordinary man sitting on a park bench."

"Until somebody took a closer look at him," I said.

"That's right, until then." Don looked over his shoulder at his assistant, Mark Nells. "Go ahead and bring the gurney in."

"Right away."

Don stood and folded the stool. "If there's nothing more you need from me, I'd just as soon get the body back to my office and take care of that tox screen."

I nodded and looked at how the bench was mounted to the sidewalk. We would probably need somebody from the maintenance department of the county park system to come out and remove the bolts since we didn't carry maintenance tools with us to crime scenes. I made the call and was told that someone should arrive within a few hours.

"That gives us time to scour the park and look around for security cameras," Henry said.

"Sure, go ahead and get started on that. Frank and I will

catch up as soon as Don leaves with the body, and I still have to update Lutz." I stepped away and found a different bench to sit on while I called our commander.

"What have you got, McCord?"

"A dead man on a park bench just like it was called in, Bob. He looked to be somewhere in his early sixties, dressed in business casual attire, and until Don tells us what the tox screen shows, there was no identifiable cause of death noticed. Because the man was fully dressed, we didn't see any tattoos, scars, or birthmarks. We'll know more after Don gets the deceased on the table."

"So his teeth were damaged and his fingertips were cut off. Is that correct?"

I rubbed my forehead as the image popped into my head. "Yeah, his teeth looked like somebody took a hammer to them, and his fingers? Each one was cut off at the last knuckle."

"Jesus." Silence filled the line for a few seconds. That was Lutz's way of telling me his wheels were turning. "I'm wondering why someone would go to the lengths of essentially removing somebody's fingerprints and dental records if it was a random killing. Why would they care if the person was identified unless there was something that could lead back to the killer?"

"And that's another avenue to investigate, Boss. Henry and Potter have started looking for surveillance cameras, and we have a handful of officers canvassing the neighborhood, primarily at the apartment buildings whose windows face the park. You never know."

"Right. Anything else?"

"Yeah, Danny and Mike are bringing the park bench back to the lab with them as soon as a county worker shows up to detach it from the sidewalk."

"Okay, and you and Frank are pitching in with the interviews?"

"Yep, that's the plan." I was about to hang up when Lutz began talking again.

"One last thing."

"Shoot."

"Was there anything in his pockets? Anything at all?"

"Nope. Not even a stick of gum."

Chapter 4

"What are you doing, honey?" Janet turned off the television that was usually playing just to provide background noise. Neither she nor Gail watched TV on a regular basis since their recent tasks occupied a good portion of their free time and were far more satisfying.

The chair screeched against the tile as Janet pulled it out and took a seat at the table. She cozied up to her daughter's left shoulder and stared at the laptop.

Janet kept her voice just above a whisper—the walls were thin in their temporary apartment space. "Looking for a different park?"

Gail nodded with a look of determination. "There are hundreds in the Chicagoland area. That's for sure. Three months here and then I'll transfer somewhere south during the wintertime. We won't miss a beat."

"Any park in particular come to mind for Mr. Hennessey?" She glanced over her shoulder at the unconscious man tied to the iron radiator.

Gail pointed at Washington Park. "It's close by, it's large, has a lot of entry points, and plenty of tree cover. It'll do just fine, but you have to keep up, Mom."

Janet rubbed her hands together then lit a cigarette. "I will. I promise. When are we going to make the drop?"

"I only work a half shift today, so late tonight would be the smartest. Law enforcement will still be preoccupied with the Bixler Park situation. Don't forget, to be the most effective, we have to hit quickly, and then when the cops think they have it figured out and start surveilling all the parks in their district, we'll go to parks in a different area."

"Maybe we should change it up altogether and dump the men in a vacant building or something of that nature."

"Maybe, but let's see how this goes before rushing to change things. Remember, this isn't our first rodeo." Gail tucked her mother's stray hairs behind her ear and noticed a Band-Aid around Janet's finger. "What happened there?"

Janet brushed invisible crumbs off the tablecloth as she dismissed the question. "It's nothing. Just a small cut, and I needed to stop the bleeding. You know my blood is thin." She rose from her chair and walked to the sink, where the pruning shears lay. "Got to give these a good scrubbing. Can't mix blood from man to man."

After following Janet to the sink, Gail plugged the drain and filled the bowl with hot soapy water. "We'll let that soak for a bit, but your comment about changing things has made me think about our process."

With the teapot in hand, Janet returned to the table and filled both cups. "What do you have in mind?"

Chapter 5

It was closing in on noon, and other than several apartment tenants telling us they'd seen dog walkers and joggers before daybreak that morning, nobody had noticed suspicious activity in the park. I assumed that even though the park was a relatively small area, the killer had chosen it—and the early hour—because the tree cover would help hide the activities within its borders.

I stood on the path in the most open area with nothing but grass surrounding me. Making a slow three-hundred-sixty-degree turn, I looked for lights. A street lamp at the end of the cul-de-sac was all I saw other than wall-mounted lights on the neighboring apartment buildings. At best, they might illuminate as far as the sidewalk along the park, but the park itself would likely be pitch-black until the sun broke the horizon. I was sure our killer was also aware of that.

"What are you thinking?" Frank caught up to me and stood at my side.

"Just how dark the park must be before the sun comes up." I pointed at the streetlamp to my right. "That's the closest street light, and it's on the other side of the park from where our vic was found."

Frank frowned as if he were giving that some thought.

I checked his expression. "What?"

"Just wondering what time the sun actually rises in September. Enough to see without a flashlight, I mean."

I huffed. "I've already checked the charts. The sun rises at six fifteen this time of year, but unless we're out here and actually in the park ourselves, we won't know what people can or can't see from their windows."

"And that isn't taking the trees into account either."

"Right. We've got nothing more than dog walkers and joggers, and they'd be on the sidewalk, anyway, where there's ambient light." I jerked my head toward the group of officers who had just come out of the twelve-story apartment building that bordered East Fifty-Sixth Street and the park. The building's south-facing windows on the higher floors would have an unobstructed view of the park and playground. "Let's find out if they had any luck."

We followed the path that led to the building's entrance on East Fifty-Sixth Street and met up with officers heading our way.

Frank called out to them. "Anything that can help us?"

Tillson shook his head. "Same old story. Until the sun comes up, this park is pitch-black. Nobody saw anything, and the people who are actually up before daylight were likely getting ready for work, not staring out the windows into blackness."

I tipped my chin toward the patrol cars lined up along the curb. "Good point. Okay, head back to the precinct. The park itself has been thoroughly searched? Especially on the southwest side near the benches and playground?"

The response was a unanimous yes. Frank and I returned to the scene, where Mike and Danny had just loaded up the bench in the back of their van.

Henry called me over. "Since you're the lead detective here, I wanted you to know that the county worker needs a signature that the bench will be returned to the park once Mike and Danny are done with it."

"Yep, okay." I greeted the man in the orange vest and signed the form he passed to me on a clipboard. "Thanks for your help. The Chicago PD appreciates it."

We walked to the forensic van just as Mike slammed the rear doors closed. "Nothing suspicious in the immediate vicinity?"

Mike wiped his forehead with his sleeve and sighed. "Warmer than usual today, and no, we didn't find anything that didn't belong on the ground in a park. The bench will get a thorough inspection, though. There could be threads that caught on the slats, perspiration DNA, and so on, but of course, that evidence doesn't tell us who the perp is. Those clues, if found, could belong to anyone."

I nodded with the knowledge that anything found on the bench would be a long shot in connecting it to a suspect. What we needed was a witness or camera surveillance that showed movement in the area—which we didn't have. I looked from face to face. "I guess we're done in the park for now." I cocked my head toward the entrances. "Jefferson, go ahead and pull the tape down then tell those officers they don't have to patrol the sidewalk anymore." I watched as Jefferson trotted away.

"Ready?" Frank shook a cigarette out of his pack as we walked to the cruisers that had been sitting at the curb for hours.

Henry turned and grinned at me before climbing into their car. "Glad I'm riding with Shawn."

Frank flipped Henry the middle finger and got comfortable outside the driver's-side door. He slipped on his sunglasses and pulled the car keys from his pocket. I glanced at my watch with impatience.

"Yeah, yeah, give me another minute. I'm almost done."

My phone rang as I paced. I fished it out of my pocket, and Lutz was calling. I swiped the green arrow and asked, "What's up?"

"I want you four to stop in my office when you get back. How much longer at the scene?"

"We're done and should be back in ten minutes or so."

"Good enough."

Clicking off the call, I walked up to Henry and Shawn's cruiser. "Lutz wants us in his office as soon as we get back."

"That's if Frank doesn't light up another cigarette," Henry said.

I gave the doorframe a slap. "I'll work on him." I returned to our cruiser. "Let's go. Right now. Lutz wants to talk to us."

Frank flicked the butt then climbed in behind the wheel. He pulled out after Shawn. "What does Lutz want?"

"He didn't say, but we ought to know in a few minutes."

It was twelve thirty by the time the cruisers were parked and we entered the back door of our building. That entrance was the fastest route to the Violent Crimes division, and we took the stairs with Henry in the lead. He palmed the reader then pulled open the door, allowing us to pass through. Lutz's office was three doors beyond the bull pen on the left side of the hallway. Looking ahead, I saw his door was halfway open. Henry gave it a knock out of courtesy to our commander, and Lutz called us in.

"Have a seat, guys."

That meant two of us would sit and two would stand. I remained on my feet, and Henry did as well. Shawn and Frank took the guest chairs.

"What's on your mind, Bob?" I asked.

Lutz rocked back in his chair and squeezed the sides of his head. "I've been doing some investigating, which led me to reach out to the police departments in Charlotte, North Carolina, and Sacramento, California."

I frowned with no idea of where the conversation was going. "About what?"

"We don't know the manner of death in the man discovered. Yet. Don will have a good idea once the tox report comes back, and he said he'd put a rush on it. There are two things we are certain of, though, and that's the telltale signs left behind."

"The bashed-in teeth and the snipped fingertips," Frank said.

"Exactly. Why the killer wouldn't want the victim's identity known raises a few questions."

"Such as?" Shawn asked.

"Could learning the victim's identity lead us back to the killer, as in someone he knew? Could the killer have been a scorned lover? Or could the killer be targeting a group of like-minded people, and he began the killing process somewhere else?"

"You mean a group of people that the killer hates because of their race or their sexual orientation?"

"Possibly, but at this point, it's only speculation." Lutz blew out a hard sigh. "Like I said, I researched the national database for murder victims that had either or both features—the removal of fingertips and bashed-in teeth."

"And you got those two hits—in North Carolina and California?" I asked.

Lutz locked eyes with me. "That's correct, and both happened within the last year. Unfortunately, the killer or killers were never apprehended, so they could be traveling from city to city and state to state."

"Shit. How about leads, eyewitnesses, or camera footage?" I asked.

Frank piped in. "Were the other victims men, and were they identified?"

Lutz raised his hands for us to take a breath. "All good questions, and I'm tasking the four of you to work this case exclusively. I've requested the police folders from Sacramento and Charlotte."

I crossed my arms over my chest. "That's a good start. Maybe we'll find a clue that connects today's murder to those two cases."

"Except."

My eyes narrowed as I raised a brow at Lutz. "Except what?"

"Except it was actually three murders in California and two in North Carolina."

"So the man from this morning was vic number six?"

"If the cases are connected, yes. The autopsy and crime lab reports are being forwarded to us too. Everything has to be compared to the information we have once Don and Forensics have completed their reports."

"Humph."

Everyone looked at me and waited.

"Go on with your thought, partner," Frank said.

"Well, if it's only the four of us working this case, then who will be working the scenes?"

Shawn frowned. "Sounds like you're expecting more murders."

I gave him a head tip. "If the cases are connected, then the signs point to more than one murder in each city."

Lutz pushed back his chair and stood. "I need coffee." He jerked his chin toward the door. "Go back to the bull pen, organize how you'll divide up the investigation, and I'll have to give your question some thought, Jesse."

I had plenty of questions as I plopped down at my desk minutes later. I was going to be a desk jockey for the foreseeable future instead of out on the streets where I belonged, solving crimes. I tapped the end of my pen against the blank sheet of paper in front of me. First and foremost, we needed to ID our vic. He was an older man and dressed nicely. What did he do to piss off somebody, what was his name, and why hadn't anyone reported him missing? We needed to get his face on the air as soon as possible.

Henry rapped his knuckles on my desk. "Should we head to the back table and divide up the tasks? We'll be closer to the coffee station too."

"I suppose." I whistled and caught Frank and Shawn's attention. They grabbed their supplies and joined us near the back wall. Loaded up with full cups and with a new pot of coffee brewing, we began bullet pointing what we knew up to that point—which was very little.

Chapter 6

Bob joined us ten minutes later. "I've been thinking." He pulled out a chair, sat down, then blew over his coffee. "Jesse, you're my senior detective and second in charge. You need to be on the streets."

I quietly breathed in relief. I was sure Frank would be discharged from the time-consuming task of digging through paperwork and looking for a common thread that would tie our new case to the old ones from other states.

"Frank, since you and Jesse are partners, you'll be on the streets too."

"Thanks, Boss."

Lutz turned to Henry. "Kip and Tony will join you and Shawn on the paperwork end of the investigation. You need to research where the man's clothing came from and go through the missing persons files to see who has recently been added. The man in the park could have come from a nearby town or even a different state. Maybe that's why nobody has called our precinct and reported him missing."

Henry took notes while Lutz talked. "We need to get his face on the air, sir."

"And we will as soon as Don gets the man's information to us. We need a picture that's mild enough to air on TV, so Don will have to clean up his face first. We also need an age range, his height and weight, eye and hair color, that sort of thing." Lutz yelled across the bull pen. "Kip and Tony, come over here."

Both detectives rose and joined us in the back. "What can we do for you, Boss?"

"You're going to take part in this investigation. You two, Henry, and Shawn, will work solely on following the killer's trail on paper with whatever we learn from California and North Carolina. We have to know if there's a connection. We should be getting the police reports within the hour. Put your heads together. Jesse and Frank will work the streets."

"Didn't we finish at the scene earlier?" Kip asked.

"Yep, but there's a good chance that old guy won't be the only victim."

I remembered a question Lutz hadn't answered when we were in his office earlier. "About the other vics. Were they identified?"

Lutz fell silent for a few seconds before responding. "Only one was."

"Only one out of five? Why?"

"The others were in the elements for weeks and were too decomposed when found. If these cases are related, it's telling me that the killer has taken on a whole new persona and is becoming far more brazen."

"What about the vic who was identified? Who was he?"

Lutz took a gulp of coffee before answering. "He was a well-known and easily recognized politician from Sacramento who had recently announced his engagement."

Frank raised a brow. "So?"

"It was to another man."

I raked my hair with both hands. "And that, my friends, just opened up a whole new can of worms. Maybe we are looking at a hate crime after all."

Bob knuckled the table and stood. "I'll let you know when the police reports hit my in-box. Until then, work together on a plan of action."

I stood and crossed the bull pen. "I'll check in with the boys downstairs."

I entered our medical examiner's office first since Don had left with the body much earlier than our forensic boys had left with the park bench. Peeking around the second door that stood ajar, I saw Don at the autopsy table. A sheet was draped over the man's body and covered him from his feet to his shoulders. He lay on his side, I assumed because he was still fixed in that bent-knee position. It appeared that Don had already started the preliminary exam.

"Can I enter?" I thought it was more respectful to ask than to barge in.

"Sure. Nobody in here is going to object."

Don tried to add a little humor to his job on occasion, and I appreciated his attempt.

"Got any preliminary information for us? We'd like to get this man's face and description on the news as soon as possible. Since we have nothing yet, we'll be leaning heavily on the help of the public."

"Understood." Don stared at the man then rubbed his chin. "I can give you a guestimate on his height. It'll be off a little because he isn't exactly prone."

"Sure, whatever you think." I pulled my notepad from my pocket and grabbed a pen from the back counter.

"I'd put him between five foot ten and six foot but not more. His weight is one hundred eighty-six pounds. Salt and pepper hair, but mostly salt." He shot me a quick smile, which I returned. "Dark eyes and a scar on his right shin."

"Really? Enough to be considered an identifiable feature?"

Don tipped his head toward the body. "Here, have a look." He lifted the sheet from the man's legs and pointed at the front of the right leg, about four inches below the knee. A sizable scar, about two inches long, covered a vertical area of his shin.

"Humph. What do you think that's from?"

Don shrugged. "It isn't surgical, so it could be from anything. He could have fallen off his bike as a kid or gotten into a car accident as an adult."

"Or he could have tripped over something."

"Exactly. It's noteworthy, though, especially to anyone who may be looking for him."

I breathed deeply. "Okay, no tattoos, piercings, or birthmarks?"

"Nope. Clean as a whistle."

"How about the tox report?"

"Should have it by tomorrow afternoon."

I gave Don a nod of thanks, left the autopsy room, and headed for the crime lab. Through the double glass doors, I saw Mike and Danny inspecting the bench they had placed on a workstation table.

I walked in and got a head tip as I approached the guys. "Find anything we can use?" I was hopeful.

"Not sure, but we'll test it. There's a blood smear on one of the bottom slats but away from where the man's hands were positioned," Mike said. "A smear doesn't fit with the scene of blood dripping from the finger wounds."

I rubbed my chin as I processed that detail. "So blood transfer, maybe from transporting the body?"

"Possibly. We'll definitely test it to see if it belongs to the vic or somebody else."

"Can you make that a priority?"

Mike shrugged. "Sure, if that's what you want."

"Was there anything else? Caught fibers in the bench, something like that?"

"No, can't say we found anything like that, just the smear along with the blood that pooled under the vic's lap."

"Okay, and how long will that take?"

"I'll call you when we've got something. Give us an hour."

"Good enough. Thanks, guys."

I passed Lutz's office on my way to the bull pen. "Boss, got a second?" I popped my head through his half-opened door.

He looked up from his computer, took off his glasses, and rubbed his eyes. "I think I need a stronger prescription. Damned old age."

I chuckled. "I hope that's not me in fifteen years. Anyway, I got some information from Mike."

I had Lutz's full attention. "Yeah? What did he say?"

"They noticed a blood smear on one of the lower slats on the front of the park bench. The fact that the man was placed there after death, and the only wounds that would have dripped would be from his missing fingers, wouldn't result in smears being on the bench."

"Unless the perp accidentally transferred blood from the dead guy's clothes or wounds to the bench when he moved him. No prints in that smear, though?"

"Nah, just the smear."

Bob jotted that down. "So only an observation, or what?"

"Mike said he'd test it against the vic's blood to make sure it was his."

"Okay, keep me posted."

I gave the doorframe a smack with my open hand. "Will do." I returned to the bull pen and joined the guys at the back table. "Figure out how to divvy up the paperwork?"

Henry responded. "There are four of us assigned to compare the police, autopsy, and crime lab reports, and six vics in total. We'll divide up everything the best we can."

"Sounds good. Frank and I will tell the news channels what we have on the Bixler Park case and give them the dead man's description. I have everything I need from Don except the facial shot, and I'll have Danny run over there and take a decent picture for us. I'll see when Don will have the vic ready. We need to set up a few dedicated call lines, and unless another victim is discovered, Frank and I will man the phones. We'll have to interview people that sound credible, whether it's about knowing the deceased or seeing something suspicious in the area of the playground. A witness could have driven by and noticed something that looked off, so we'll see what shakes out."

Chapter 7

"Help me get the funnel's tube down his throat," Janet said. "We need to have this done before he wakes up and fights us. If we're dumping him tonight, he needs to be stone-cold dead." She glanced at the wall clock and mentally calculated how long it would take for the full thirty-two-ounce bottle of drain cleaner to kill the man tied to the radiator. "He should definitely be dead in a few hours if we do it now."

Gail released the ropes that secured him to the radiator. Tied by his arms, Mr. Hennessey was hunched forward, his chin against his chest, which made getting the tube down his throat nearly impossible. They would waste too much time. He needed to be lying down.

"Okay, he's loose."

Mr. Hennessey fell sideways, still in the same position, but Gail, a perfectionist, placed him the way she wanted him on the hardwood floor, then she reached for the funnel at her back. In the kitchen, Janet retrieved the bottle of drain cleaner, tucked it under her arm, and went to the hall closet and grabbed a towel. She assumed if any liquid ended up on the floor, it would destroy the clear finish, and they'd be billed for the repair. As she draped a towel over her arm and closed the closet door, the scream to her right caused a head jerk in that direction. With his back to Janet, the man had his fist balled and his arm cocked, as if ready to deliver a blow to Gail's face. Grabbing the eight-pound antique flatiron used as a doorstop, Janet bolted down the hallway, and just as he turned, she slammed it into the side of his nose. Blood erupted from his face, and if that didn't kill him, she would do it again.

"Screw the drain cleaner. You're about to take your last breath right now, you son of a bitch!"

Rolling out of the way in the nick of time, Gail watched as her mother pounded the iron weight into the man's skull. Blood ran down the walls and pooled on the floor. With the back of her hand, Janet wiped the blood spatter from her face then dropped the iron. She knelt over the man and jabbed his chest with her finger. "See, that's more proof of what I've always said. Your breed is nothing but shit and not to be trusted. If I could remove all of you from the earth, the world would be a much better place."

Gail sucked in a gulp of air as she tried to compose herself. "Thanks, Mom. My head was turned for barely a second. I had no idea that son of a bitch was awake and waiting to strike. I was sure the sleeping pills would have lasted longer than they did." Standing over the man, Gail spat on him then picked up the weight and dropped it on his head, which was now caved in.

Janet unfolded a paper drop cloth that she'd pulled from the utility closet and spread it across the floor. "Give me a hand undressing this idiot. I don't want to leave clothes behind anymore that could possibly lead to identifying the men." They dragged Mr. Hennessey by his ankles, centered him on the cloth, then disrobed him. Janet tipped her head toward the kitchen. "Grab the shears and hammer off the counter. We have to turn him into Chicago's John Doe number two."

Destroying the man's body didn't take more than ten minutes. Finding the exact location of the finger joints was easier than cutting through half-inch-thick bone. A few snips and the tops of all ten fingers were gone.

"Hold his mouth open," Janet instructed.

"Just don't hit my fingers," Gail said.

Janet smiled. "We're both pros, remember?" Holding the hammer, she directed several crushing blows to his upper and lower front teeth. After that, she slammed the hammer into each cheek, destroying the molars from the outside in.

"There. Job done, and he's unidentifiable. Nice to meet you, John Doe number two."

With the dustpan and broom in hand, Gail swept up the bloody fingertips and teeth fragments and flushed them down the toilet. It took three flushes to make sure nothing had settled at the bottom of the bowl. They rolled Mr. Hennessey and his wadded-up clothes into the drop cloth for the time being.

Janet jerked her head at the black blanket folded on a kitchen chair. "Take that with you and back up the van to the door. We'll put him inside and out of the way so we can clean up this blood before it stains the hardwood." Janet pulled out her cell phone and set the alarm. "There, that's done. At three a.m., we'll head to Washington Park and get rid of him. I will admit, though, watching him suffer the effects of the drain cleaner would have been far more satisfying. That's something I've always enjoyed seeing."

Chapter 8

We had barely made the deadline to get our John Doe's information on the six o'clock news, but we squeaked in, and the stations accepted it. A photograph of his face with some makeup magic around his mouth gave him a presentable appearance, especially for the early-evening broadcast. We included the scar on his right shin in his description. If anyone was looking for him and knew him well, they would probably be familiar with that scar. All we needed was a name, then we'd take it from there. We would offer a few vague details in hopes of drawing in the killer. Oftentimes, they inserted themselves in investigations by pretending to be caring citizens who only wanted to help. We'd say the deceased man was discovered in a Chicago park, but we wouldn't say which one. To a friend or family member, the location wouldn't matter much, anyway, but the killer would want every detail known as a way to frighten nearby residents. We wouldn't identify how the man had died, and at that moment, we had no idea, but even when the tox report came back, that information wouldn't be shared. Only law enforcement and the killer would know John Doe's manner of death.

I wasn't sure which way the tip line would go. Either we would be flooded with calls, or I would be home by dark, but regardless, the doggy door Frank had installed and Bandit's self-feeding and watering bowls were a godsend. My guilt had subsided during grueling cases, and Bandit and I had grown accustomed to our new normal. It was working okay for both of us, and when I was home, I lavished him with love.

I took my seat after powering up the TV in our conference room. All of the detectives tasked to the John Doe case—along with our commander, Bob Lutz—were in attendance. Two phones had been set up for tip-line calls, and if it turned out to be too much for Frank and me, we'd have more phones brought in, and officers would lend a hand. If our John Doe wasn't a well-known figure or a local resident, I wasn't expecting more calls than Frank and I could handle.

With an elbow to my ribs, Frank tipped his head toward the TV, which was already turned to our favorite news station—Channel 7.

The evening anchor, Charles Landry, began with breaking news, which pertained to our John Doe. The broadcast was right on target. Our John Doe's face, his height, weight, eye color, hair color, and the long shin scar on his right leg were all mentioned. A photograph of his shirt and description of his pants, along with the sizes and brand names, were also described. Charles said that the man currently known as John Doe was found deceased in a local park with no identification on him. We made sure to gloss over the part where viewers would wonder about fingerprints and dental records, and we had the anchor say only that fingerprint and dental records provided nothing useful to the police department. In a roundabout way, that was true. The segment was only two minutes long, then the banner with the tip-line number ran across the bottom of the television screen. They moved on to the regular evening news after that.

I slapped my hands together after shutting off the TV. "Well, now it's a waiting game. Either I'll be here half the night and Bandit will have to fend for himself, or I'll go home, throw a steak and a potato on the grill, and have dinner an hour later."

Frank pressed his temples and chanted, which entertained all of us. "I'm feeling a sort of psychic power taking over my mind."

I grinned. "Then work your psychic magic and solve this case."

The rest of our team broke out in laughter as Frank continued. "I'm thinking dinner is going to consist of a vending-machine sandwich, a bag of chips, and a soda."

The phone on the left rang, and our entire group groaned.

"You may be right." I picked up and had my pad and pen ready to go. "John Doe tip line. This is Detective McCord speaking. Do you have information for us?" I jotted down what the caller was saying.

Both phones rang nonstop for two hours. At eight o'clock, I had Henry plug the vending machines with dollar bills and bring back two turkey club sandwiches, two bags of corn chips, and two sodas for Frank and me. It was nearing nine o'clock when the calls subsided. Both phones had recording devices connected to them, so we could go through each call at a slower pace and decide in what order of importance they would land. I wrote brief notes to myself about what time the calls came in to help me track the ones I wanted to give another listen to.

I looked over my notes, which I could barely read. My penmanship was poor at best. With a scratch to my forehead, I glanced at Frank. "Did you get anything that needs a second look?"

"Some. How about you?"

"The same. Let's listen to the calls again and decide in what order of importance or urgency we need to address them."

Frank found the first call he thought was important and backtracked to the fourteen-minute mark.

"Give me a synopsis of the call."

"It was a woman who said the guy is her dad and that he's been missing for two weeks."

I grimaced. "Not sure about that one, buddy. Why would anybody hold on to a man that long without a good reason? Did she say there was a ransom demand?"

"Nope, just that he's been gone."

"So he and his killer hung out and played cards for two weeks? It isn't like he was tortured. There were no clear injuries on his body except—"

"Yeah, except the ones that were right in front of us, and I'd consider having your fingers snipped off and teeth smashed down your throat as torture."

"I meant to say signs of torture over a period of several weeks. Did she mention his scar?"

"Nah, let's move on. I'll get back to her and insist she email us a photograph of her dad."

We returned to our lists and calls then chose three people to connect with that night. One was a woman who thought the man looked like her old neighbor. He was a widower and had never had children. Maybe that was why nobody was looking for him. The lead had substance, and the woman lived only fifteen minutes from our station. We would visit her first. The second caller we wanted to check in with said he saw something strange as he was driving home from the airport. He said he took a red-eye flight from Miami. Although the vic's location was never revealed, we learned the man's home was only four blocks from the playground. Asked what he saw, he said two people were pulling what looked to be a wagon. He admitted they remained in the shadows as he drove by on East Fifty-Seventh Street, but it was four thirty in the morning, and although he thought it odd, he chalked it up as being a couple of homeless people.

"That one totally sounds legit," I said. "Let's visit him first instead of the woman."

Frank agreed. The last man said he would be bowling until eleven and his team always stopped at Gilda's Pub afterward. I said we could meet him there after eleven.

"And what was the story behind his call?"

"He thought the man looked just like a mom-and-pop bookstore owner who ran a shop about a mile west of Washington Park. He said it's been closed for several days now, which is unusual."

"Hmm. Still in the general vicinity and could hold merit.

Okay, let's head out. You have all the addresses?"

"Yep." Frank handed me the sheet. "You guide, and I'll drive."

Chapter 9

The digital readout on the cruiser's dash showed it was 9:35.

"Damn it, maybe we should have gone to that woman's house first," I said after realizing we wouldn't get to her until ten thirty or later.

Frank waved me off. "If she didn't want to talk, she wouldn't have made the call. She's doing her civic duty, so time shouldn't matter."

I laughed. "Says the guy who hates door knocks or phone calls after nine." I checked the address I'd written down then told Frank to pull over. We had arrived. "That's the house." I pointed at the white two-story with the well-groomed lawn and porch light on.

Frank dipped his head and peered out the passenger window as he slowed against the curb. "Looks like a decent place."

I raised a brow. "Meaning he's more legit?"

"Probably. Let's find out."

We exited the cruiser and took to the brick sidewalk that led to the porch. Frank pressed the doorbell. I glanced down at the slip of paper again to see the man's name—Tom Greenwood.

Seconds later, the door swung open, and a middle-aged man about my size reached out and introduced himself with a handshake. "Tom Greenwood here. Detectives McCord and Mills, I presume?"

Frank nodded. "You'd be correct. I'm Detective Mills"—he shot a thumb in my direction—"and he's McCord."

"Good, good. Come on in." Tom led the way through the foyer and into a cozy-looking den. "Have a seat. Care for anything to drink?"

"Nah, thanks. We're good." I wanted to get down to business.

"Sure thing." Tom took the chair with the ottoman, and Frank and I shared the couch.

I waited until he looked comfortable before beginning. Frank pulled out his notepad and pen.

"So Mr. Greenwood, you said you saw something unusual this morning. Go ahead and walk us through it, starting at the point when you got back to this neighborhood."

"Sure. Like I told Detective Mills on the phone, I had a red-eye from Miami, and by the time I got back here, it was around four thirty a.m. Because of the late hour"—he smiled—"or early hour, I finally went to bed. I had a vacation day today. From what the news described and what I saw with the police presence at the playground, I put two and two together."

"You drove past the playground today?"

He nodded. "I needed groceries. I've been away for a week on a work conference, and the refrigerator and cupboards were bare. I didn't mention it during the phone call, but I'm a bachelor and don't have a wife or maid who does the grocery shopping."

"Got it. Thanks for the clarification. So describe to us everything you can remember about the people pulling a wagon."

"Yeah, that's what it looked like. I mean, it was still really dark outside, and if it wasn't for my headlights illuminating that corner of the sidewalk, I would have missed them altogether. It wasn't much more than a quick glimpse, but it was definitely two people, and they weren't pushing a grocery cart. They were pulling something. What else would you pull other than a wagon?"

I rubbed my chin. "That's true. Did it look like something was inside?"

"Sure, but I figured it was their belongings. You know how homeless people collect things." He furrowed his brows.

"Think of something?" Frank asked.

"Just that I've seen hundreds of homeless people during my travels, and either they carried nothing more than a duffel bag, or they pushed grocery carts because they're easy to steal. I've never seen anyone pull a wagon."

I gave Frank a sideways glance. Tom had a point.

"Could you tell if the people were men, women, or one of each?"

"Nope, too dark outside, and they were wearing black or navy-blue clothing, probably to blend in with the night."

"Did you notice their hair? Long or short?"

"I didn't." Tom put his legs up on the ottoman then pinched the bridge of his nose. "If I recall correctly, the few seconds I did see, I think they were wearing hoodies."

Frank jotted that down then tapped his pen against the pad. "What street were they on, and which direction were they going?"

"They had just turned north on South Dorchester Avenue. That's how my headlights caught them for a split second."

I thought out loud. "Okay, so they entered the park from the east."

Tom pulled back his head. "So you think that dead guy was in the wagon?"

I stood, and Frank did the same. "It's early in the investigation, Tom, and we can't speculate. It could be just like you thought, two homeless people walking by." I knew he wasn't buying what I was selling, but we couldn't confirm anything at that point, anyway. We gave him our cards, and I reached out for a handshake.

"You've been very helpful, and we may need to contact you again."

"Not a problem. Happy to do my part."

Back in the car, I checked the time—10:19. We were off to the house of the woman who thought John Doe looked like her old neighbor. I gave her a courtesy call to say we were en route.

Frank pulled into her driveway at 10:40. She lived in a modest-sized single-story house that didn't appear to be more than a thousand square feet, and I assumed she lived alone. With a couple of short raps on the screen door, we waited. A woman who looked to be in her early sixties peeked out the sidelights, which was smart on her part given the hour. We already had our badges exposed to give her peace of mind. She nodded and opened the door.

"Detectives, please come in."

We thanked her, introduced ourselves, and apologized for the late hour.

"I'm Lois Porter, and it's okay. I'm retired with nothing better to do in the morning except sleep in. Right this way. We'll sit in the kitchen."

Frank and I followed her then pulled out chairs on one side of the table, and she faced us from the other.

"We don't want to keep you too long, so we'll get right to it, okay?"

"Sure thing. Go ahead and ask your questions."

"Appreciate it, ma'am."

"Just call me Lois."

I nodded. "What makes you think John Doe was your old neighbor?"

"Simple. Because he looks like him. Granted, the deceased had his eyes closed in the photograph, but the description was on the money. I don't know what brand of clothing he wore"— she smiled—"it wasn't like we were ever talking about clothes, but the picture of his shirt and description of his pants seemed like the type of outfits he wore."

"What was his name, and why did he leave the area?"

"His name was Miles Jamison, and he was from England originally. When his wife Patrice died of cancer four years back, he left the neighborhood and moved to an apartment building. I guess living in the same home that they shared for twenty years was too painful for him. Since then, we lost touch."

My mind flashed to my own home, the one I'd grown up in. It held wonderful childhood memories, but a few years after my parents died, I had the entire house remodeled. I believed it was because I couldn't face those memories every day. I needed a fresh start but kept some of the home's features that were near and dear to my mom's heart.

"Do you have any photographs of Miles?"

She excused herself momentarily then came back carrying a photo album. "I'll admit, the pictures are old. I mean, nobody uses cameras or stores pictures in albums anymore."

I thought of the totes full of albums in my basement. "May we?"

"Sure." She slid the album across the table then came around and leaned over our backs. "That one there was from a neighborhood block party about fifteen years ago. Miles is the man in the red polo shirt."

I pulled my reading glasses from my inside jacket pocket and put them on. A side view of the man wouldn't help, and being fifteen years older made a huge difference in a person's appearance. "Do you have any of Miles looking directly at the camera and possibly a bit newer?"

"Well, let's see. Go ahead and flip the pages. I'll tell you if I see him again."

Feeling deflated, I didn't have faith that we would see any up-close headshots of the man in question. She found one more picture in the album, a straight shot, but Miles was still across the yard at a picnic table with a half dozen other neighbors. It looked to be about the same decade too.

"Sorry I don't have anything better than these, but as soon as I saw that news segment, my mind went immediately to Miles."

"Do you know what apartment complex he moved to?"

She shook her head. "We were acquaintances, not best friends. Back then, when people moved, they just said their goodbyes and left. He didn't have family in the area, but he hoped the activities offered at the apartment complex would help him make new friends."

We thanked Lois, gave her our contact information, and left.

"I'll pull his name when we get back to the station, and maybe an address will pop up. If it does, we'll bang on his door tomorrow and see if anyone answers."

Frank fisted his eyes. "One more interview and then I'm done. It's lights out for me."

"Yeah, I'm pretty beat too." I thought about Bandit, and the guilt began to creep in, but I knew he was likely asleep on the couch and dreaming about chasing squirrels.

We headed to Gilda's Pub, where we would talk to our last caller. I pressed the map light to get a look at his name— Gary Fowler.

Luckily, when we arrived, Gilda's had only about twenty people inside. A neighborhood establishment, it wasn't the type of bar that served martinis and Jell-O shots. It was a beer drinker's pub and the kind of place I'd probably frequent myself. We approached the bartender to ask who Gary was, but as two men in suits, we couldn't help standing out. Gary easily found us.

"I'm Gary, and you must be the detectives."

Frank chuckled. "What gave it away?"

Gary shook our hands and pointed at a vacant bar table. "Is that okay?"

"Sure, it's fine," I said, "and it helps that you can actually hear yourself talk in here. So what leads you to think John Doe is the bookstore owner?"

"To be honest, I'm a struggling author and stop in there often. I read books in my genre to see how other authors write. Maybe I'll learn a few things on how to improve my style. Plus, the shop is within walking distance of my house. Convenience, I'd say, more than anything else."

"Sure, and he hasn't been around lately? That's why you called?"

"Well, that and the fact that John Doe looked a lot like Conrad Beaumont."

I made sure Frank wrote down the name. A quick internet search would tell us where he lived, and he would get a door knock tomorrow too.

"Any idea if Conrad had plans to go on vacation? Maybe a note on the bookstore's door?"

"Nope, nothing like that. Just a gut feeling on my part, I guess. Normally, he's closed on Sundays and Wednesdays, but the shop hasn't been open since last Tuesday."

"Okay, so in a regular week, the doors would have reopened on Thursday?"

"That's right, and now it's the following Monday night. Can't figure it out unless it involves foul play."

Frank smiled. "What genre do you write in, Gary?"

"What else? Crime fiction."

Chapter 10

The buzzing alarm startled Janet awake. She picked up the phone and squinted at the screen—two forty-five. It was time to get up and rid themselves of Mr. Hennessey's body that lay covered in the back of the van. She slipped on the clothes she had worn earlier and headed to the bathroom. A quick splash of cold water on her face would wake her up. Janet called out to Gail, who slept in the small second bedroom, as she made her way down the hall.

"Get up. We've got to go."

They had things to do and places to be. Coffee and breakfast would be enjoyed at their leisure after the drop and once they were safely home.

"Move it. We're leaving in three minutes."

"I'm coming, Mom. Can I at least put on my shoes?"

"Yes, but do it quickly. Is the wagon in the van?"

"Of course, just like always."

"Put on your hoodie." Janet zipped hers up to her throat and grabbed the keys.

They were fortunate to have an end unit on the first floor. Having the van backed up to the apartment, and with both rear doors open, kept people from seeing them load a body into the vehicle. Janet double-checked the contents then quietly closed the rear doors. She took a seat behind the wheel and inched out of the driveway, then the headlights went on a block later.

"Have you decided on the entrance into the park?" She glanced at Gail, who was studying a map on her phone.

"Yeah, give me just a second to make sure." Gail spread the image with her fingers to enlarge the photograph of the park. "Let's take East Sixtieth to Best Drive. There are dozens of small roads weaving through the park in that area. We'll follow the one that goes out to the peninsula. Water is all around it, there's a ton of trees, and it's a safer choice for us, off the beaten path, so maybe we can move a little slower." She gave her mom a quick smile.

"That sounds good. It shouldn't be long now, ten minutes tops."

Janet turned onto Best Drive and went right. She cut the headlights and used only the fog lamps going forward. Several hundred feet ahead, Gail pointed to the left.

"Turn there. That'll take us to the peninsula."

They continued on and went deeper in until the road was no wider that a golf cart path.

"That should do it." Janet pulled under a large oak and parked. Gail leapt from the passenger side, rounded the van to the back, and opened the double doors. With a couple of snaps, the collapsible wagon was locked in the open position and the body dropped into it. They covered him with the black blanket and pulled the hoods up on their sweatshirts.

"We better not lollygag after all," Janet said. "It'll take a solid five minutes to get out of the park. Now I'm wondering if cops patrol this area."

"I'm sure they do." Gail scanned their surroundings then grabbed the wagon handle and walked at a quickened pace into the tree cover. She was thankful that Janet matched her stride. "Hit the light, Mom, so I can see how it looks back here."

A couple of on-and-off bursts with the flashlight showed them enough. The body would be well hidden, but if vultures circling the area eventually raised the curiosity of people in the park, then so be it. The man was unidentifiable, anyway.

They tipped the wagon, rolled him out, and covered him with twigs and branches.

"Let's go." Gail pulled the wagon to the path and then folded it into the collapsed shape.

Janet quietly chuckled as they walked to the van. "The cops will be going in circles. One guy in plain sight and another hidden deep in the woods. They won't know if they're working with one killer or if a copycat has joined in on the fun." She brushed the dirt and twigs from her clothes, and Gail did the same before they climbed into the van.

"Wait. We have to get rid of the drop cloth and his clothes." Gail walked to the back of the van and jammed the white sheeting and his shirt, pants, and underwear into a plastic trash bag they'd brought along. Janet drove, and several miles away, Gail pointed at a random dumpster on a side street. "I'll throw it in there."

Janet rolled to a stop, and Gail jumped out and stuffed

the trash bag deep into the bin. They continued on until they reached the safety of their apartment, where the next items on their to-do list were breakfast, strong coffee, and planning the abduction of another man.

Chapter 11

Taking the steps two by two, I headed to our lower level as soon as I arrived at work, anxious to find out if Don had gotten the toxicology report back. A short knock on his office door announced my presence, and he turned his head away from the computer and tipped his chin at me.

"Come on in, Jesse. I'm sure you're here about the tox report, right?"

"Did you get the findings yet?"

"They just arrived in my in-box. Let's take a look together, and then I'll print out a copy for your department."

I scooted the roller chair next to Don's desk and took a seat. He slipped on his reading glasses, I did the same, then he opened the attachment.

"Uh-huh. That'll definitely do the job. A combination of sodium hydroxide and benzodiazepine."

"Layman's terms, please."

"In simple terms, it's sleeping pills and lye, as in drain cleaner. I imagine the man was either forced to swallow drain cleaner, or he was already unconscious from the sleeping pills when it was poured down his throat."

"Whoa." I shook my head in disbelief. The killer was far more vicious than I'd originally imagined. Removing fingertips and smashing teeth to the point of making a person completely unidentifiable was already a sadistic act, but pouring drain cleaner down someone's throat was beyond evil. "So which do you think came first?" I realized it didn't matter in the end, but I was curious.

"Probably the drain cleaner so the victim would either be dead or near death when the perp destroyed his teeth and fingers. The killer wouldn't be able to complete those steps unless the victim was somehow subdued."

I gave Don a concerned stare. "We really need to find that maniac and quick. I just hope John Doe wasn't a preview of what's still to come."

Don hit Print then spun his chair and retrieved three copies of the tox report he'd printed out for me. "Give one to Lutz and keep a couple for your files. Now I can go ahead with the full autopsy. The effects of the drain cleaner should show in his esophagus and stomach lining and will substantiate that lye was the cause of death."

I thanked Don and headed upstairs, taking the back way to our bull pen, but stopped at Lutz's office first to give him a copy.

Good, his door is open.

After rapping on the doorframe, I entered. "Hey, Boss." I slid the sheet of paper across his desk.

"What's this?"

"I stopped in Don's office before coming upstairs. He just got the tox report back."

"Really?"

I followed Lutz's eyes as he skimmed the report. "Holy shit." He rubbed the wrinkles that had just popped up on his forehead then scrunched his face at me. "Drain cleaner?"

I shrugged in disgust. "Apparently, and it takes a certain kind of evil to be that sadistic."

Lutz stood. "Have the John Doe team meet me in the conference room in ten. I want to hear how the tip-line calls went, anyway."

I was about to recap our interviews for the commander, but I would save that for the whole group to hear. After our powwow, Frank and I would drive to the addresses on record for Miles Jamison and Conrad Beaumont to see if anyone was home.

We entered the conference room carrying our necessities and then took our usual seats. A cup of coffee sat in front of each of us along with a notepad and pen. Lutz had conducted a short roll call and updates with the rest of our unit, then he walked in and sat at the head of the table.

"Okay, a quick update for all of you as well. Don received the tox report this morning, which confirmed the COD as drain cleaner. He'll conduct a full autopsy, and the damage to John Doe's stomach lining and throat will definitely tell him that lye passed through the deceased's mouth and traveled to his stomach. There may be more when the urinalysis report comes in, but that's yet to be seen." Lutz gave Frank a glance. "What have you got, Mills, as far as tip-line leads?"

Frank balled his hand into a fist, held it to his mouth, and cleared his throat before speaking. "Jesse and I were pretty busy answering calls last night for, what, a couple of hours?"

I nodded.

"We chose a handful as the most credible calls, and of those, we went out and interviewed three people before ending our work night. There was one more caller who said the missing man was her dad and that he'd been gone for several weeks."

Lutz scratched his cheek. "Not sure about that one, Frank."

"Right, and that's why I called her back and requested she email me a picture of the man in question, which I haven't yet received."

Lutz turned to me. "Okay, Jesse, take it from there."

"Sure thing. We interviewed a man who at four thirty yesterday morning saw two people pulling a wagon alongside Bixler Park."

Lutz's eyes lit up. "And?"

"And although he thought it odd, he chalked it up as homeless people walking from one squatting location to another."

"Hmm… I suppose it could have been. How about a description?"

"Nothing. He said it was too dark, and the only reason he saw them at all was because his headlights caught them for a second as they were turning the corner. He said they were both wearing dark-colored clothing and hoodies, essentially only looking like moving shapes in the night."

"Not very helpful but still interesting. Why was he driving around at that time?"

"Red-eye from Miami. He was just getting home and said he only lived four blocks from the park. He saw the police presence later when he went out to get groceries, put two and two together, and then called the tip-line number after watching the news broadcast."

"Got it. What about the other two?"

Frank shuffled his notes and began. "We talked to a woman who thought the man was an old neighbor of hers. He was a widower and didn't have any family in the area, which would explain why a missing persons call never came in for John Doe. He moved away after his wife died, and the woman who made the call lost touch with him. We're going to follow up and bang on his door as soon as our meeting is over."

Lutz wrote that down. "Good, and the last person?"

I finished our findings. "That was a guy who thought the victim looked like a bookstore owner. Guess the caller frequents the place often and said it's been closed up for nearly a week. No notes on the door as to why the store is closed. We're going to give his residence a check too."

"Okay, conduct those follow-ups and let me know. Henry and Potter, I want you to walk the route those people with the wagon took. Look for evidence on the ground and cameras on buildings." Lutz turned to me. "Give Henry the street they were on before you guys head out."

"Roger that, Boss." I jerked my chin at Frank. "He's got the route in his notes."

Chapter 12

After our meeting ended, we parted ways with the group. Frank, Henry, and Shawn discussed the direction the people with the wagon had come from and turned on when the witness saw them, then we left. As I sat in the passenger seat, I checked my phone for the addresses of the two men in question.

"Looks like Conrad Beaumont's home is the farthest away. Let's hit his place first and then cut back."

"Roger that."

I stared out the window as Frank drove. We were both quieter than usual.

"Something occupying your mind?" I asked.

"Yeah. Just wondering what kind of trigger sets crazy in motion. I mean, isn't it usually a traumatic event that turns a person into some kind of bloodthirsty lunatic?"

I sighed with a shrug. "Statistically, yes, but that doesn't take into consideration the most well-known and notorious killers in the historical archives. The majority of them killed simply because they wanted to know what it was like and decided they enjoyed it. Some people, as the movie says, are natural-born killers."

"True, but that story was about guys who had traumatic childhoods."

"I'm going by the title only since it was a movie and a fictional one at that." I glanced down at the phone on my lap. The GPS was guiding us closer. "Turn north two blocks up on South California Street and then go about a half mile. The address is just north of Kelly Park on West Fortieth Street."

"Got it."

Moments later, we arrived at an attractive redbrick upper and lower duplex. From the address we'd found for Mr. Beaumont, his residence appeared to be the lower unit. Frank parked along the curb in front of the home, and we took the short sidewalk to the stoop. We gave the door several knocks then waited.

After the second round of knocks went unanswered, I craned my neck past the shrubs and toward the living room window. "Doesn't seem like he's home. Maybe Gary Fowler was right." I smirked. "I guess it's that crime-fiction-writer instinct." The words were barely out of my mouth when the door to the second floor creaked open.

"You looking for Conrad?"

I thought it a strange question since there was no other reason we would be knocking on Conrad's door, but I replied politely that we were.

The woman who came down to check our intentions introduced herself as Judy Compton. She pointed above her head. "I live upstairs."

Another obvious statement.

"Conrad isn't home."

We waited for something more, but I saw that wasn't going to happen without some prodding. We didn't have time for back-and-forth one-liners.

"Ma'am, we're detectives from the police department. Do you know where Conrad is?"

"Sure. I took him to the airport myself last Wednesday around seven p.m. His daughter went into labor two weeks early and had complications, so he left for Pittsburgh that night."

We thanked her and took the sidewalk back to the cruiser. That bit of information had just eliminated Conrad Beaumont from the pool of John Doe possibilities.

With a grunt, I settled into the cruiser's passenger seat and fished my phone out of my pocket. "Okay, let me pull up the address for Miles Jamison." I plugged that into the GPS map route, and we were off to the Royal Arms apartment complex three miles south and a mile east.

Fifteen minutes later, we arrived at the four-building complex, each holding twelve units. Another building centered between the apartments appeared to be their recreation center, and bocce ball and shuffleboard courts were located next to it in a covered area outside.

"Is this a fifty-five-plus apartment complex?" Frank asked.

"Don't know, but it looks like one." I glanced down at the address then checked the letters above the entrance to each building. I pointed at the second building on our left, the closest one to the rec center. "He lives in that one, in apartment number three. I guess the *B* represents building number two."

Inside the front door was a vestibule holding a wall-mounted intercom with each tenant's call button. I looked at the third one down—Miles Jamison.

"This is it. Let's see if anyone answers." I pressed the button, and seconds later, a man's voice asked who was there. I shook my head—another dead end. We introduced ourselves and asked for a minute of his time. I wanted to see how closely Miles resembled our John Doe. It would give me an idea of other people's perception of facial similarities and could possibly keep us from running in circles.

Mr. Jamison said he would come to the vestibule. I couldn't blame him and didn't expect him to let two strangers in without proof that we were the detectives we said we were.

It took only a second before a man who looked very similar to our deceased showed up in the hallway and walked toward us. At the glass door, he asked to see our IDs before opening it. We complied, and he pulled the door toward him and allowed us through.

"Less crowded here if somebody needs to get in." He pointed at a small loveseat against the wall across from the bank of mailboxes. "What can I help you with, Detectives?"

"First and foremost, thank you for giving us a few minutes of your time," I said. "Just to be sure, you are Miles Jamison, correct?"

"I was the last time I looked in the mirror." He grinned.

Other than his eye color and the fact that he appeared a few inches shorter than what Don had documented as John Doe's height, I could see how Lois Porter might have thought

Miles was our deceased man. "You know Lois Porter, right?"

"Lois, yes, of course. She used to be my neighbor. Did something happen to her?"

Frank picked up where I left off. "No, she's fine. Actually, she thought something might have happened to you, so we stopped in to do a welfare check."

He looked puzzled. "Why would she think that?"

We didn't want to tell him she thought he was dead, so I just said she had a concern since they never talked anymore.

"Well, that was really nice of her, and maybe I should give her a call. I appreciate you taking the time to stop by, and as you can see, I'm doing okay."

Frank pulled a card from his pocket. "If you ever need the police, Mr. Jamison, we're here to help. Thanks for your time."

With a handshake, we left and returned to the cruiser.

"Guess that puts us at zero leads," I said as I buckled my seat belt. "Let's go back to the station and review what we do and don't have."

Frank snickered. "That'll take all of two minutes."

Chapter 13

My desk phone rang just as I stood to walk to our cafeteria. The vending-machine lunch I had in mind was only minutes away, but I plopped back in my seat and answered the phone instead.

"McCord speaking."

"Jesse, it's Bob. We've got a problem in Washington Park. Another body with the fingers removed was just discovered."

Our commander went on to tell me about the call he'd received from our dispatch operator just minutes earlier. A husband and wife riding bikes through Washington Park happened to smell the odor of decay. The message relayed to the 911 operator was that the husband—a detective from Charlotte—was biking through the park with his wife and caught a whiff of the smell. While investigating farther into the woods, he discovered the body of a nude male with a severely crushed head and missing fingertips.

"Get your team out there right now," Lutz said. "Patrol is already on site, and I'll head out as soon as I get word to Don, Mike, and Danny."

"Got it, but do you know where everyone is? That park is

damn near four-hundred acres."

"The caller said they were on the peninsula at the lake."

"Okay, we're on our way." I hung up and got the attention of our John Doe team. "Another body was found in Washington Park with the same MO as the one in Bixler. Lutz wants us out there now."

Shawn, Henry, and Frank leapt from their chairs, gathered what they needed, and were at the door within seconds. Tony and Kip stayed behind to answer calls.

"Same as always," I said. "Frank and me in one cruiser"— I pointed at Henry and Shawn—"and you two in the other."

We took the back stairs to the side exit, where our cruisers were parked. I told Henry to stick to my rear bumper. The scene was on the peninsula at the lake.

Since the north end of the park bordered the same street as the police station, we had only a short six-minute drive. From East Fifty-First Street, we headed south on Dr. Martin Luther King Jr. Drive to Best Drive—it was the fastest way to reach the area where the body was discovered.

Patrol was already on scene, and three squad cars sat lined up nose-to-bumper along the road leading onto the peninsula.

Taking the lead, I started by telling Henry to have the officers close off every path that led in, which included one main road wide enough to drive a car on and two narrower paths for walkers and bicyclists. We were led to the scene by Officer Jackson, and as we walked, I saw to my right the man who had made the call. I knew I'd get a good recollection from him. Lutz had learned the man was a Charlotte, North Carolina, detective and in Chicago with his wife on their honeymoon. He, his wife, and their bicycles sat on the grass some hundred feet away. I walked over, introduced myself, and told the husband—a detective Chuck Donahue—that I'd be right back after taking a quick look at the body.

Frank, Henry, Shawn, and I continued on with Jackson to the location where the deceased lay. Among the thick undergrowth, he was partially covered with leaves and twigs in what appeared to be an attempt to hide the body until it decomposed. That would have had a good chance of success if it weren't for the odor of decomp wafting past the nose of a person familiar with that smell. We got within five feet of the body but made sure not to disturb the scene. Don and the crime lab needed it to remain as pristine as possible until their investigation on site was complete. I shined my flashlight at the spots most important to me in that moment—the man's hands and mouth. From where I had crouched under the trees, I saw the missing fingertips, but with his mouth closed, I had no way of knowing whether his teeth had been shattered. That would be left to Don to find out. Everything so far led me to believe the killer was the same person as at Bixler Park—except for the fact that John Doe had been displayed prominently, and the body I was looking at was so well hidden he might never have been found. I wondered if we had a copycat killer on our hands but quickly dismissed that idea. John Doe's manner of death, including the fact that his fingertips had been snipped off, had not been released to the press, telling me a copycat killer wasn't possible. Even so, there were similarities and differences between both men. The most obvious was that the man I was staring at was nude and had his skull so badly crushed that it was no longer round, yet John Doe's skull didn't have any blows inflicted on it at all. I wondered if the killer's rage was increasing or if he was changing up his MO with hopes of throwing law enforcement off his trail. I jerked my head at Shawn.

"Get a couple of quick pictures, and then we'll leave the scene as is until Don arrives."

I glanced across the open space, and the detective from North Carolina was pacing a rut into the grass. I knew how he felt. I had been in the same predicament a year earlier when my sister, Jenna, was murdered in Wisconsin. I was out of my jurisdiction and legally had to take a seat on the sidelines during that investigation.

"Let's have him walk us through the last forty-five minutes."

Frank and I headed in his direction while Henry and Shawn waited for Lutz, our medical examiner, and the crime lab team to show up. We approached the couple again.

"I hear Chicago was your honeymoon destination. Sorry about the speed bump, folks. We have a beautiful city here, but we also have our fair share of crime. Times ten."

Frank found a large rock to get comfortable on and pulled out his notepad. "Why don't you walk us through what happened after you crossed over to the peninsula."

"Sure. Stacey and I were riding our rented bikes and had been out for about a half hour. Right, babe?"

She nodded. "About that."

"I checked the map of the park last night and knew the

route we wanted to take. We came in on Best Drive and followed that to the road that came onto the peninsula. The plan was to have coffee here, walk around a bit, and then continue north to Payne Drive and take that to East Fifty-First Street, where we'd find a spot for breakfast."

Frank wrote that down. "Sure. So you reached this spot around when?"

The detective scratched his head. "I'd say around seven forty-five. Our plan was to be at a restaurant by nine, but when we got to this point, I caught a whiff of decomp." He shook his head. "Once that's smelled, it can't be unsmelled. I didn't have a choice. I needed to investigate further. I'm sure you understand."

"We do and appreciate your work ethic even when you're on your honeymoon." I gave both of them a nod of thanks. "You didn't touch anything on the deceased, did you?"

"Nope. I've been on the force for nine years and know crime scene protocol."

"What division do you work?" I asked.

"Just started in Homicide a few months back. Before that, I was in Gang Control."

I tipped my chin at him. "That's quite a transition."

"Not as much as you'd think. I worked side by side with the homicide detectives on a regular basis since most of the gang violence led to bloodshed, anyway."

"Where in North Carolina do you live?"

"We live in Gastonia, but I work in Charlotte. Unfortunately, we have our fair share of murders too."

At the sound of people talking behind me, I looked over

my shoulder. Lutz and Henry were walking toward us. I made the introductions, Lutz thanked Mr. and Mrs. Donahue for calling it in, then he excused himself to join our medical examiner, who had just arrived.

I returned my attention to the newlyweds. "How long are you going to be in Chicago?"

"We're heading back to Charlotte on Saturday," Chuck said.

I pulled two of my cards from my pocket. "Would you mind writing your cell number on the back of one in case I need to contact you again?"

"Sure, not a problem."

Frank handed his pen to Chuck, who scribbled his phone number on the card. He handed the card to me and the pen to Frank then put the second card in his wallet. I noticed from the frown wrinkling Chuck's brow that something was weighing on his mind.

"Is there something else you remembered?"

"Not pertaining to this scene, but several similar murders took place last winter down in our neck of the woods. I remember Charlotte was on edge when murdered men were found without fingertips, but maybe that's just something killers are doing these days. No identity, no ties."

"Interesting that you mentioned it since Commander Lutz just found that information yesterday in the nationwide database. And the killer was never apprehended, right?"

"That's correct."

With a handshake of appreciation, I told them that was all the questions we had at the moment, but I called out to

Chuck as they rode away. "I have a feeling we'll be talking again."

Henry, Frank, and I returned to Lutz's side, where Shawn was already standing. From the twenty-foot perimeter that Don, Mike, and Danny needed to conduct their field examination, Lutz asked his usual questions.

"When do you think the victim was dumped, Don?"

"Definitely during the night since there's morning dew on the body. It seems that our killer has an aversion to daylight hours."

I snickered. "Yeah, since it's easier to get caught in broad daylight."

Chapter 14

Lutz jammed his thick fingers into his pocket and jangled his keys—a habit he often displayed when agitated. "All of you go back to Bixler and dig deeper. Expand the search to a ten-block perimeter around the park. Look for every building-mounted camera you can find. There has to be a camera somewhere that caught those two people with the wagon. I'll get the okay from Adams to have Patrol canvass the entire peninsula, the road leading out, and to look for cameras along the streets that enter the park." He flung his hands into the air. "Now go!"

We turned back the way we'd come in and walked to our cruisers.

"Jesus, he's got his boxers in a bind," Shawn said. "I don't think I've ever seen him this uptight."

I had to agree. As soon as the media caught wind of a second murder, they would push the serial-killer theory and say whatever they could to drum up higher ratings for their network. We had to stay tight-lipped about the brutality of both murders.

I called Tech as Frank drove to Bixler Park. "Hey, Todd,

it's Jesse. I need a ten-block perimeter around Bixler Park mapped out and sent to my phone. Yep, appreciate it." I clicked off the call. "We'll divide up and plan our route as soon as I get the street borders from Todd."

Frank gave me a side-eyed glance. "What's your take? Is it the same killer, or are you of the mind-set that the detective from North Carolina is?"

"Depends. Which mind-set are you referring to?"

"Where he said that cutting off fingers and removing identifiable features from the victims could be a new trend with murderers."

I blew out a puff of air while I thought about Frank's question. "I really don't know. If it's what they're all doing, then there's a good chance that the two killings aren't related, but short of removing somebody's head, the victim could still be identified from his description and a facial photograph."

"Be careful what you say, partner. Anything is possible."

We reached the park at two thirty. Todd sent over the names of streets that encompassed a ten-block perimeter around Bixler Park. If the two people with the wagon were spotted on camera, we could backtrack their route and find out where they came from. Since it was the only lead we had involving a middle-of-the-night sighting, especially with a potentially suspicious wagon involved, we had to follow up on it and see where the trail led. Besides, Lutz was on the warpath to find the killer or killers before they struck again.

We gathered at the park entrance, and I went over the route with the detectives.

"All you need to do is look for cameras. If you see one,

71

write down the address and continue on. We'll go back to each location when we're finished canvassing the neighborhood and see what we have. Don't bother chatting it up with the home or store owners who have cameras. There's time for that later when we're done. Everyone have paper and a pen?" Sometimes the most obvious assumptions were what stalled our investigations.

With everything we needed in our pockets, we headed in different directions. We would reconvene at the cars at four o'clock and compare notes. I yelled out before turning the corner. "Call me if something important comes up."

I took off going south and would continue that way on South Kimbark Avenue, just like the others were doing in their own directions. Looking over my shoulder, I saw Frank follow the path through the greenspace to South Kenwood Avenue, where he would head north. Henry turned onto East Fifty-Sixth Street and went west, and Shawn turned on East Fifty-Seventh Street and headed east. With an hour and a half to locate as many sidewalk and street-facing cameras as possible, we needed to come up with something. We had a commander to report to later.

Starting out I was hopeful, since there were plenty of apartment buildings in the immediate area to check out. I planned to cover a four-block grid east to west and then from the south back north on a street parallel to the park. I noticed cameras along several apartment buildings, wrote down the addresses, and continued on. If the rest of the team had similar results, we'd need extra help from our officers to view all of the camera footage.

As I walked, I noticed dozens of sidewalks and alleys that zigged one way and zagged another. If the two individuals with the wagon were trying to stay hidden until they reached the park, my chances of catching them on camera might have just diminished substantially. By the time I got to our cruisers, I had spotted fourteen cameras on numerous buildings throughout the grid, but none of the alleys that I'd seen had cameras at all. Pushing back my sleeve, I checked the time—3:56. I saw Henry first then Frank. Shawn took up the rear and returned to our group a few minutes after four. We placed the slips on the trunk of our cruiser and counted our results. Between the four of us, we had written down the addresses of fifty-three cameras. With that many, there had to be a camera somewhere that caught the people walking by. And if they were also seen in the vicinity of Washington Park, we would have them dead to rights.

Chapter 15

Janet carried two cups of tea to the table and placed one in front of Gail. They had just gotten up after napping from noon until four, since waking up in the middle of the night to conduct business often took its toll.

"Did you sleep well, honey?"

Gail shrugged. "I guess so. I think I was out by the time my head hit the pillow."

"Good. Then it's time to choose another man."

"Already?"

Janet opened the laptop and placed it in front of them. "You know it takes time to pick a man, get acquainted through flirtatious emails, and then finally set up a date. Besides that, I do have a say in your selection. He has to resemble your father, and many of those men don't want to date somebody their daughter's age."

"Then maybe you shoul—"

Janet lifted her palm to Gail's face. "Don't even say it. You know I can't go out in public, and it's cruel to even imply that as an option."

"Sorry. I didn't mean it."

Janet patted her daughter's hand. "I know, but you should consider yourself lucky. You can go out day or night since you have nothing to hide." She typed www.singlechicagoprofessionals.com into the search bar then slid the laptop over to Gail. "You're so beautiful, honey, any man, no matter what his age, should feel proud to have you on his arm."

Gail forced a smile and opened her online profile. "I know it's a necessary evil, but it doesn't mean I have to like being with those old geezers."

"I'd do it myself if I could." Janet leaned in and tapped on the message alerts. "Look, you have four new communication requests. They have to have salt-and-pepper hair."

"Yeah, I know what guidelines to use, Mom."

The parameters she set up stated that every man had to live within twenty miles of downtown Chicago, he needed to be under sixty-five, and he had to be single. Nothing else mattered. Janet and Gail's goal wasn't about being gold diggers. It was about being gravediggers.

Chapter 16

A meeting was set up for five o'clock at our district. Word from Lutz was that Patrol had found building-mounted cameras, and although they weren't within Washington Park itself, several of them faced the roads that led into it. A camera was located on an apartment building at Sixtieth and St. Lawrence Street and another at the intersections of Best Drive, Sixtieth Street, and South Dr. Martin Luther King Jr. Drive. Every vehicle that entered the park would be caught on surveillance and also written down on the list our officers compiled.

According to Don, the victim was dumped after midnight but before six o'clock in the morning. Those parameters gave lividity time to settle in and rigor, too, which had already begun. We would start by viewing the vehicles that had entered the park at the midnight mark.

Lutz wanted all of us—including every district officer and patrol unit that had worked the Washington Park scene—to join in. We had to compare notes.

Men in both suit jackets and uniforms filled the conference room. Lutz, along with Commander Abrams from Patrol, sat side by side at the head of the table, and officers lined the wall.

Lutz slipped on his glasses and coughed into his fist, his way of calling the meeting to order. A hush fell over the room.

"Sounds like we may have leads to follow. One of the callers to the tip line mentioned seeing two hooded figures walking toward Bixler Park with a wagon in tow at four thirty yesterday morning. It's obviously a long shot since we don't have an ID as to whether they're male or female, old or young, nor do we have a vehicle. *But* in order for the man found in Washington Park to get to the location where he was discovered, there would have to be a way to transport him there too. That path isn't wide enough for a typical vehicle to drive all the way to the dump site, and we didn't see tire tracks in the dirt or grass. That leads me to believe the second John Doe could have been taken back there in a wagon. I'm confident the two-person theory is correct." He checked all of our expressions then continued. "I'll admit, one very strong man could probably drag the vic back into the woods, but it was a good twelve hundred feet from the point where a car can't go any farther to the place where he was found. A tough job at best, and Forensics didn't see any drag marks." Lutz turned the meeting over to Commander Mark Abrams, who nodded a thank-you and began.

"My patrol units discovered several cameras, spoke with the superintendents of the buildings, and asked that the footage be sent to the Second District Violent Crimes Unit. What I will say is I have patrol officers who are willing to put in OT and help review the footage." He looked directly at me. "Jesse, I've heard you and your team have located over fifty cameras in a ten-block grid around Bixler Park."

"That's correct, sir."

"And it's a time-consuming project to review every camera for a glimpse of two people and a wagon."

I had to agree.

He went on. "Our officers can start with the Washington Park footage and document every vehicle that entered after midnight. Hopefully, you'll catch the people with the wagon in the Bixler Park area and be able to track them to a home or vehicle, but if it's a vehicle, we could possibly have a match to ones that entered Washington Park. We have to start somewhere."

Lutz took over. "Especially when those other two leads that seemed promising fell through. Both men were alive and well."

Kip Murray asked for permission to speak, and Lutz nodded.

"We still have tip-line calls coming in on the first John Doe. What are we going to do about the second one?"

"Good question, Kip, and I think the commander can answer that for you." Lutz gave Abrams the floor again.

"My units will start patrolling parks around the clock. That's a huge endeavor, so we'll have to start with the parks in the Second District since the two that were hit are within your borders. We'll see what happens and whether the killer catches on or not. If they do, they may move farther out. For now, let's take it one step at a time and see what we find on surveillance."

Next, Lutz addressed all of his officers and detectives. "Go over what you have with the night crew. They can get started and hopefully make a dent in it."

The meeting adjourned, and most of us headed to the bull pen. Our night shift detectives and officers would start trickling in any minute. As I compiled notes to go over with them, my desk phone rang.

Pinching the receiver between my ear and shoulder, I answered. "McCord speaking."

"Jesse, it's Mike."

"Yep, buddy, what's up?" I couldn't remember why Mike would be updating me on anything unless it pertained to the victim found in Washington Park that morning.

"You aren't going to believe this."

I was dead tired but chuckled, anyway. "Yeah, try me."

"Remember that blood smear I told you I found on the bottom slat of the bench?"

I remembered now. "Yep, sure do. Did it belong to the vic?"

He huffed. "Not even close. It was from a female."

"Son of a bitch," I yelled out, "that changes everything!" I slammed the phone down on the base and raced to Lutz's office. He wasn't there, and that was likely the reason Mike had called me instead. I spun on my heels and headed to the conference room. Inside, Lutz and Abrams sat alone while reviewing the meeting notes.

"Boss!"

They both jerked their heads in my direction.

Lutz furrowed his brows, and a look of concern spread

across his face. "Jesse, what's wrong?"

"Mike just called. The blood smear they found on the bench from Bixler Park belongs to a woman, not John Doe."

"Holy hell!" Lutz said. "We need to come up with a different mind-set and damn fast. We have no idea who we're looking for." He leapt from the table and headed toward the door. Abrams was right on his heels. "We have to put together some type of profile." He jerked up his sleeve and checked the time. "Another meeting in the bull pen as soon as everyone from the night shift is here. Until then, the first shifters stay put."

Chapter 17

After reviewing each profile and reading the messages they sent, Janet was enthusiastic about a man named Cliff Howard, and at sixty-one, he was the perfect choice for Gail. He boasted about his financial status, but that was of no concern to them. He wouldn't need money much longer. Reading between the lines, they learned that Cliff exhibited an air of superiority. He addressed Gail as "little lady" and made it perfectly clear that he could spoil her as long as she complied with his wishes. They both knew what that meant.

"What a piece of shit. He's just right." Janet turned the notebook's page to a clean sheet. "We have to draw him in quickly since men like Cliff have no right to be walking this earth." She pointed at the half dozen pictures he'd posted of himself on the website. He stood next to a new sports car and a Jeep in one, was beach lounging with a cocktail in hand in another, and vacation shots were in the rest. "He's definitely full of himself and views women as nothing more than arm candy without brains, but the deciding factor in choosing him over the other fools is his hair."

Gail agreed as she lifted the pen to write her response

before posting it. "I know. It's just like Dad's."

Janet stood and paced—it helped her think. "Okay, tell him you find him very attractive and love the photos he posted. Say how older men are more handsome and wiser, that you enjoy beach vacations, and add that the fact that he's willing to spoil you is a bonus. Stroke his ego for the short time he has left to live. By this time tomorrow, not only will he be begging, but he'll literally be dying to meet you."

Gail jotted down everything Janet had said then typed a response to Cliff Howard's message, making sure to sign it as Lynn. Now all they had to do was wait. Men like him needed that constant attention and approval from beautiful women. It made them feel young, vibrant, and desirable—none of which Janet and Gail cared about. Putting an end to his life was all that mattered.

After reviewing what she had written and with her index finger hovering over the send button, Gail gave Janet a questioning look. "All good?"

"All good, and now we wait for his ego to hit your message box."

Chapter 18

Ten detectives, seven officers, and two commanders took seats in our bull pen wherever they could find a spot.

Lutz led the meeting for the second time that evening. Abrams sat in to gather information for the patrol units that had offered to lend a hand by putting in extra hours.

"Okay, everyone," Lutz said, "in the last few minutes, it has come to our attention that the blood smears Forensics tested from the Bixler Park bench happen to belong to a female." He raised his hands when the muttering began. "Let me finish, and then we'll open the room to discussion and suggestions. It's already been confirmed that the blood is fresh and hasn't been on that bench any longer than the victim's blood. So, we have several scenarios if, and only if, the people with the wagon are our suspects." He scratched the top of his balding head and looked from left to right. "Who's taking notes?"

A half dozen people scrambled to pull pens and paper from their desk drawers.

"That's better. Okay, here's how it is. We've either got two women or a man and a woman involved in these murders. I'm leaning toward it being a male-and-female team. The man would have the brute strength to heave dead weight around, and the woman could be the one organizing the abductions and murders. The wagon would come in handy if the man wasn't particularly strong enough to carry that dead weight long distances."

Abrams took his turn. "My patrol units will monitor the park systems twenty-four seven, and the recent murders are leading us toward thinking the killers are only active at night."

I piped in. "They're cloaked from head to toe in dark clothing according to the witness. Going under the cover of darkness with very little moonlight, committing the crimes in remote parks, and doing it when most people are fast asleep is the perfect way to go unseen and literally get away with murder."

"Agreed," Lutz said. He twisted the cap off one of the five water bottles that always sat as extras on my desk. "So now, who specifically is their target, and why do they want to kill them?" He stood, rolled his neck, then cracked it. "Take a five-minute break, and when we resume this discussion, we're going to put together a profile. It's time to alert the public that the deceased man in Bixler Park was actually murdered, and the second man found in Washington Park met with foul play too. The citizens of Chicago need to know that it might be the same killer in both cases."

"I'll have units stationed at all the parks in the Second District, and they'll cover them from ten p.m. to six a.m. every day until the perp is caught," Abrams said.

Lutz shook Abrams's hand. "Okay, take that break, guys, and then we're putting together a profile when everyone is back in their seats. I need something to give the press in the morning."

I was joined by Henry, Frank, Kip, Tony, and Shawn at the coffee machine.

"Who would have thought a woman could be involved?" Kip quietly whistled. "Aren't women supposed to be obedient, nurturing, and motherly?"

I chuckled. "Maybe in the eighteenth century. Say that too many times in front of the wrong woman and you might find yourself on a park bench minus ten fingertips and a bunch of teeth too."

He grimaced while double-checking his surroundings. "Good thing there aren't any ladies present."

Frank's eyes widened. "I just thought of something."

I gave him my attention. "Yeah? We can use some enlightenment."

"It's something I'll have to run by Don to see if it's even possible, but what if—likely under a microscope—he could tell if the cuts were the same between victim one and two? Whatever was used to remove the fingertips cut through joints and possibly bone. There could be some kind of similarity, almost like striation marks, if the same tool was used in both homicides."

"Great idea, partner. Bring it up when we get back to the bull pen." I rubbed my forehead as I thought. "I'm trying to remember the names of the man-and-woman team that crisscrossed the country about ten years back and killed people just for fun."

"Look online," Henry said. "I bet you'll find it."

I glanced at the wall clock. "Let's head back and put our thinking caps on. We need to come up with a logical profile for the press."

Returning to our seats, Lutz suggested we brainstorm profile suggestions and reasons for the murders and go from there.

Frank began. "This isn't a profile idea, but it's a possible way to confirm both murders were done by the same perp."

"Sure," Lutz said. "I'm listening."

"If the same tool—whether it be a knife, snippers, shears, a hatchet, or whatever—was used to cut through the fingers of both vics, wouldn't there be similar markings on the edge of the bone that was cut?"

Lutz rubbed his chin. "Good question. I don't know if the finger bones are large enough to see a repetitive pattern, though, like a serrated knife or a hatchet with a nick in it. Give me a second." He picked up the receiver from the phone base on my desk. "Keep running ideas by each other while I see if Don is still here."

He gave us a nod that Don had answered while we continued talking among ourselves. After a few minutes of back-and-forth between them, Lutz hung up and rubbed his brow. "Okay, Don doesn't know if he'll see any similarities, but he's going to check it out. He'll let us know his findings in the morning. So ideas, opinions, suggestions?"

"I understand the male-female perp idea, but unless they're just cold-blooded killers who are choosing random older men simply because they can overpower them, what the hell would be the motive? The only thing I can think of other than joy killing would be if the female was fooling around, the man found out, and he made her help kill the guy she was messing with as a warning to her. That seems pretty complicated to me, though," I said.

Henry added his two cents. "What about the hate crime angle we talked about? That politician in California publicly announced his engagement to another guy and was killed shortly after that. Maybe the perps are on the rampage and working together to kill every gay man they can track down."

Lutz frowned. "I'm not sure. We can hit up a few gay bars with the facial photo of the first vic to see if anyone recognizes him, but it's taking away from actually tracking down the killers."

Kip suggested checking the database for people arrested for hate crimes. It could be a faster process.

"We'll look into that. What about the two-women theory?"

"That also could be a type of hate crime," Shawn said. "Scorned lover or abused wife, maybe even several ladies working together, because killing and transporting men is tough work for one woman."

"Right, and not a bad idea, but we can't give the press a bunch of theories to choose from. Why change MOs?"

"Mixing it up," I said. "Possibly to throw us off their track and make us think two different killers are committing the crimes."

"I'm almost certain the perps are the same," Lutz said. "Nobody was told about the fingertips being cut off, yet in both cases, they were. There's some kind of connection between the victims and the killers, and the perps don't want the murders to lead back to them." The commander let out a frustrated-sounding groan. "Guess we need to hold off with the profile until we have more." He turned to Abrams. "I need your guys to view those surveillance tapes around Washington Park right away. They should document every vehicle that passed those cameras and entered the park last night after midnight. Once we have that list is when we're going to need your help the most since we have fifty-some cameras around Bixler Park to go through."

"Whatever you need, Bob, and I know my guys are reviewing that footage as we speak."

Lutz rose from my guest chair. "Day shift guys, go home. You'll have plenty to keep you busy tomorrow, and I don't want anybody falling asleep while they're reviewing those fifty surveillance videos. For now, the night crew can contact the building managers and make sure the cameras are actively filming whatever it is they're pointing at and that none of them are taping over themselves."

Abrams rose too. "I'll have that list of vehicles ready for you first thing in the morning."

"Appreciate it, Mark." Lutz pointed at the door. "Go on, first shifters. Head home and get some rest."

Chapter 19

With Bandit's head nestled in my lap and my computer on the arm of the couch, I searched female murderers in the United States during the last thirty years. The most famous female serial killer was Aileen Wuornos, but that was likely because a movie was made about her crimes. There were a handful of female killers here and there, and the majority of them were women who snapped for one reason or another and killed their own children, yet the cold-blooded—the kill-for-the-sake-of-killing type—were a rare breed. My temples began to pound, and if I didn't let go of work issues, I would never get any rest that night.

After moving my pup's sleeping body to the side, I crossed the living room and opened the upper kitchen cabinet then shook four ibuprofen into my hand. I cracked open a can of beer and used it to gulp down the tablets then returned to the couch, where Bandit resumed his earlier position.

Needing a distraction, I began a search of dating websites. I'd been thinking about jumping into the pool of the unknown for months but had never pulled the trigger. Work always gave me a good reason to hold off, but work would be there until I retired, and I wasn't sure I would feel like entering the dating scene at seventy. I focused only on the first page since sites beyond that wouldn't be something I'd investigate, anyway. It seemed that the first few were the swipe-left-or-right sites popular with the teen to twenty-something crowd—far from my recently turned thirty-seven-year-old mind and body and something I had neither the time nor the energy for.

The fifth site down piqued my curiosity. It was a dating website for professional singles, and although no age ranges were listed, I felt a site like that would serve me better. I set up an account, and while it was free, charges kicked in when messages were exchanged. Still, I could set my search parameters and browse for free. I figured a half hour of seeing the type of people in the dating world was better than dwelling on work issues that I couldn't solve from home, anyway. Several women's profiles caught my eye, but being the skeptic I was, I wondered if they were pumped up with false bravado. I was sure many had fake jobs, fake body parts, and fake ages. I'd heard horror stories about dating sites from some of my college buddies. Still, reading how every woman loved dogs, was a great cook, and enjoyed walking hand in hand on the beach—a phrase that had gone stale years earlier—made me chuckle. I powered off my laptop, woke up the pup, and headed down the hallway as I looked forward to dropping my head on my pillow and falling asleep.

Chapter 20

Lutz called out to me through his half-opened door as I passed his office that next morning.

"Jesse, we have news."

His comment was music to my ears, and I popped my head in.

"Have a seat. I'm going to update everyone during roll call, anyway, but since you're here…"

I sat on his guest chair, folded my hands on his desk, and leaned forward. I was excited to hear what he would say.

"I've already spoken to Abrams this morning and have a list of vehicles that entered the park after midnight, and there weren't many."

"Good to hear, and I imagine the fact that the park is patrolled every few hours keeps the riffraff out."

"Exactly." He looked at his notes. "According to the surveillance cameras at the two entrances, his patrol officers caught nine vehicles that turned in. Some may have exited elsewhere, but the streets that enter the park off of Sixtieth are the closest to the peninsula where the body was dumped."

"Sure. Were they able to make out any plate numbers?"

"No, too far away, but they did identify most of the makes and colors."

"Nice. That should help out quite a bit, but most of the work still lies ahead of us."

"Reviewing footage on fifty or more cameras?"

I raised my brows. "It *is* a lot of legwork, but since the witness was dead set on it being around four thirty a.m., that should reduce the amount of time we're at each location. I'd suggest starting with the cameras nearest the park and then backtracking since we have no idea where they came from other than the man saying they turned left off East Fifty-Seventh Street and went north on South Dorchester. What we need to do is map out each camera location and see if a route emerges."

Lutz pushed back his chair, grabbed his coffee cup, and tipped his head toward the door. "Let's get roll call out of the way and put that map together. I either want to see the building those two individuals came out of or what kind of vehicle they were driving." He shook his head. "What I really want to know is why nobody has reported those men missing."

As we walked side by side, we discussed what we had up to that point. A breakthrough could very well be on the horizon.

Roll call was the same as always. Names were yelled out, and the corresponding officer or detective responded. The normal updates followed, but that day was different—we finally had something to work with.

After reading off the makes and colors of the nine vehicles

spotted in Washington Park, Lutz gave everyone an assignment. The cars needed to be plugged into our database to see how many of those particular vehicles were registered in Chicago and to whom. That job was handed off to the officers in our precinct. Henry, Shawn, and Kip were to head to the Bixler Park neighborhood and start going through footage that might show the two people walking or any of those nine cars driving by. Every task that day would be time consuming. I reminded Lutz that the detectives needed to visualize how the cameras along that ten-block radius lined up before they headed in that direction.

"Okay, everyone get busy and find out who owns those types of cars. Narrow it down to the most logical suspects and make sure you're going by color as well. That'll help lessen the number you're looking at." He jerked his head toward Henry, Kip, Tony, and Shawn. "You four join us in the conference room in five."

I arrived before the rest of the team and hooked my finger through the ring at the bottom of the roller map of our district. I pulled it down and, in the cabinet to my right, found a plastic box filled with red and yellow pushpins. With the box of pins and the sheet of camera locations in the ten-block radius, I used the red pushpins and began mapping out each spot where a camera was located. With the yellow pins, I marked the streets where our witness briefly saw the two people with the wagon.

Minutes later, the rest of the group arrived and funneled into the conference room. Lutz, with a handful of papers, took up the rear. I stopped what I was doing and found an empty seat so the commander could lead the meeting.

As he made his way to the head of the table, Lutz passed out the sheets of paper. "Okay, guys, what you have in front of you are the makes, models—to the best of our knowledge—and color of the vehicles that entered Washington Park after midnight. There aren't a lot, so if any are seen on the footage from the Bixler Park area, it better raise a bright-red flag with you." He turned to me and tipped his chin. That was my cue to go ahead with what I was doing. I rose and went back to the map.

"I've started marking every location where a camera faces the street or sidewalk in that ten-block area we searched." I pointed. "Those are the red pins. The yellow ones mark where our witness saw the people with the wagon."

Kip spoke up. "So they were walking east on Fifty-Seventh Street, turned north near the east edge of the park, and then went north on South Dorchester?"

"That's right, but our witness continued east on East Fifty-Seventh toward his home. He only saw them for a few seconds before they were out of eyeshot. We don't know where they entered Fifty-Seventh Street from, so I'd suggest checking cameras in that area first and then backtracking their route if they're seen on the footage. It'll be the fastest way to locate them since they had to have passed a camera along East Fifty-Seventh somewhere." I turned to the map and tapped three spots. "These cameras should be checked first, and then follow a logical route in that general area before spreading out." I finished adding all the pins to the map, took a picture of it, and sent the image to Kip, Henry, and Shawn's phones. "There, now you have all the cameras mapped out. Look for the two people, or one of those cars on your list, and then work in reverse."

"Any questions?" Lutz asked.

"Nope." Henry looked at his teammates. "I think we're ready to roll."

We exited the conference room and headed to the bull pen, where Frank and I would pitch in with the database search for those nine vehicles.

Chapter 21

During our search, we had eliminated one car simply because it was a small sports car. It wasn't physically possible to fit two people, one dead man, and a wagon in that vehicle. Now we were down to eight. I studied the list while the others worked the database. Any one of the remaining cars would do. There were two SUVs, three midsize sedans, one large twenty-year-old Buick, one van, and a pickup. I tapped my pen against the desktop as I thought about the vehicle that would be the easiest to get a body in and out of. I wrote down the van as my first choice, followed by the two SUVs and then the pickup, although a truck would be risky—no place to actually hide the body.

"Got anything on the van yet?"

"There are two hundred late-model light-blue Toyota vans in the city," Frank said. "Brian in Tech thinks it's a Sienna." He raised a brow at me. "Is the van calling out to you?"

"Sort of. Easy in, easy out, and plenty of room. Keep in mind, if those individuals are the same ones who are responsible for the murders in California and North Carolina, then they needed to move some of their belongings with them whenever they traveled to a new location." I squeezed my head and groaned.

"What?"

"Damn it! If they're the same people from those other crimes, they wouldn't have Illinois plates on the vehicle. I'm afraid we may be spinning our wheels."

"So now what?"

I picked up the receiver, dialed Lutz, and pressed Speakerphone. "Hey, Boss. Did you ever get the copies of the police reports from California and North Carolina?"

"I did, but nothing stood out except for the fact that the reports were damn near identical to our own."

"Then that in itself stands out. Those crimes had to have been committed by the same killer, but we need to have more. Eyewitness accounts, a car speeding away, somebody trolling the neighborhood, that sort of thing."

"Sounds like something is percolating in your mind."

I wrote notes to myself while I thought. "I realized we're looking in the Illinois database for a car that may be registered in California or North Carolina or none of those states if the killer is traveling from one to another. What's funding them if they're the same perps?"

"Good question, McCord. First, we have to know beyond a shadow of a doubt that the murders are at the hand of the same person. I need to contact the coroners in Sacramento and Charlotte to see if they did tox and urinalysis reports on the victims. I'll let you know. Meanwhile, get in touch with Chuck Donahue and see if he can shed some light."

"Roger that." I hung up and told our officers to check in with the detectives to see if they needed any help. I pulled open my center desk drawer and took out the card that Chuck Donahue had written his phone number on and dialed it. Just the thought of interrupting a man's honeymoon was cringeworthy, but he was a cop, and I was sure he understood. For the greater good, he'd probably made plenty of calls in his life that were unavoidable too. I listened to ringing on Chuck's end as I pulled paper and a pen out of my desk drawer. My phone was pinned between my ear and shoulder, which usually resulted in a neck cramp. I dreamed of having an earbud that was compatible with my desk phone since using Speakerphone wasn't always the best alternative. As I was about to hang up, I heard a raspy *hello* on the other end. Now I was really cringing.

"Chuck Donahue?"

"Yep, who's this?"

"It's Detective McCord from yesterday."

"Oh, sure, give me a sec."

I heard silence for thirty seconds or so before he returned to the phone.

"Okay, just needed a drink of water. I was out for a run. What can I do for you?"

I quietly sighed in relief. "Is there any chance of you coming down to our precinct? We need more input on those similar murders that happened in Charlotte. Anything you can tell us would be appreciated. Since your police reports were almost identical to our own, we didn't get that sudden epiphany that we were hoping for after reading them. I guess what I'm asking for is behind-the-scenes chatter, anything along the lines of witness accounts, a vehicle that was noticed, or tip-line statements—that sort of thing. Commander Lutz is reaching out for the autopsy report too."

"Yeah, sure. I came to Homicide on the tail end of that case and then the perp just up and disappeared, but I'm sure I can add something that'll shed some light. Give me an hour to shower and change, and then I'll be there. Stacey has a spa afternoon scheduled, anyway."

"Great, and thanks. We're the Second District precinct on Wentworth and Fifty-First. See you soon." I ended the call and dialed Lutz's phone. "Hey, Boss."

"What's the word? Did you get ahold of Donahue?"

"I did, and he's stopping by in about an hour when his wife leaves for a spa treatment."

Lutz sounded relieved. "Good. Hopefully, he'll have something we can use."

I hung up and called Debra Blake, our desk sergeant at the front counter, where all the incoming action took place. "Hey, Deb, can you lead a detective named Chuck Donahue back here when he shows up? It'll be in about forty-five minutes. Yep, appreciate it." One last call to the crime lab would give me a good forty-five minutes of paperwork to review before Chuck arrived. I wanted to see if anything found at our first murder scene was similar to anything from the second. At least it would make me feel proactive.

"Is anyone still working the call lines?" I asked.

Tony said he was, although the calls had diminished significantly. Without a chance in hell of airing victim number two's face, we knew the only tips that would be relevant had to come from John Doe number one. I jotted notes to myself as I waited for the crime lab reports to hit my in-box. We needed to know how the killers were funding their travels and where they were staying if they were the same people from California and North Carolina. We also needed to know why nobody was searching for our vics. They had to have family somewhere who noticed their absence, didn't they? A new idea popped up in my mind, and I called out to Frank.

"Hey, partner. Do me a favor and see where the nearest hotels, motels, or flop houses are in the Bixler Park area, especially along East Fifty-Seventh Street west of South Dorchester."

"Yep, on it."

An alert on my computer indicated a new email had come in. I clicked on the first message, downloaded the attachments, and hit Print. I liked having hard copies since they would go in the case file, anyway.

I read and reread the reports but didn't find the smoking gun I had hoped for, and there was no mention of anything found that didn't belong in nature—other than a dead body tucked away under last winter's fallen leaves and tree limbs. I huffed my disappointment and cracked my stiff neck. Dialing up Don Lawry, I glanced at the time. If Chuck was prompt, he would be arriving any minute.

"Hey, Don, it's Jesse. Did you send for a tox and urinalysis screening on vic number two?"

"I did, and the results should be available tomorrow. Of

course, the blunt force trauma to the man's head would have definitely killed him, anyway."

"Yep, that's a fact, but it would be interesting to know if drain cleaner shows up in his report too. Okay, thanks." I clicked off and added that to my growing list of notes.

Chapter 22

Frank walked to my desk. "Here are the hotels you wanted. Most are over two hundred bucks a night except one two-star unit on East Pershing and South Michigan."

I scratched my cheek as I thought. "Nah, that won't work. I doubt if anyone, even if it *is* four thirty in the morning, would be stupid enough to drag a dead body in a wagon for two and a half miles to Bixler Park. The killers live somewhere in the area, maybe in a weekly or monthly rental since that would be more affordable, but I'll give it more thought."

My phone rang seconds later, and before I picked it up, I told Frank to check with Henry and the guys on their progress. I added one more note to my sheet of paper before the thought evaporated from my mind. I needed to find jobs—possibly targeting females—that gave employees the opportunity to travel and have their rent covered as part of the benefits.

"McCord here." I snugged the receiver against my ear.

"Jesse, Detective Donahue just arrived. I'm bringing him back."

I thanked Deb and hung up. I had a list of questions for

Chuck to see if I could jog his memory. If that didn't help, maybe he had a way to find out more for us than what was on the police reports.

Deb walked into the bull pen with Chuck at her side. I thanked her, and she left. With my hand outstretched, I shook his, and Frank followed suit.

"Let's have a seat back there and talk." I tipped my head toward the six-person table and chairs that sat next to our coffee station.

Chuck gave each of us a glance. "Making any progress?"

"Hell yeah," Frank said. "One step forward and two steps back." He sighed. "At least there aren't any family members breathing down our throats."

A surprised expression crossed Chuck's face. "Really? That's either a deliberate act on the perp's part or a very unusual coincidence. Nobody ever came forward in the two murders we investigated either. The cases eventually lost momentum and press interest, so to speak, even though it's only been a few months."

I opened the folder with my notes. "So the California murders happened in February, your murders happened in May, and now they're happening here in September."

"Every three months or so," Frank said, "but the number of murders differed between California and North Carolina."

"How many were in California?" Chuck asked. "Actually, I didn't know about the California connection, maybe because I came in when the case had already started to stagnate."

"Three, and one was a well-known politician. He openly

announced his engagement to another man, and within days, he was murdered."

"Hate crimes, then?"

I shook my head. "Who the hell knows. The other two were never identified, so we don't know their background."

Chuck's forehead wrinkled. "Same in Charlotte."

I tapped my pen against my open hand. "Did your PD ever put together a profile?"

"Not the best one, but at least it's something."

"Let's hear it," Frank said.

I offered a round of coffee before Chuck began, and I thought it best to see if Lutz wanted to sit in on our conversation. I poured the coffee while Frank called our boss, and Lutz said he was on his way.

Several minutes later, our commander entered the bull pen. A handshake of appreciation was all that was needed, then Lutz took a seat across from Donahue. "Okay, where are we?"

"I was about to describe the vague profile the Charlotte PD put together on the killer. Honestly, by the time I transferred to Homicide and was brought up to speed on the case, they still didn't have much to work with."

Frank snickered. "That sounds familiar."

Chuck blew over his coffee, took a sip, and began. "We always thought it was two individuals committing the crimes simply because of the physicality of it. The first victim was found along the shore of a remote lake that was surrounded by private property. He would have never been found if it wasn't for the owner of the land deciding to spend a week there fishing, and he saw the body tangled in the weeds from his jon boat. Our coroner said the body had been partially submerged for weeks."

"Jesus," Lutz said. "And you're thinking there was no way one person could have dumped him back there alone?"

"Yep, that was the conclusion the detectives came to since it would have been quite a hike back to the water."

"What if that person had a wagon?"

Chuck rubbed his chin. "That could change the dynamic considerably, although the terrain wasn't conducive to pulling a wagon back to the water. I guess a wheelbarrow could have worked, but the dead man was a hundred seventy-seven pounds on the autopsy table. That was several weeks after his death, so his live weight had to be ten to fifteen pounds heavier. It seems like a lot for one person to handle unless the killer was a very strong and determined man. We figured him, or them, to be risk takers to a degree because of the crimes in general but also elusive because they wanted to hide the bodies where they wouldn't be found."

I glanced at my colleagues then back at Chuck. "Our forensic team determined that a blood smear found at the first scene belonged to a woman."

Donahue whistled as if surprised. "Wow, that's a new one. Maybe it's a man and woman committing the crimes and they're taking turns, like in your case. One body is prominently displayed because one killer likes taking risks, and the other is hidden because that killer likes to remain safe, like in your second case and ours as well. They're a psychotic couple that travels the country and kills older guys who don't seem to have family in the area. The victims could be widowers or new to the neighborhood, but the killers are definitely seeking a certain type of man. As long as they remain careful, they can get away with their crimes if they're moving from one location to another every three months or so."

That information still stuck in my craw. There was a reason the killers moved at regular intervals, other than just being cautious. My focus returned to Lutz when he asked the next question.

"How about witness statements, forensic evidence, a car seen in the area, that sort of thing?"

Chuck swatted the air. "Nah. Two weeks later, people aren't going to remember the night of the dump. We don't even know for sure when the victim was left there, only the approximate length of time he'd been dead and in the elements. There wasn't any forensic evidence to gather either, especially since it was an outdoor dump."

"And you couldn't put a photo of him on the news. Was a description aired?"

Donahue turned to me. "Yeah, but it wasn't helpful. The weather and critters did a number on the poor guy. The only thing I can tell you for sure is that the dismemberment and crushed teeth were the same as in your cases."

Lutz nodded. "That pretty much sums it up. Because the MO is the same, the killer continues to do what works for them."

Frustrated, I sighed. "We don't have answers to many of our concerns and possibly never will. It seems that unless the killer is caught in the act of moving the victim to the dump site, we'll never know where a body will show up next."

Chuck echoed my sentiment. "The sad thing is, there could be more victims out there that haven't been found."

I stared down at my list of concerns. "So we don't know the means of transportation the killer or killers use to get from one state to another. We don't know where they stay while in the area, and we don't know how they're supporting themselves while traveling."

"Whoa… hold up a minute." Chuck rubbed his forehead. "My sister-in-law is a traveling nurse. Stacey always teases her about having it made in the shade. She gets free rent and a stipend for food and a rental vehicle while she's in the area she's assigned to."

Lutz's eyes lit up. "How long is her normal gig?"

"Not sure, but Stacey would know. I believe they can choose anywhere from a month to a year depending on what's available in the area they're looking at."

I was chomping at the bit to check that out as soon as our meeting was over. The female in the two-person killing team could have a similar job, and the husband, boyfriend, or brother could be nothing more than the muscle needed to complete the act. If she worked during the day, that could be another reason the dumps happened at night. It was definitely a possibility.

We thanked Chuck for his input, and he left. I felt guilty enough the way it was for having him help in our investigation during his honeymoon.

"What do you think, Boss? Should we call the guys back

in or just tell them to focus their efforts on watching for the couple with the wagon?"

"They should keep their eyes peeled for the people," Lutz said. "The car isn't going to matter after all, and it's doubtful that it's even a vehicle registered in Illinois—"

I interrupted with a sudden epiphany. "What if it is a rental and the person using it is a traveling nurse or has a similar job with rental-car benefits? The state the vehicle plates are registered in doesn't matter. What does matter is who rented it and for how long. The guys can keep looking for an SUV or van that matches the ones that drove into Washington Park. We'll start calling car-rental agencies to see if anyone rented one of those vehicles for an extended period of time. We're looking for a light-blue Toyota van, possibly a Sienna, and a tan Subaru and a red Mazda SUV, both unidentified models, but we'll ask what each agency offers in that make as rentals. If we get a hit, we'll take it from there."

Lutz rose from the table and slapped his hands together. "Then let's get after it. I'll call Henry and go over everything with him while the rest of you hit up car rental agencies in Chicago. Start with the airport first. If the killers flew here, they'd likely get the car at O'Hare. Check Midway after that and then find agencies in the Hyde Park area near our crime scenes."

Chapter 23

We had our work cut out for us, but my enthusiasm and hope were restored. I had something to work with, and if the guys could find one of those three vehicles passing by any of the cameras surrounding Bixler Park, we could narrow down what and hopefully who we were looking for.

Frank, Tony, and I jumped on the rental-car-agency angle. A dozen facilities were within the airport itself and another five or six in the surrounding area. We would introduce ourselves as the Chicago PD to get our foot in the door faster, then we'd ask about SUV or van rentals lasting more than a month. We'd whittle down the possibilities one agency at a time.

"How far should we have them go back?" Frank asked.

"Hmm, that's a good question. I doubt if they've been here very long if the murders just began."

Tony huffed his opinion. "*If* is the unknown word. We have no idea *if* the killings just started, or *if* there are more bodies out there that we haven't found yet."

"True enough," I said. "Let's ask them to go back the full three months to be on the safe side. Between the three of us, and since the search should only consist of a few keystrokes on their end, we should be able to knock out the airport agencies in less than an hour."

I glanced at my computer's clock. It was a quarter after three, and I hoped to have a few leads before our shift was done.

We dug in and divided up the agencies within the airport. We would compare notes to see if anything struck a chord before continuing on with Midway. Between the four agencies I'd called, I had only one possibility, and that didn't even seem likely. A couple had rented a Subaru Outback for three weeks and asked for two child seats to be included. The best lead after that involved a single woman wanting a ten-day rental of a RAV4, which wasn't on our list. I hung up and felt my shoulders automatically slump.

"You two get anything?" I asked after realizing fifty minutes had passed.

Neither of the guys were told of any rentals extending past two weeks.

"Maybe they're playing it safe and changing up the cars," Frank said.

I didn't think so. This wasn't their first time killing, and I was sure by now, they had a good routine working for them.

"Let's move on to Midway. Who knows? It's a hell of a lot closer to this neighborhood than O'Hare is, and if a company is footing the bill, anyway, then it wouldn't matter if flying into Midway costs more. Convenience is what counts."

We started over with the same parameters we'd used for the calls to the rental agencies at O'Hare. With Midway having only six rental car counters within the airport, we'd knock them out in no time.

Less than ten minutes into our calls, Tony began waving his hand wildly above his head and caught our attention. I ended the call to the last company that didn't have anything for me, and hung up. I jumped from my chair, crossed the bull pen, and read over his shoulder as he wrote something down. Frank stood at his left side.

"Uh-huh, the Sienna was reserved by a Cornerstone Medical Staffing Service out of Kansas City, Missouri. The person who provided their driver's license at the time of pickup was a Janet St. James. Her address is listed as what? A post office box out of Grants Pass, Oregon?" Tony looked at us and shook his head. "Okay, slowly, please, since I'm writing this down. What? Yes, that would be very helpful." Tony gave us a thumbs-up and rattled off his email address. "I'll stay on the line until it hits my in-box." He waited only a few seconds, and a new email popped up. Clicking it and giving us both a grin, Tony maximized the screen. Staring us in the face was the contract between the rental agency and Cornerstone Medical Staffing Service. "Yes, I have it, and thank you very much." He hung up and slapped the desk. "This has to be it. A light-blue Sienna was rented two weeks ago, and it isn't scheduled to be returned until the end of November."

"Print that out," I said. "I don't want to read the details over your shoulder."

"Sure thing." Tony hit Print, and at the back wall, the printer whirred to life.

After grabbing one of the five copies he made, I filled my cup with two-hour-old coffee and returned to my desk. I needed to absorb every word on that contract to see what I could get from it. I called out to Tony. "Give Lutz a buzz, tell him what you found out, and see if he wants to sit in on our powwow."

Within minutes, Lutz charged through the door with a bag of chips still clutched in his hand. "Let's see that contract." He took a seat on my guest chair and read the document as I noted the important parts of the copy I was holding. I wrote down names and locations as I went through it. Grants Pass, Oregon, post office box. Janet St. James, possibly from Oregon. Cornerstone Medical Staffing Service. Rented Sienna fourteen days prior and had it until the end of November.

Lutz finished reading before me and called out to Frank. "Pull up that name in the DMV database and see what you get."

Frank jiggled his computer's mouse and typed the DMV's web address into the search bar. Once in, he typed Janet St. James and waited for the results to populate.

"Shit, in a nationwide search, there's forty-two women named Janet St. James."

"Narrow it down to Oregon."

Frank did and came up with the same post office box number in Grants Pass. "This is the woman, but the picture is so dark you can barely see her features. I've never seen such a poor-quality driver's license in my life, and how do you get a post office box number to show as an actual address?"

Lutz grumbled that there were ways to get around the

system. Gathered at Frank's desk, we crowded in and gave the driver's license photo a closer inspection. I frowned with uncertainty.

"Can that really be who we're looking for?" I pulled my phone off my desk and calculated her age. "She's fifty-seven. Do staffing agencies actually have revolving nurses that old?" I wasn't really expecting an answer.

Lutz pointed at Frank. "Call them and find out. My gut says that license is phony."

After pulling up the name of the staffing service, Frank found the one with their headquarters based in Kansas City. "This must be it." He dialed the number and pressed the button for Speakerphone.

The usual gatekeeper answered, and like most, she tried not to connect us to a person of importance until Frank said it was the Chicago police calling and he needed to speak to the person in charge of temporary staffing immediately. That didn't give the gatekeeper much to work with as a redirect.

"That would be Gary Alcott, but—"

"Ma'am, may I have your full name, please? This is a matter of life and death, and I want to know who the person is that's holding up an official police matter."

Her aggravation clearly came through the phone line. "One moment while I connect you."

Frank winked, stood up, and turned over his phone and chair to Lutz. The commander would take charge from there.

Seconds later, Mr. Alcott answered and asked why the Chicago police needed to speak to their company in Kansas City. Lutz explained that a rental car had been reserved for a three-month stint in Chicago by a client of theirs who traveled as a temp, and that person was a fifty-seven-year-old woman named Janet St. James.

"That's highly unlikely since our normal age for traveling nurses is from their mid-twenties to late thirties. We rarely have a travel request from anyone in their forties, let alone fifties. There must be a mistake."

"How about checking that name in your database, anyway."

"I can assure you, sir—"

"It's Commander Robert Lutz, and I'm in charge of the Second District Violent Crimes Division."

"We have over seventy temporary people staffed in Chicago at this moment, Commander."

"We're only looking for one—Janet St. James."

He sighed. "Give me a minute while I check our Chicago list."

We listened to hold music while he looked up her name. Mr. Alcott was back on the line seconds later.

"I'm sorry, Commander Lutz, but nobody by that name comes up in our database."

"Anyone at all with the same last name?"

"No, sorry. Is that it, then?"

"Not yet. I'd like for you to email me a list of the people in Chicago who are staffed by your company, where they're staying, and what kind of vehicle was reserved for them."

We heard a huff through the phone line. Lutz was wearing on his nerves.

"I believe you'll need a warrant for that information."

"Not a problem. While I'm waiting for that warrant, I'll make sure our local news airs your refusal to help with the investigation of two murders in Chicago that were likely committed by some of your temporary service providers. I guess that means you don't vet the people you send all around the country. Is that correct?"

"Fine. What is your email address, Commander Lutz?"

Chapter 24

Gail had just gotten home from work and entered the apartment's small kitchen, where Janet sat at the table. Hooking her purse over the chairback, she took a seat and leaned in next to her mother, who was preoccupied with the computer. "I'm beat. What are you so fascinated with?"

"Cliff messaged you and wants to meet tonight, so you need to perk up." Janet rose from the table. "I made coffee."

Gail groaned. "When does he want to get together?"

"At seven o'clock for drinks."

Janet filled two cups and handed one to Gail. "You still have a few hours to liven up and take a shower. You choose the place but make sure it's close by. You'll cozy up to him and flirt over a few drinks because that's what he wants, anyway, then invite him back here afterward. I'll take care of everything once you get him through the door."

"What if he says no?"

Janet laughed. "He wouldn't have contacted you if he wasn't interested. He expects you to fawn over him because he thinks he's a big shot. You know how to play the game and draw men in, so play it." She smiled lovingly at her

116

daughter. "Who would say no to you? Have you looked in the mirror lately?"

Gail blushed. "His message said I was hot."

"And you are, so let's look online for a place to meet, and then you can message him back."

Not knowing the area or any of the local hot spots, they chose a bar close to their neighborhood. That would be a good reason for Cliff to stop in afterward since they lived only a few minutes away. They chose Woodland Tap, which seemed nice enough, and Gail returned a message that she was excited to meet him.

Janet's eyes lit up when Gail pressed Send. "That ought to get his arrogant juices flowing. I think you should wear that same black dress you wore for Mr. Hennessey." She chuckled at the thought. "Remember? He told you it was to die for."

Chapter 25

The email the commander received contained a gold mine of information. It listed every hospital, clinic, and in-home health care location that the employee worked at, along with the name of the extended-stay apartment or hotel they temporarily resided in, and the type of vehicle they'd requested. The only problem was narrowing down the list of seventy-five to a more manageable number of names that could be relevant. It still didn't explain the blue Sienna seen entering Washington Park and the fact that an identical vehicle was picked up at Midway by a fifty-seven-year-old woman named Janet St. James.

My confidence was fading, and I felt like we were barking up the wrong tree. Why would she attack, kill, and cart away men in her same age group? I doubted she had the physical endurance to commit the crimes to begin with, and maybe the whole thing was a computer glitch.

Lutz pointed at our laptops as he scooted the guest chair to my side of the desk. "Each of you take twenty-five of those names and plug their addresses into your computer's map of the area. I want to know who lives the closest to Washington and Bixler Parks. Tony, you take the first twenty-five, Frank, the next, and Jesse, the last batch. Call me as soon as you have the search results for anyone who lives within that ten-block perimeter of Bixler or near Washington Park. Once we have our best selection of people, we'll station patrol units outside their homes and watch their movements."

Lutz walked out, and we began the task of searching for addresses that could be in our own backyard. I checked the time before plugging street names and apartment numbers into the search bar. It was now four thirty, and my thoughts of going home, playing with Bandit, and possibly checking for messages on the dating site had gone straight out the window. I would probably be working until after the night crew showed up, especially if we found a promising lead.

"Don't get tunnel vision, guys, since men can be nurses too. We need to check out every male name and address on our sheet," I said as I crossed off the second name on my list.

By five fifteen, we had all the addresses that were near both parks. We sat at the back table with our new list of fourteen people, three of them men.

The door to our bull pen opened, and Todd Jacobsen, the lead analyst in our tech department, walked through with a rolled-up paper map of our area.

"Hey, guys, I hope this will work for your needs." He unrolled it and taped the corners to the table.

"It's perfect," I said. "Thanks, buddy."

With Magic Markers, we spent the next twenty minutes placing red dots at every address where a temporary worker lived. Three of those fourteen lived within seven blocks of

Bixler Park, and the rest were spread out between both parks.

I jabbed the map in those three locations. "We should focus on these first. I'll call Lutz and see if he wants to take a look."

Sitting next to us moments later, Lutz looked over our results then compared them to the names on the list.

"So, we have one male and two females who live in the general vicinity of Bixler Park— John Merring, Gail Fremont, and Leah Standish. Have you done background checks on them yet?"

"Not yet." Tony rose from the table and crossed the room to his desk, where he unplugged his laptop. Back at the table, he typed the first name, John Merring, into the DMV database to narrow down the search by state in case there were multiple people with that name.

The results showed John was from Memphis, Tennessee. With that information, we pulled a background check on him, and he came up clean.

"Let's move on." I nodded at Tony.

He typed Gail Fremont's name into the DMV database. "That's weird. She only has an ID, not a driver's license."

"Where's she from?" I asked.

"Petaluma, California."

"Maybe she gets a stipend for the city bus unless her job is close enough to walk to work. See if she has a criminal record."

Tony entered her name, and just like John, she came up clean.

"Okay, one more."

Tony checked the DMV for Leah Standish and found that her hometown was in North Carolina. "Whoa, what's this? Our last woman is from Asheville, which is only a few hours from Charlotte." He plugged her name into our background-check software and told us she had a misdemeanor charge five years earlier for assaulting a patron at a bar.

"She could be the one," Lutz said. "I'll get Patrol to sit on her residence and watch her comings and goings."

"But if it *is* her, then who's her partner? A woman who's five foot two and one hundred ten pounds, according to her driver's license, can't overtake, murder, and transport a body all by herself," Tony said.

I added my two cents. "And a good reason for Patrol to follow her movements for a few days. Maybe she has a partner who lives right here in Chicago or comes on their own once she's established in the city she's working at." I double-checked the car she was given to drive during her stay. "The sheet shows she picked up a cream-colored Forester at Midway, which *is* a Subaru, and whether the vehicle is cream or tan is open to opinion. That's like arguing about something being fuchsia or magenta. It's the same damn thing."

Lutz grabbed my desk phone, pulled it closer to him, and dialed Abrams. "Mark, it's Bob Lutz. We have a possible suspect in our recent murders that we need units to sit on for a few days. Yep, I'll forward all the information to you. Appreciate it, pal." Lutz hung up and blew out a long breath. "Okay, keep plugging away at the rest. I'll call Henry and have them come in. There may be other people we need to keep our eyes on too."

Chapter 26

With the curling iron in hand, Janet wrapped sections of Gail's long blond hair around the barrel and pressed the mist button. That little bit of moisture would set the ringlets in place, and the curl would stay longer.

"You look beautiful, honey. Now put on your makeup and earrings while I get your dress and heels out of the closet."

Minutes later, Janet checked the time—6:59. "You should go now. By the time you get there, find a parking spot, and go in, it'll be ten after seven. You want him to know you aren't a pushover, and that'll make him try harder to impress you." Janet handed her daughter the keys. "Remember, make him unable to resist you and find a way to text me when you're heading back."

"How do I look?" Gail asked as she walked to the door.

"You look like the kind of woman that most men would do a double take over. Go knock them dead and make Mr. Hotshot jealous right out of the gate."

A twelve-car parking lot sat behind the apartment building where Gail lived temporarily. Cornerstone had no idea Janet lived there, too, but with everything paid for by the employer, it was very affordable for them to travel from state to state together and accomplish their main goals of eliminating everyone who reminded Janet of her former husband, David.

Gail walked outside and clicked the key fob. The Sienna's lights flashed in the first space to the left of the door. Inside the van and behind the wheel, Gail pulled up the map to Woodland Tap and hit the blue start button. The map's audio assistant guided her there—a short five-block distance. She circled the block twice before she found a parking spot then slid in easily only three buildings away from the bar. Using the visor's mirror, she gave herself one more application of lip gloss before exiting the van. It was time to impress Cliff Howard. Gail quickly texted Janet to confirm that she'd arrived, and a thumbs-up text came back. It was nine minutes after seven.

After slipping her phone into her purse and making sure it was set to vibrate, Gail climbed out of the van, smoothed her dress, and locked the doors at her back. Cliff's demise was right around the corner, and in an hour or two, it would be over. He wouldn't see it coming.

Gail entered the bar and immediately heard a band playing a sultry blues tune. She remembered reading that one of the draws to that neighborhood tap were the weekly bands that frequented the establishment. It was the perfect ambience for that night. She scanned the bar and bar tables, then she saw him. Cliff sat on a small loveseat near the corner stage and only feet from the musicians. Luckily, they played softly. He immediately locked eyes with her when she crossed the room, and he gave her a slow up-and-down once-over. It made her skin crawl. He patted the cushion at his side and puckered his lips. Cliff Howard definitely needed to die.

She reached out to shake his hand, and he pulled her in for a kiss. Gail turned her head, and he got her cheek.

Cliff laughed. "Spunky, aren't you?"

Gail took a seat next to him. "Actually, I'd call it proper. I don't even know you yet."

"Well"—he licked his lips—"we can certainly fix that. Let me tell you all about myself."

Gail smiled. "I'll have a glass of Malbec first. I wouldn't want to interrupt your story."

At eight o'clock, Gail excused herself to go to the ladies' room, where she called Janet. "I'm on my second glass of wine, Mom, and he's still bragging about himself."

"Has he made any subtle suggestions?"

Gail snickered. "Believe me, that jerk is far from subtle, but yeah."

"What has he been drinking?"

"He's had two glasses of Scotch on the rocks, and he's becoming more disgusting as time goes on. I hope you have a plan in mind."

"I have a wonderful plan, honey, so don't you worry about it. Have one more glass of wine and then suggest continuing the evening at your apartment. Make sure he rides with you. Tell him you'll drop him off at his car later."

"Okay. I better get back out there, and I'll text you when we leave."

Returning to the loveseat, Gail saw that Cliff had already

ordered another Scotch during her absence. That was fine with her since his reaction time would be greatly reduced if he was half in the bag. She would pass on that third glass of wine, and as much as she despised doing it, she needed to get the seduction ball rolling.

"I have to admit, Cliff, you really intrigue me." She tried to blush. "I believe I'm smitten with you already. I can tell you're a man who has a lot to offer a woman." She parted her lips then ran her tongue across the bottom one. "You're so handsome, and I can't believe your physique, so strong and muscular. You're amazing."

"Well, Lynn, you haven't seen the half of it."

She squeezed his leg. "I bet I haven't, but I'd like to."

His eyes lit up. "So what are you proposing, little lady? Want to check out my bachelor pad?"

She raised a brow toward the door. "I have a better idea. I only live a few blocks from here. I'll drive and then bring you back to your car later. Unfortunately, all the parking spots at my apartment are designated spaces for tenants only."

"It would be much more convenient to come to my house. It's very inviting, plus I'm a great host."

She held her ground. "I'm sure you are, but I don't go to men's houses on the first date."

He groaned. "Fine, and you don't mind driving me back?"

"Of course not. I won't regret inviting you over, will I?"

He snickered. "I can show you things I bet you've never experienced."

She gave him her most seductive smile. "And I can too. Shall we?"

"Give me a minute to settle the bill."

"Sure, I'm not going anywhere." Gail waited until he was at the bar with his back turned before texting Janet.

"We're leaving in a few minutes. Everything is good to go."

A return message popped up just before Gail dropped her phone into her purse.

"I'll be waiting with the lights dimmed, and make sure he walks in first."

When Cliff came back her way, Gail stood. "Ready?"

"I'm always ready, babe."

She led the way out the door and pointed at the Sienna parked three buildings down. "That's me."

He laughed. "A van? Hell, we don't even have to go anywhere. Just lay down the seats."

She snapped her head toward him. "Are you looking to date somebody or just hook up?"

Cliff huffed. "With my money and swag, most women would be proud to tell all their friends they hooked up with me."

"Well, I'm not most women. You'll find out soon enough that I'm far different than everyone else."

"Good." He pulled open the passenger door. "That's exactly what I wanted to hear. I can't wait to walk through your door."

Gail sneered. "I can't either."

Chapter 27

It took only five minutes to get home. Gail clicked her blinker and turned in to the parking lot of the Parkview Arms. "This is it." She killed the engine and climbed out. "Home is where the heart is."

Cliff rolled his eyes. "I always thought the phrase was, 'Home is where the bed is.'"

"Whatever." Gail pointed at the first door beyond the parking lot. "This is it, right here. I've got the first apartment on this side."

He did a three sixty. "Guess you don't have much of a view being on the bottom floor."

"Oh, you'd be surprised, and you'll see once we're inside. There's a view to die for." Gail slipped her key into the knob and turned it to the right. She swung the door inward. "Guests first."

Cliff took two steps in and was met with a butcher knife to the chest. He yelled out and stumbled forward, giving Gail just enough room to pass over the threshold and lock the door behind her.

"We have to shut him up before somebody hears his

wailing!" Gail darted around Cliff and raced to the TV. She turned it up louder than normal but not enough to warrant complaints.

Janet pulled the knife from his chest, and it slid out with a sucking noise. She swung her arm and lunged the knife into the back of Cliff's neck. He swatted at it but collapsed to the floor before he could do anything to protect himself. He jerked a few times as he lay face down then went still.

Gail stared at his lifeless body. "Damn it. That wasn't very satisfying for the hour and a half I had to spend listening to his bullshit. I like the old way better. The men really need to understand why they were chosen instead of being blindsided and killed immediately."

"Next time, honey. Now go change out of those pretty clothes while I get the drop cloth and snippers ready. You don't want to get blood all over that dress."

Gail called out from the bedroom. "We need to find the perfect dump spot for him."

"I already have, and you'll love it, but first we need to bring his car here to the apartment. What did he drive to the bar?"

Gail walked out of the bedroom in black sweats and a matching hoodie. She shrugged. "I didn't ask him. Check his pockets for the keys."

Janet dug into the dead man's pockets and pulled out everything. She looked at the fob that was attached to the key ring containing a half dozen keys. "Who the hell needs this many keys?"

"He has a lot of toys, remember? So what kind of vehicle emblem is on the fob?"

Janet held it out for Gail to see.

"A Jeep. I need to check his profile pictures again so we know what we're looking for. I don't remember if I saw a picture of it or not. Gail logged in and pulled up the twenty-plus-picture gallery Cliff had posted on his profile. She pointed. "This has to be it, a bright-orange Jeep Rubicon, right next to the sports car. That shouldn't be too hard to find. So where are we leaving him?"

Janet laughed. "Since he's such a dog, let's leave him in the local Humane Society parking lot."

Gail grinned. "Not a bad idea, and I doubt if they have parking lot cameras. I imagine the county park system is being surveilled by the cops, anyway." She glanced at Cliff, who had a substantial blood pool forming beneath him. "Let's throw him in the tub for now, and we'll deal with him after we find that Jeep."

Janet stared at the floor. "What about the blood? That's undisputable evidence if we were ever found out. That's what Luminol is all about, you know."

"Yeah, you're right. Let's mop it up quick and then bring his vehicle back here."

The dark-pink water from the mop bucket was dumped into the toilet and flushed, then they repeated the mopping process two more times. When they were finished with the floor, Gail filled half the bucket with water and the other half with a bottle of bleach then set the mop inside to soak.

"Okay, let's go find that Jeep, bring it back, and then we'll wait until the middle of the night to move him." She headed to the bathroom.

"What are you doing?"

"I'm pretty sure he had false teeth. They looked way too perfect. If we don't take them out now, rigor will make it impossible to open his mouth later."

Chapter 28

We completed the background checks on the rest of the fourteen people who were residing in temporary lodging near both parks, and they all came up clean. Our focus would remain on Leah Standish. I sent a text to Chuck Donahue, thinking a text was less intrusive than calling him at nine o'clock in the evening. I asked if the name Leah Standish had ever come up during the murder investigation in Charlotte. I knew it was a long shot, but it was worth sending a text to find out.

A response came back right away. His wife must have been busy at the moment since his eyes were clearly on his phone. He said the name didn't sound familiar, but he would fire off a message to his partner and ask him. I was grateful to have Chuck ready and willing to help in any way he could and texted him my thanks. With my phone back in my pocket, I signed off for the night. The second shift crew was more than capable of handling anything that could possibly go wrong that evening. As I walked the hallway past Lutz's office, I saw his light was still on. I rapped on the door, and when he called out for me to come in, I entered.

"Still working, Boss?"

He leaned back and stretched. "Just wrapping up the day, and then I'm heading home. Looks like you've finally decided to call it a night."

"Yep. Just wondering how Patrol's surveillance is going on Leah Standish." I tipped my wrist and checked the time. "Maybe too early?"

"Yeah, dead quiet, excuse the pun. Tillson said Leah hasn't left her apartment since she got home from work."

"No surprise there since their preferred MO is to prowl around late at night." I knuckled the doorframe. "Okay, see you in the morning."

"Yep, and thanks. I've got quite the team."

It was nine thirty by the time I settled in at home. Bandit got the first half hour of my time, and we sat comfortably on the couch together, my laptop in front of me and the pup curled up at my feet. I logged on to the dating website I'd joined the previous night and saw three messages. I had to decide whether to pay to play or delete the account and save my dating efforts for another time. I was able to read the messages and see who'd contacted me, but I couldn't respond unless I plugged in my credit card information. Since I hadn't dated anyone in years— many years—I was hesitant. My college buddies and work friends filled that bonding void when I had free time, and with Bandit as my constant companion, I was still on the fence about dating. I would read the messages, check out the profiles, and decide tomorrow. My life wasn't bad, and in that moment, I just wanted to watch the ten o'clock news, have another beer, then hit the sheets.

Later, as I lay in bed and felt myself dozing off, the vibration of my phone perked me up. I swatted the nightstand to feel for its familiar shape and grabbed it. I squinted at the screen, trying to see if it was a call or a text. An orange number lit up on the text thumbnail. A message had come in, and I didn't have to talk to anyone. I was thankful—I needed sleep.

I slipped on my reading glasses and took a look. The text, from Chuck, said nobody had ever come across the name Leah Standish as a person of interest in the Charlotte murders. I fired off a response and thanked him for checking into it, then I set the phone on the nightstand and closed my eyes. I felt myself relax, and the next thing I heard was the annoying buzz of the phone alarm.

No way. I just went to sleep, damn it.

I rolled over, looked at the transom window above the blinds, and saw that daylight had shown up and was peeking in. Groaning my displeasure, I felt like I hadn't slept more than a few hours, but coffee would fix that—maybe even an espresso. I trudged down the hallway to brew a strong cup to drink while my shower water heated. An excited Bandit waited at the patio door to go outside, and I watched as he walked the fence line, sniffing the plant life like he did every morning. When the coffee was ready, I poured a cup and thought about work. Maybe that day would be different and we would put an end to the crimes committed by our mystery killer. I would know more after roll call, when we got our updates.

At the precinct, I entered the building and headed for the

cafeteria before going to the bull pen. I knew I would find half of our squad in there, anyway. Looking around, I saw Henry and Frank staring at the few choices left in the vending machine. I asked if they'd heard anything about last night's surveillance, and they said they hadn't. Two hallways later, as both men chewed on their muffins, we arrived in the roll call room and joined the rest of our department. We chatted with each other while waiting for Lutz to appear. Five, then ten minutes passed, and people began to shift in their seats as they stared at the door.

"Where the hell is he?" Frank asked.

"I don't know, but he's usually the first person here. I'll go check his office."

I excused myself and walked out. Out of eyesight of the rest, I stepped up my pace in the hallway. Something was wrong, and I intended to find out what it was. Lutz was normally prompt when conducting roll call. Seconds later, I reached the commander's office to see him and Abrams involved in an intense discussion. I raised my fist to knock, but Bob waved me in.

"Jesse, I don't have time to conduct roll call, so I need you to take care of that for me. Nothing else, just roll call. Send everyone back to the bull pen afterward."

"You got it, sir." I turned around without asking questions. I had been instructed to conduct a task. Questions had their time and place, and this wasn't it.

Twenty minutes later, a bull pen jammed with detectives and officers—some leaning against the wall—awaited Lutz's arrival. More than one set of footsteps sounded in the back hallway, telling me Abrams was likely joining Lutz for an important update, and the churning in my gut told me it wasn't anything good.

"Okay, boys and girls, I need everyone's attention." Lutz reached out, grabbed a bottle of water as he passed my desk, and didn't miss a beat. He stood with Abrams at his side near the back table, then he stuck a fist in front of his mouth and cleared his throat. He cracked open the bottle and took a gulp. "It's come to our attention through a 911 call we received fifteen minutes ago that another body was discovered, this one in the parking lot of the East Chicago Humane Society."

"What the—"

Lutz raised his hand. "Hold up, Frank. Just let me get through this update, and then there'll be time for questions afterward. The unidentified nude and fingerless man was discovered inside a light-blue Sienna. We were told there's a lot of blood, but until Don gets there to inspect the body, we don't know the cause of death."

"Son of a bitch!" Frank yelled out. "We know the name of the woman who rented that vehicle, so why aren't we picking her up?"

"Okay, okay, take it down a notch, Mills," Lutz said sternly. "We have an APB out for a Janet St. James. The driver's license and address provided on said license are fake. We've made the necessary calls, and that address is just a reroute from a digital mailbox provider. It's highly unlikely that the woman is from Grants Pass, Oregon, or that her name really is Janet St. James. Forensics and Don are en route to the Humane Society. Hopefully, they can pick up some viable prints that are in the system." Lutz nodded to the group. "Okay, let's hear the questions."

I began before Frank took over the entire question-and-answer session. "It isn't a question, but there must be some relevance to the dump site since the other two bodies were found in parks."

"Maybe they're erring on the side of caution," Henry said.

"How is killing, transporting, and dumping a dead body the least bit cautious?" Frank asked.

Abrams spoke up. "I would venture to say they know we're patrolling the park system. Hell, they may even have a police scanner for all we know."

"Who found the man?" Kip asked.

Lutz took over. "The receptionist is always the first to arrive. She opens up the building and begins feeding the animals. When she pulled in, she noticed the vehicle in the parking lot, which immediately raised a red flag with her. She said she was apprehensive to approach, but by the time she was within ten feet of the van, she could see the man wasn't wearing a shirt, and blood covered his chest and back. She ran inside the building, locked the door behind her, and called 911."

Abrams added more. "Our patrol units arrived within four minutes and secured the vehicle. They had to break a window to open the doors because they were locked."

"Meaning the perp has the key and probably that man's vehicle."

Lutz nodded. "Most likely. Forensics will go through the Sienna from top to bottom and look for anything of evidentiary value."

Tony asked the next question. "You mentioned the signature removal of fingertips, but what about the broken teeth?"

"Don't know yet. His mouth was closed according to my officers," Abrams said.

Frank stared at me with raised brows as I jotted down everything I could think of in that moment. I needed to know why the killer chose the Humane Society—or as we called it as kids, the dog pound—as the place to leave the latest victim. Was the man a dog, meaning a dirtbag toward women, or was he in the doghouse for some reason? But that would indicate they knew him, meaning it wasn't a random killing. The more I thought about it, the more baffling it became. Why would the killers flip the script and take the chance of leaving evidence in the vehicle Janet St. James drove off in two weeks earlier? None of it made sense unless, like Lutz said, everything about the mysterious Janet St. James was fiction.

"Jesse, I want you, Frank, Henry, and Shawn to head to the scene and start looking for cameras a mile out in every direction. They had to have a vehicle to drive away in, and it was likely the victim's. It's probably our only chance to find out who that man is unless we can get his face on the news."

Frank grumbled. "That hasn't helped with the first victim yet."

Henry grabbed his jacket off the chairback. "Let's go, guys."

Lutz continued. "Tony and Kip, scour the grounds at the facility and then start knocking on doors. It isn't a residential neighborhood, but we still need to know if anyone saw anything throughout the night. It's worth a shot."

When we arrived, the scene was already secured. Officers stationed at the entrance let only employees through to care for the animals. Business was closed to the public until the parking lot and perimeter of the property were cleared and released back to the Humane Society.

We parked outside the yellow tape then dipped under it. The Sienna was a hundred feet in front of us, and Don, already there, was looking at the deceased.

"What have we got, Don?" I asked as we stood back five feet.

He looked over his shoulder at us. "Morning, guys. Guess we're getting an early start today."

I shaded my eyes as I tried to see past him. "Looks that way. Same MO as the others?"

"Yes and no," Don said. "We have the missing fingertips. No broken teeth, because the man wore dentures, but they're gone, and it looks like two large stab wounds were inflicted on him. One to the chest and the other to the back of the neck. Either one would have killed him, so it doesn't really matter which came first. They were within seconds of each other."

I rubbed my neck as I thought.

Drain cleaner killed John Doe, multiple blows to the head killed victim number two, and now this guy has been stabbed.

"Weapons of opportunity?" Henry asked.

Don shrugged. "Or the killers just like mixing it up."

"Did you get the tox report back on the second victim?" I asked.

Don nodded. "Came in just before I left work yesterday. No drain cleaner in his system, but alcohol did show up in his urine."

"Over the legal limit?"

"Too much time has passed to be that precise. He may have had three or four drinks prior to being killed. Alcohol dissipates in blood within six hours but is detectible in urine for up to twenty-four hours. My guess would be possibly. Maybe that's how the killers are able to overpower their victims."

"Interesting." I pulled out my notepad and wrote that down. The killer or killers might have had drinks with the victims, made sure they were drunk or well on their way, then overpowered them or coaxed them to their place to kill them. That took me back to the California politician who was murdered after announcing his engagement to another man. Was it that type of hate crime, or was it a crime committed by a woman who coaxed the victim to her place with the intention of killing him? Still, I would consider that a hate crime too—a hatred for men in general. "Come on, guys. Let's start pounding the pavement and look for cameras. You know the drill. Start close and work our way out." Our forensic team showed up, and I walked over to talk to them. "Mike, Danny. Staying busy, huh?"

Mike nodded. "Damn straight. Same as the others?"

"Pretty much. Kip and Tony will be here any minute to walk the grounds and then start knock and talks. We're heading out to look for cameras in the area. Keep us posted and make sure that vehicle is taken to the evidence garage."

"Sure thing, Jesse."

I called out to Don before we left. "We're going to be out in the neighborhood, so give Lutz the updates when you have them."

Don waved then stuck his head back in the van's door.

Luckily, because we were in a predominantly commercial neighborhood, finding cameras wasn't nearly as tough as it was in residential areas. The ones on the streets surrounding the animal shelter should give us the answers we needed. We each took a street that ran parallel to the shelter and began walking the block. I found a camera immediately—my lucky day, as I'd hoped. Mounted above a corner door, it could possibly catch a portion of the intersection in both directions. I entered the accounting office and asked to speak to the person who owned or managed the company. I assumed the first individual who spoke up was that person, and it was. A friendly-looking woman said she was the senior employee and asked what she could help me with. I showed her my badge and said we needed to see the footage from the camera above the door.

"I'm sorry, Detective, but we don't own the building. We just lease the space. You'd have to contact the owner about the camera, but I believe the footage is stored off-site since we don't have any equipment within our office space."

I thanked her and got the contact information for the building's owner and called him as soon as I stepped outside. Robert Dolan answered on the second ring and gave me the name and address of the company that stored the surveillance footage and said it was on a weeklong loop. It recorded over itself every Sunday night beginning at 11:59 p.m. He told me the only reason there was a camera at all was that they'd had a break-in at the accountant's office last year. He didn't want the firm to move out since they were good tenants, so he had the camera installed.

"Is there a chance you could call the storage company and give the okay for me to view last night's footage?"

"Sure, but you know they'll need to see your credentials."

"Of course, and it's mandatory on our part, anyway." I thanked him, said I was on my way, then hung up and called Frank. "Having any luck?"

"I'm looking at the footage from last night at a deli on the street west and parallel to the animal shelter. Haven't seen that Sienna, though."

"Okay, watch it until eight this morning. If you don't see the van, we'll know they didn't come from the north or south on that street. I'm heading to a video storage facility that has the footage from the accounting office near the driveway to the animal shelter. I think it's our best bet. Tell the guys to keep looking on the surrounding streets and I should be back by midmorning."

"Roger that."

I programmed the address into my phone and checked how long it would take to get there. Because morning rush hour was over, it looked like I would arrive in just under a half hour. I set the GPS and took off.

I chuckled when I stepped out of my cruiser and read the sign for Backup Plan Storage in a suite of office buildings—a catchy name, I had to admit. I walked the hallway to Suite 19, where the facility that stored cloud and video data was located. When I walked through the glass door, the buzzer sounded. At the counter, I introduced myself, which appeared to ring a bell with the receptionist, Marilyn. She said Robert Dolan had called, explained that I was on my way, and told them what I needed. She asked to see my badge, which I showed her, then she escorted me to the second room on the right, about halfway down a long hallway.

"We already queued up the footage from last night for you. All you have to do is press Play, and use the forward and backward buttons to advance, slow down, or reverse the footage."

"Great. Very efficient and sounds simple enough. Appreciate it."

Marilyn smiled and said to give her a shout if I needed anything else. With that, she walked out, closed the door, and left me to it.

Chapter 29

I didn't have the luxury of fast-forwarding through the video since I had no idea when the killers had entered the Humane Society parking lot. I set the recording to begin when the facility closed last night at seven o'clock and would watch until the time the receptionist pulled in a few hours ago. I was sure I could speed through the footage when I didn't see headlights or movement in the area. I settled in and hit Play.

It felt like hours had passed when I pushed up my shirtsleeve and checked the time—I'd been there only forty-five minutes. I sighed deeply and continued watching, speeding up the footage every chance I could. Vehicles passed, then there were lulls, and as intensely as I watched, it was almost hypnotic. I paused the recording at eleven o'clock and called Lutz with an update.

"Hey, Boss, I just wanted to tell you I'm still staring at cars passing back and forth on the screen, and none of them are the Sienna. How is it on your end?"

"Don is back with the body and did an initial table exam. He said the implement was likely a butcher knife, nothing fancy, and probably a weapon of convenience. The wound in the back of the neck severed the spinal column, which led Don to believe the first thrust was to the chest."

"So the perp was facing him? That's a daring move."

"Or the perp caught him off guard and lunged forward from a hidden position."

"I guess. Any news from the guys?"

"Frank didn't see anything on the deli footage and has moved back another street. Henry and Shawn struck out with some of the cameras. Either broken or only there as a deterrent but not actually operable. That sort of thing, but they're still plugging away."

"And Forensics?"

"Nothing at the scene. The van is already here in the evidence garage, and Abrams has patrol units on foot scouring the area and helping Kip and Tony with knock and talks."

"Okay, I better get back at it, then. Actually, I was almost falling asleep and needed a distraction for a few minutes." I hung up and resumed my position in front of the monitor with my fist propped under my chin.

Minutes into staring at nothing, I nearly jumped off the chair when the footage reached the one a.m. mark. I saw the Sienna turn in to the lot and slow down. "Whoa! There you are. Now let's see what kind of vehicle is following you." I perked up, my face within a foot of the screen, and watched, but no other vehicle appeared. "What the hell!" Were they that smart, that cunning, and that experienced to know exactly what to do and what not to do? I slammed my fist on the table out of sheer disappointment. I was pissed off and frustrated. I returned my focus to the Sienna and backed up the recording to when they turned in. Slowing down the speed, I watched each second pass. Brake lights flashed, and the van stopped. Somebody cloaked in dark clothing climbed out from behind the wheel, then I saw movement at the sliding side door. I leaned in closer but couldn't make out much—the van blocked my view of that side. The driver remained in place, then movement caught my eye at the front passenger door. The person who had exited through the sliding door must have opened it.

Both individuals busied themselves with something in the front seat. I assumed that was when they pushed the victim to the driver's side. The logic of that act escaped me since nobody would believe the victim drove himself there with two fatal wounds to his body, yet no murder weapon was found at the scene. It took a good five minutes for them to complete the task, then both doors closed, the person on the passenger side rounded the van, and they both walked away together but not before I saw the van lights flash. They locked the doors, headed east, and disappeared on foot. I stood and pressed my temples. Again, they got the best of us. They knew what they were doing and were experienced at it. I regained my composure before talking to anyone. I had sat in that space and watched a computer screen for a good three hours just to walk out without that *gotcha* moment.

Back at Marilyn's counter, I asked for a copy of the footage. "Not sure how you transfer cloud-stored videos, but I'll need to have a copy sent to my email address."

"Sure, Detective McCord. That won't be a problem."

"Good." I handed her my card listing my email address, thanked her, and left before heading back to our station with hopes that Tech would be able to enhance the images on the footage.

A drive-through at a fast-food restaurant beat anything available in our vending machines all day, every day. I made a quick detour and grabbed a double cheeseburger, large order of fries, and an iced tea, then continued on. There wasn't time to go out to lunch. We needed to find out where those two killers went and what kind of vehicle they drove off in. Without the vehicle, or unless somebody reported the man missing, we would never know who the latest victim was—just like the others.

When I arrived at the precinct, I made a pit stop at Lutz's office. "Got a minute?"

He waved me in. "So you struck out too?"

"Yes and no."

Lutz gave me *the look*. "You do realize I hate that phrase. Either you struck out, or you didn't."

"Sorry. I heard Don say that earlier, and it seemed fitting in the moment."

"Go on."

"The recording is being sent to my in-box so Tech can go over it. I saw the killers—"

"What!" Lutz rose to his feet. "And you didn't think to call me that very second?"

"That's where the 'and no' part comes in. They turned in, parked, and moved the vic to the driver's seat." I shook my head. "That still doesn't make sense to me. Anyway, they were both in dark clothes, fully covered from head to toe, and unidentifiable by gender. They clicked the fob, the headlights flashed, and then they walked off into the night."

"That's it? There's nothing more to the story?"

"Sorry, I wish there was. They walked east, so we can look for cameras on the eastern streets, but going in that direction may have been a ruse. I'm sure they were aware of the neighborhood cameras, and they could have cut back in any direction, through dark alleys and parking lots."

"It's still worth a shot. I'll get everyone working the streets east of the animal shelter. They had to pop out somewhere, even if it was only to cross the street."

I jerked my head toward the door. "I'm going to check my in-box to see if that video arrived yet. If it has, I'll forward it to Tech and ask if there's anything they can do to enhance the killer's images." I groaned. "That parking lot only had one overhead lamp, and they deliberately parked away from it."

"Go ahead and let me know what they get."

I slapped the doorframe as I walked out. "I will, and I'll stop in by Don too. We need to get that man's face on the news."

It seemed odd to be alone in the bull pen, but everyone else had taken to the streets. I woke up my laptop and logged in to my email account. A message had come in from Back Up Plan, and an attachment was included. The video had arrived, and I forwarded it to our tech department. I pushed back my chair, grabbed my drive-through iced tea, and headed downstairs to go over the video with Todd and Billy.

Through the glass doors, I saw Todd sitting at his computer. He must have noticed the email I'd just sent. I walked in and headed in his direction.

"I'm reading your email," he said as I pulled the roller chair alongside his desk. "There's an attachment?"

"It's the camera feed from the accounting firm across the street from the Humane Society. Don't know if you were aware that another body was found this morning."

He rubbed his forehead. "Jeez, and no, that news hadn't filtered down here yet."

"Anyway, the video caught the vehicle driving into the parking lot and the perps getting out and walking away. Wondering if there's any chance of enhancing what we have."

"Let's take a look. Do you know the time they arrived?"

"Yeah, at one in the morning. I fast-forwarded through the footage until I hit seven o'clock—the time the facility closes. That's when I began paying attention. The time stamp on the footage was at the one-hour mark for today, give or take a few seconds. The footage starts over at midnight every night, and they pulled in at one a.m."

"Got it. Let's take a look." Todd advanced the scrubber bar through the hours of footage I'd watched until it rolled over to the current date. Then he slowed it down until he reached a few minutes before one a.m.

"I'll start it five minutes early so we can take a closer look at everything in the immediate area. Possibly people walking by, someone trolling the neighborhood in a vehicle, that sort of thing."

"Good idea." I watched with keener eyes that second time

around and took notice of any movement in the area surrounding the driveway to the shelter. All I saw was a feral cat scurry across the street and random cars pass by. None of them showed up multiple times.

"Okay, I didn't see anything that stood out. Let's continue on."

When I saw the Sienna, I pointed. "That's it, and it's about to turn in."

Todd slowed the footage even more and tweaked the clarity the best he could. "It's tough working with night images, especially when the only light is on that one pole in the parking lot."

I nodded. "And they made sure to park far enough away from it too."

We watched as the scene played out again. The driver parked and climbed out. The sliding side door opened, and seconds later, the front passenger door did too. The scene remained that way for five minutes.

"What the hell are they doing?"

"Pretty sure they're moving the body to the driver's seat. It takes them a few minutes and is quite a risk in my opinion."

Todd frowned. "No kidding, right? Okay, and now the passenger walks to the driver, who clicks the fob after closing the doors, then they disappear into the darkness." Todd leaned back in his chair while Billy watched over our shoulders. "That's brazen."

"Or just stupid," Billy said.

"Nah, they're brazen. I realize they're both wearing dark

clothes and hoodies. No distinguishable features to tell us if they're male or female or even get a height and weight."

"We might be able to sharpen their shapes, but I can't guarantee it. What we can get is their height based off the height of the van. That should give us something as far as the odds of them being male or female."

"Great," I said, "since the van is in the evidence garage right now."

Todd pushed back from his desk and grabbed a laser tape measure. "Let's go take a look."

Chapter 30

I joined Todd and Billy in the evidence garage, where Mike and Danny were deep into their inspection of the van.

"Find anything of value?" I asked as we approached.

"Actually, I think we have."

I perked up. "Really, what is it?"

"Other than the blood-soaked front seats from the most current victim, we've found small amounts of dried-blood evidence in the back area. We'll take samples of the stains and compare it to our other victims' blood and see if there's a match."

"Great. The evidence is mounting that we have two serial killers loose in Chicago. We just don't know who they are. How about something personal they've left behind?"

"Nothing yet, but we'll check every nook and cranny."

"But they've had that van for two weeks. They had to leave fingerprints somewhere."

"And we'll enter all of the viable prints into the database, but if they're not in the system, they won't help."

I was fully aware that fingerprints couldn't help us if the perps had never been arrested, but I was grasping for straws.

At least the van had been reserved for three months. That meant the forensic team could take their time with it and hopefully find something the killers had left behind, even if it was a single strand of hair.

Todd pulled out his tape measure and checked the height of the van—70.5 inches.

"I'll enter it into the computer as seventy and a quarter inches since the weight of a dead body would lower it slightly. I'll plug that number into our software program and measure it against the height of the two perps. The difference will show up on the screen."

"Perfect. By the way, what is the average height for men and women?"

"In the US, it's just under five foot four for women over the age of twenty and five foot nine for men of the same age."

I rubbed my chin as I thought.

No woman in her right mind would wear anything other than flat shoes on that type of mission, would she?

I turned back to Todd. "Can you tell if they're wearing flat shoes?"

"Yeah, I think so. Ready to head back?"

"I'm going to check in with Don, but let me know what you come up with."

"Will do."

I took a different hallway to get to Don Lawry's office and morgue. Out of courtesy, I knocked before entering. He yelled out loudly—likely from the autopsy room—for me to come in.

"Hey, Don, it's Jesse."

"I'm in the back with this morning's vic. Give me a second to cover him up."

I waited a good twenty seconds then entered. "Got a few questions for you."

"Yep, shoot."

I approached Don, who had just draped a white sheet over the man lying on the autopsy table. The only thing exposed on the deceased was his face, and it appeared normal, other than the grayish tint. The perps had been kind enough to give us something to work with.

"We need to get his face and description on the news as soon as possible." I gave Don a quick smile. "No pressure."

"Not a problem. As a matter of fact, I've already documented everything, and he looks relatively clean. Mike can work his camera magic and tint the vic's face to look a little less gray. PG for TV, right?"

"That's right. Can you have that ready for me in, say, thirty minutes? I'd like to get it broadcast on the early-evening local channels."

"Shouldn't be a problem, and I'll call you when everything is ready."

I thanked Don and headed upstairs. At my desk, I organized the information I knew up to that point. Each location where a body was found had been documented. The clothing, or lack thereof, was described and written down as well as the approximate age and general description of the men. Coincidentally, the three men looked almost the same. They all had salt-and-pepper hair, styled similarly, and each one's height and weight was nearly identical.

The last and likely the most important common denominator was that no close friends or relatives were looking for them. I finally had my aha moment. Those particular men were chosen deliberately and ahead of time, but how, and even more importantly, why? I dug deep in my mind. If nobody was looking for them, what could be the reason for that? Did they live far away from family, or were they estranged from them? Were they widowers or maybe lifelong bachelors? Were they married to their jobs, or were they wealthy playboys with a different woman on their arm and in a different city every night? Why was the first man clothed and the other two nude?

I tapped my pen as I pondered that question. I remembered airing on the news a photograph of John Doe's shirt and a description of his pants. That meant the killers had clearly watched the broadcast and were honing their skills to always be one step ahead of us. Could the other two have been dressed for a night on the town, possibly giving away what they'd last done? Or because the killers elected to display John Doe in a public playground and park, could they be showing an ounce of dignity for the dead and also for the small children who might have been present when he was discovered?

I read over my notes, and everything held merit. I would present my thoughts when the guys returned to the bull pen and open it up for discussion.

The part about the men looking similar intrigued me, and I wondered where the killers would find such people. An elderly group maybe, or possibly people who had just lost their mates? The killers could pretend to have the same loss and befriend those men, and that would definitely lean more toward them being women.

I called Frank's cell phone. Either they were heading back soon, or I could go lend a hand. Sitting alone in the bull pen was unproductive. He answered on the third ring.

"What's up, buddy?"

"Have any of you seen them slinking around in the dark?"

"I'm striking out, plus it being nighttime and them wearing dark clothing isn't going to help the cameras catch their movements."

"How about the others? Have you talked to Henry?"

"Not in the last half hour, but Lutz gave us until two o'clock, and then it's on to something else."

"Okay." I glanced at my wrist and realized it didn't make sense to join them for less than an hour before they headed in. "I'm going to put something together for a news broadcast and run it by Lutz. The latest victim has a clean face, and I want it on the air as soon as possible. Maybe the third time is the charm and we might get a legitimate lead. I'll talk to Lutz about searching the nationwide missing persons database again, too, since it may have been updated during the last few days."

"Sounds good."

I placed the receiver back on the base and rose from my chair. I would walk my sheet of paper down to Lutz's office and let him look for himself. Everyone needed to throw out ideas on how these victimized men were connected, since the more information we had the luckier we'd get.

I rapped on Bob's door. "Got a minute?"

He removed his reading glasses, pinched the sides of his

nose, and pointed at his guest chair. "What's on your mind?"

"I'd like you to read these thoughts I've jotted down. I plan to run them by the guys when they get back too. We need leads, Boss, and the more ideas to follow, the better."

"Agreed." He perched the glasses back on the bridge of his nose and read the few paragraphs I'd written down. "Following the common thread between the victims could be the only way to catch the perps, especially since we don't have names to attach to the men. I like that. Check out bereavement groups, over-fifty-five clubs, that sort of thing."

There were plenty of organizations in the Chicagoland area that catered to the over-fifty-five crowd, and we would have our work cut out for us, but the idea was a good one. It made me think the killers were targeting men who reminded them of a particular individual, maybe somebody and something in their past that they couldn't let go of.

"Don is working with Mike on a facial shot of this morning's vic. He already has all the vital information put together for a news broadcast, and it should be ready any minute now."

"Good. Email it to me as soon as he sends it, and I'll take care of contacting the news channels." Lutz slid the paper back to me. "I just spoke with Henry. It doesn't sound like they're having luck seeing those two on camera."

I grumbled. "Frank echoed the same sentiment."

"Okay. They should be back soon, and I want everyone working on a connection these men may have had to each other. Somewhere, there's a common thread that the killers are using to choose their prey."

Chapter 31

I had passed Don's information on to Lutz, and the picture of the deceased provided by Don and Mike looked good enough to air on the local channels. The man's approximate age and description was sent along, and the commander would get it on the news as soon as possible.

The bull pen door opened, and five detectives poured through, each carrying packaged sandwiches and chips from the cafeteria as they prepared to eat lunch at nearly three in the afternoon. They placed their food on the desks and plopped down in chairs, grunting as they took their seats.

"No luck on any cameras?" I asked.

"Nope," Shawn said. "They slithered away and probably made a point of staying in dark alleys where they couldn't be seen."

"Yeah, probably. Go ahead and eat, and then we have work to do. I've written down questions we need to address, and I want opinions and ideas from all of you. Lutz wants us to start investigating clubs for the over-fifty-five age group too."

"That'll take forever," Frank said. "It would be too

obvious if they belonged to the same club and all went missing in the same week."

That thought hadn't entered my mind yet, but Frank was right. It was going to be a time-consuming process, but we had to weigh all possibilities.

"We can't drop the ball on Leah Standish, though. She needs to be interviewed. She's staying in the area, has been arrested for assault, and is from North Carolina."

"But she didn't leave her apartment last night according to Patrol, and she leased a tan Forester, not a blue Sienna," Tony said.

"You're right, but I'll see what Lutz thinks. It doesn't hurt to talk to her, and that way, we can cross her off our person of interest list."

While the guys were eating, I called Lutz. He said the news would be airing the latest victim's information on the five o'clock broadcast. I mentioned interviewing Leah Standish, too, and Lutz agreed.

"Check that sheet of temporary employee work locations, and then you and Frank pay her a visit. Abrams can put his patrol units to better use if she isn't deemed a person of interest."

Back in the bull pen, I gave the guys the sheet of ideas I'd thought about. "Go ahead and brainstorm your own ideas and write them down. We'll go over them later. Right now, Frank and I have to interview Leah Standish. Either she'll be crossed off, or we'll dig deeper into her past."

Frank grabbed a can of soda on our way out and already had a cigarette in hand when we hit the parking lot. He would have time to smoke only half of it before we left.

Fifteen minutes later, we reached the Oakview Clinic, where Leah was a temporary employee. The large three-story facility in front of us housed twenty-six doctors in various fields, a lab, a radiology department, and its own pharmacy. The main reception counter was directly ahead as we crossed through the automated doors.

Frank took the lead as he flashed his badge and introduced both of us then asked to speak with Leah Standish.

"Certainly, Detectives, I'll page her. It shouldn't be but a few minutes."

We thanked her and took seats in the waiting area, where newspapers and magazines filled the racks and coffee tables. A few minutes passed, then I noticed a thirtysomething brunette with her hair pulled back in a sleek ponytail walking toward us. The name tag on her lab coat read Leah S. We stood and introduced ourselves.

"Is there a place where we can speak to you privately, Miss Standish?" I asked.

"What on earth is this about?" Her eyes darted from Frank to me. She seemed petrified. "Did something happen to a family member of mine?"

"Not to our knowledge, ma'am. Our questions for you are related to recent crimes committed in Chicago."

"How would I know anything about crimes in Chicago? I've only been here a month."

"Ma'am, this conversation is better suited away from other people's eyes and ears."

She glanced at the relatively full waiting area. "Fine.

There's a small conversation pit down this hallway."

Frank and I followed as Leah led the way. At the end of the corridor sat a small grouping of four chairs and a round table centered between them. We took our seats.

She wrung her hands, and a look of anxiety mixed with aggravation crossed her face. "I really can't sit here long, so can you get to the point? I seriously have no idea what you're talking about. I'm from North Carolina, I work for the country's largest medical temp service, and I travel to different states every three to six months. Why on earth would my name come up in anything?"

I pulled my phone from my inner jacket pocket and located the file we had put together on Leah. "You're from Asheville, North Carolina, only a few hours from Charlotte. Is that correct?"

"Yes, but apparently you already know that."

"And you had charges filed against you a few years back for assaulting a patron in a bar?"

"It was a misdemeanor offense, and I made my restitution and paid a fine. That was five years ago, too, and I haven't had any altercations with anybody since. I mind my own business and go to work every day."

"Where were you last night?" Frank asked.

"At my apartment like most other nights. I got home, ate dinner, and watched TV until I went to bed at ten o'clock."

"Can anybody verify that?"

"No, other than a call from my mom at seven thirty while I was eating pizza for dinner. The delivery receipt is in the garbage can in my apartment, for God's sake."

"Is there a GPS system in the Forester you're leasing?"

"Yes, but how do you know what I'm driving?"

I ignored the question. "When does your term at the clinic end?"

"In two months."

"Do you have any reason to leave Chicago before that?"

"No. I work five days a week. I'm not going anywhere."

"Okay, that's all we have for you right now." We stood, and I handed my card to her. "We may need to contact you again. One more thing."

She stood and put my card in her lab coat pocket. "What's that?"

"Have you made friends with any other temp workers since you've been in Chicago, and do any of them work here?"

"I've made friends in the department I work in, which is phlebotomy, but I'm the only temporary employee here and filling in for a woman who's on maternity leave."

I nodded. "Sure. Thanks for your time."

Frank and I left, but instead of exiting the building, I headed to the reception counter again.

"Now what?" he asked.

I tipped my chin toward the same woman I'd talked to earlier. "Excuse me again. I'd like to speak to somebody in your Human Resources department."

"Certainly, unless there's something that I can help you with."

"We need to know if Leah Standish has missed any work or has come in late since she began her employment here."

"I can pull up her file since she isn't actually one of our employees. I wouldn't be overstepping that confidentiality clause. Give me just a second, please."

I watched as she tapped the keyboard on her side of the counter.

"Okay, here we go. Leah has been working with us for a month now, and it doesn't look like she's missed any days or come in late. A model employee by all appearances."

I patted the counter. "Okay, appreciate your help."

We walked out the same way we'd come in and I slipped my sunglasses over my eyes as we crossed the parking lot.

"So what's your gut feeling?" Frank asked.

I swatted the air. "She didn't have anything to do with the murders. She's petite, hardworking, and it doesn't sound like she knows anyone in the city other than her coworkers. I'd feel okay about crossing her off our list. She isn't the person we're looking for, and she doesn't have an accomplice."

We were back at the precinct in time to watch the five o'clock news. The first segment began with the news of another older man found dead in Chicago. That wouldn't necessarily raise suspicion with anyone since murder in the Windy City was a daily event, but these were older gentlemen and ones who hadn't been reported missing. His description and a facial photograph were shared along with the same tip-line number as before. Once more, it would be a waiting game with hopes of getting a viable lead.

Chapter 32

When Gail walked in, Janet craned her neck around the corner. "Hurry and sit down." She patted the spot on the loveseat. "The news is airing a segment about Cliff Howard."

Gail tossed her purse on the kitchen table and took a seat next to her mom. "How much did I miss?"

"None. They were leading into a commercial, showed his face, and said that segment was next. You're right on time." Janet scrunched her face into a scowl. "Makes me think, though."

"About what?"

"Missing fingers and teeth slow down the identification process to a degree, but if they're still recognizable, then it doesn't help on our end. From now on, we'll destroy their faces, too, just like—"

"I get it, Mom. With their faces destroyed, even if they are reported missing, nobody will know for sure if it's the right guy short of a DNA match. The news certainly can't air a headshot if it's completely mangled. We were lucky with Mr. Hennessey because his head was caved in, and so far, no news has come in that Robert Smith has been identified. I guess we'll see with Cliff." Gail scratched her chin. "There's always that learning curve to deal with."

"Or we can stop leaving the bodies where they'll be found. Hell, there's plenty of country lanes and back roads once you get away from big cities."

"True enough." Gail squeezed her mother's arm. "Here we go. The news is back on."

They watched eagerly as the anchor announced the discovery of another body, found that morning in the East Chicago Humane Society parking lot. The man's face was shown, and they gave his description as well. The anchor said the man had no identification on him, but if any viewers recognized his face, they were to call the toll-free tip-line number that went directly to the Chicago PD, and as always, the caller could remain anonymous.

Another commercial aired, then the segment went to the weather report.

"I guess that was it. Sounds like the PD is staying tight-lipped about the cause of death and the similarities between each man."

Gail chuckled. "Of course they are. Only the real killer and the police have that information. It's their way of weeding through the wack-a-doodles that want their fifteen minutes of fame."

Chapter 33

I pointed the remote at the TV and powered it off. "That's all we can do until the phones start ringing and hopefully with something promising. You four look online for local clubs that cater to the over-fifty-five crowd and start making calls while Frank and I man the tip lines."

Our group of detectives headed back to the bull pen. We would try to narrow down clubs that might be a good fit then send them photos of our first John Doe and the latest victim. If we were lucky, the men would be recognized, and that would give us names to work with.

The tip-line phones were located at the back of the bull pen with their own extensions so they wouldn't tie up our desk phones. They began ringing as soon as we crossed the threshold into the bull pen.

"Looks like we're going to be busy for a while." I picked up the receiver of the phone whose light was flashing red. "Chicago PD tip line, how can I help you?"

With paper on our desks and pens in hand, Frank and I began the long process of taking down information from every caller, legitimate or not, but without knowing who might have a lead, we had to take each one seriously. At seven o'clock, over a hundred calls had already come in, and by then, Shawn was on board to help lighten the load. It would take days to substantiate the calls to see whether any held merit, and the night shift guys would need to start on that as soon as they came in.

By eight o'clock, I was ready to call it a night since the twelve-hour shifts were taking a toll on everyone. The first shift crew bowed out and handed the reins over to our night detectives. Lutz had gone home an hour earlier, and I couldn't blame him. My own thoughts of plopping down on the couch with a cold beer in hand were appealing.

Frank and I walked out of the precinct and crossed the parking lot to our vehicles. I didn't have the energy or enough ambition to keep talking while he had a cigarette, so I said good night and drove away.

Twenty minutes later and with a tap on the remote, I lifted the overhead garage door and pulled in. I appreciated my home even more on the days where I'd spent most of my time at the precinct, which brought back my doubts about ever finding a woman who would be okay with my long workdays. Homicides in Chicago were a daily occurrence, and putting in an eight-hour day, five days a week, was almost unheard of.

After tending to Bandit's needs and plating a microwave fried chicken dinner, my pup and I retreated to the couch. Bandit curled up, content, and I cracked open a beer and ate my meal. A half hour later and with my laptop powered up, I logged on to the dating website I'd joined and checked my messages—I had two. Both women sounded nice. One said she was an attorney, and the other said she was an editor for a local magazine. I still didn't think I was quite there yet, but as I paged through profiles and posts, an epiphany sprang to mind. A traveling nurse might get lonely and look at dating sites, so why not a traveling nurse who was also a murderer?

What if those men were found through dating sites?

Our victims weren't so old that the thought of jumping into the dating pool wouldn't have crossed their minds. If they didn't have close friends who could set them up, then the possibility of browsing the dating sites made sense. Going that route was much easier than hitting the local bars that catered mostly to the younger crowd, anyway. I logged off my site and searched for ones primarily for the over-fifty-five crowd, and with the handful I found, I began setting up accounts on each one as if I were a woman searching for a man. Doing that gave me the ability to look at member profiles and possibly find our first and third John Doe. It was another avenue to explore, and it would either be a success, or we would rule it out and move on. I wrote down my log-in and username for every website I'd joined, and we'd go through them in the morning. I couldn't keep my eyes open any longer, so I gave up the fight and went to bed.

Chapter 34

My night was restless as I drifted in and out of sleep—none of which was sound or rejuvenating. I woke as tired as I was when my head hit the pillow the night before, but a shower, a bagel, and strong coffee would wake me up. I was excited to dig into my dating-site theory as soon as I planted my butt in my office chair. There were only five local sites, but the large, nationwide ones could also be an option. We couldn't rule out any, so we would have to give them a look, too, but we'd start with the Chicago-based sites first.

I explained my idea to our group during the roll call updates and got the okay from Lutz to check into dating sites but not until after we exhausted the local over-fifty-five social clubs and bereavement groups. Frank and I would finish calling them while the others continued with the tip-line leads. I was chomping at the bit to get a start on the dating sites, but it was a process of elimination, and we had to work through one idea at a time.

Checking online, I found the phone numbers of four bereavement groups that were mainly focused on the elderly. I started making the calls, asking if any of the male participants had suddenly stopped coming to the meetings. Three of the responses I got were that the usual attendees were there during the previous meetings, and one said a man hadn't shown up for the last two sessions. After digging deeper, I found out from the group administrator that the man was in his late seventies. That age wasn't in the range of our victims. I struck out and took a seat in Frank's guest chair.

"How many social clubs do you have left to call?" I was becoming impatient.

He ran his finger down the sheet. "There's nine left."

"Give me four of them, and let's knock them out. I think the dating sites might be the route to go."

"Sure." Frank tore the sheet of paper in half and handed the bottom part to me.

"Any promising leads on the tip lines?" I asked as I returned to my desk.

Henry spoke up first. "A few could be worth checking into. I'm thinking we should hit the handful of them that sounded legit this afternoon."

I gave him a head tip as I picked up the receiver and made my first call to Shuffle Time—an over-fifty-five shuffleboard club. As I was sure would be the case with most places we'd call, I was told that they needed a name, which I didn't have. I would offer a photograph of the first and third victims and hope that would be enough. It would be a time-consuming attempt at making IDs, but it was all we had. I hung up after collecting the email addresses of the administrators at each facility. I'd send the photographs via email so the images would be larger than the thumbnail sent with text messaging, then I'd wait for their responses, and I mentioned that the request was urgent.

Frank tapped his pen against the sheet of paper while waiting for the last contact to pick up. When they did, he went through the same explanation he had with the others. I poured a cup of coffee and listened to his side of the conversation while I waited for the call to end.

"Yes, I can send you the photographs now in a text but—uh-huh, I understand. Give me just a second." Frank tapped the pictures and attached them to a text message. "Okay, they're going through right now. It reads Sent and Delivered on my end. Now, if you'd give both of them a very close look and tell me if either are members of your Fifty and Better exercise group. Sure, I'll wait." Frank rolled his eyes and leaned back in the chair. A moment later, he sprang upright. "What! You recognize the first man? His name is Robert Smith, and you're certain it's him? Okay, I'm going to head your way as soon as we get off the phone, Ms. Riley, and thank you. I'll be there in fifteen minutes." Frank hung up and leapt from his chair. "We've got a positive ID on our first John Doe. Let's head out."

I made a quick call to Lutz as we took the back hallway to the rear exit. He needed to know about the latest development, yet I still wasn't one hundred percent convinced that Ms. Riley had correctly identified the man. Hopefully, they kept their own copies of the photo ID cards most gyms and health clubs insisted their members have. Witnesses often mistook people for someone else or gave a completely inaccurate description. It was commonplace, and I knew human recall wasn't nearly as good as we thought it was, but we were cautiously optimistic. I checked the time as we crossed the parking lot—9:32.

Frank drove as I pulled up the address of the Always Fit location on East Forty-Seventh Street, only a ten-minute drive from our precinct. Beth Riley had explained to Frank that she had to teach a spin class at ten o'clock. We would have about fifteen minutes to spend with her once we arrived unless she could get someone to cover the class in her place.

"Stay on Fifty-First until we hit South Drexler Boulevard and then hang a left. It'll be four blocks up on the right."

"Easy enough." Frank pulled out of our parking lot and gunned it.

"Why did she answer if she's an instructor?"

"Don't know, but it had to be a cell phone she answered because I was able to text the pictures to that number."

We arrived in under ten minutes, but parking, walking in, and asking for Beth Riley ate up another five precious minutes, and time was of the essence. The receptionist paged Beth to the counter, and we paced as we waited.

A woman, likely under thirty, approached us, and she was dressed in exercise wear and sneakers. A towel was draped around her neck, and a light sheen covered her skin. I assumed it was Ms. Riley.

"Detectives." She extended her right hand. "Excuse the towel. I'm still cooling down from the hot yoga class I finished just before you called." She glanced from Frank to me then back to Frank. "Which of you did I speak with?"

Frank made the introductions and said he had called. "If

we could sit somewhere, we'd like to discuss Mr. Smith with you. It's urgent that we get as much vital information as we can before your spin class."

She waved Frank off as she led the way to one of six table-and-chair groupings in the expansive members' area beyond the entry. "Not a problem. I found another instructor to cover that class. I'm all yours until ten forty-five."

Frank and I exhaled collective sighs. We could relax and ask every question we needed to. Since Frank was the detective who'd made contact with Beth, he would be the one conducting the interview while I took notes.

"First, we want to thank you for setting this time aside for us."

She smiled.

"As I said in our phone conversation, the man you say is Robert Smith was found deceased a few days back. His face was shown on the local news, but not everyone watches TV."

She lifted her hand. "Guilty. I'm so sad to hear about Mr. Smith's passing." She frowned. "Heart attack?"

"Not exactly. We wouldn't be here if that were the case, but he was found without identification on his person. That's why we've been reaching out to locate somebody that knew him. But before we get too far, we need to see his membership ID to make sure we're talking about the right person."

"Of course. I'll be right back."

We watched as Beth headed toward the registration and welcome counter, went behind it, and opened a file cabinet. She pulled out a folder and returned to our table.

"This is the file we put together for Robert when he joined

the club. His workout goals, the membership level he purchased, that sort of thing. And yes, his photo is in there too." She slid it across the table to Frank.

Robert's photo, stapled to the inside of the folder, was the first thing we saw. He was definitely our John Doe from Bixler Park.

Frank nodded. "That's him." He continued to the gym application and located Robert's address and phone number.

"Did you know Robert well?" I asked.

"Not really. He started the Fifty and Better exercise class just a week ago after having a free week to decide. I guess he wanted to get a feel for the club before making a real commitment as a paying member. He could come as often as he liked during that time and he spoke about hoping to make new friendships."

I wrinkled my brow. "New friendships. Why?"

She shrugged. "I think he had recently moved to the area."

I looked over each line of the application, and no one was listed as a contact person. "Did he say where he was from?"

"I don't remember him mentioning that, but of course I was the instructor and focused mainly on the classes and the participants' needs."

Frank passed Robert's application back to Beth. "Can you make us a copy of this?"

"Sure thing."

I gave Frank a head shake when Beth was out of earshot. "So Robert was new in town, from who knows where, and still nobody was wondering where he went? You'd think after trying his phone and not getting him on the line, they'd wonder why."

"True, but we don't know his story. It's sad to think, but maybe he didn't have anyone who checked up on him regularly."

Beth came back with the copy in her hand. "If that's all, I should really freshen up a little before my next class."

We thanked her and left. We had plenty to do as soon as we got back to the station. We needed to learn more about Robert Smith.

Chapter 35

Lutz had sent Henry and Shawn out to follow up on the few leads they took over the tip line. That left Frank, Tony, Kip, myself, and Lutz sitting around the table at the back of the bull pen. Frank went over the information shared by Beth Riley at the gym and handed Lutz the application that Robert Smith had filled out only two weeks prior.

"Have you gone to this address yet?"

Frank told him we hadn't, but as he drove to the station, I looked up the address on my phone. I added that it was an apartment complex on Halstead.

"What else do you know about this Robert Smith?"

"Only that he's new to the area, but we don't know from where or why he moved to Chicago. That leaves forty-nine other states he could be from."

Lutz tipped his chin toward my desk. "Grab your laptop and type his name into the database." He looked at the application again. "Of course he didn't put in his middle initial. That would make our nationwide search too easy."

"With all due respect, Boss, the guy didn't know he was about to be murdered."

Bob let out a long puff of air and apologized. "Sorry, that was uncalled for. We've just hit so many dead ends along the way, and there have to be hundreds of men named Robert Smith in the United States."

I logged on to our people-search database and typed in Robert's name. I started with the entire United States to get a feel for what we were dealing with and groaned when thousands of names popped up.

"Maybe I should try the missing persons database again to see if it's been updated. At least we have his name now."

Bob nodded, meaning go ahead. I typed Robert Smith into the search bar and came up with a half dozen names—easy enough to go through in a minute. All I needed to do was compare the ages of the missing men to our Robert Smith, and I did, but none were even close. The oldest missing Robert Smith that somebody was actually looking for was forty-seven years old. I was disappointed again, and I was sure the rest of our team felt the same way. We had a name but no backstory to go with it.

"Don't let it get you down, Jesse. Maybe Henry and Shawn will get lucky. Murders aren't always solved in a day or even a year."

I raked my hair as I responded. "I know, but in the meanwhile, those killers are searching out their next victim." Just as I was about to look up information on that apartment building to find out who the manager was, one of the tip-line phones rang on the counter behind us. I pulled the receiver off the base and answered simply because I was the closest to it. "Chicago Police Department tip line, how can I help you?"

I pressed the speakerphone button and set the receiver down. A female voice spoke on the other end.

"I'm calling about that unidentified man who was aired on the news last night. I've gone out on a date with him, and his name is Cliff."

"Ma'am, what is your name, and what is Cliff's last name?" I asked.

She sighed into the phone. "I'm Liza Wakefield, and as far as Cliff goes, we didn't get that far. The man was a total jerk, so I ended the date within a half hour. All he did was talk about how wonderful he was and how every woman should be honored to go out with him. That was all I could take, and I walked out of the restaurant."

"Did you meet Cliff through a friend?" Lutz asked.

"Am I on Speakerphone? Your voice is different than the man I was just talking to."

"Sorry, but yes. This investigation involves our entire detective team, and I'm Commander Bob Lutz. Nice to make your acquaintance, Liza."

"Thank you. So, back to your question, I'm embarrassed to say I met him on a dating website."

I fist-pumped the air, knowing I had been on the right track all along. "What is that dating site called?" I asked.

"It's singlechicagoprofessionals.com. I'm forty-eight and a high school principal. I figured I'd find the perfect match there, but now I'm disillusioned about dating altogether." She paused for a second. "I'm so sorry. Here I am carrying on about myself when that man is dead."

There was no way I was going to tell three other rough-

and-tough detectives and my own commander that I was a member of that very site, but narrowing down our search to one dating site was a step in the right direction. We might not have to investigate those other websites after all.

"What was his username?" Frank asked.

She groaned. "I should have known better as soon as I saw it. He went by In-Demand."

We simultaneously groaned with her.

"Did he mention family or what he did for an occupation? Where he worked, maybe?" Lutz asked.

"He said he was an investor and had hit it big in the tech industry during its infancy. He never mentioned family or having grown kids."

"Is there anything else you can tell us about him? Did he say where he lived?"

"No, but I did see him step out of a bright-orange Jeep when he got to the restaurant. I remember seeing words on the front bumper."

"Like the model name?"

"Yes, that's probably what it was and in large black letters."

I wrote that down. "That's a big help, and it could have said Wrangler or Rubicon."

"That was it—Rubicon. I remember now. He was bragging about it being brand-new and expensive."

Bob thanked Liza and gave her his office phone number then said we might contact her again. After making sure we had her name spelled correctly and the best number to reach her at, I clicked off the call.

Lutz pushed back his chair and stood. "Now we have something to work with. There are four of you, so start tearing apart that dating site. You may have to open up your own account in order to search for Cliff's username. Meanwhile, I'll get a warrant so we can see his application. What was that company name again?"

I wrote it down on a slip of paper and handed it to Bob. "It'singlechicagoprofessionals.com."

"Right." Lutz shook his head. "Why the hell anybody would use those sites is beyond my understanding. People like that are just inviting trouble into their lives. Let me know if you find something useful."

I stared at our commander's back as he walked out. He was likely as frustrated as the rest of us. Nothing about identifying the men or where they came from would be easy. We were either missing part of their name, or as in Robert Smith's case, we had his full name yet it matched those of thousands of other men. Without knowing where the men came from, we were still spinning our wheels. We needed to know everything about them if we ever hoped to find the killers.

"Okay, all of us log in to that site and create an account," I said.

Frank smirked. "As what, a guy looking for a guy? Is that even allowed?"

I sighed, already knowing the answer since I'd checked the site the night before. It was a straight site that allowed men-to-women connections only.

"Sign up with a woman's username. You can scan the

men's profiles for free, but responding to messages is a pay-as-you-go service."

Frank scratched his cheek as his eyes bore a hole through me. "How the hell would you know?"

I waved off his question. "Jenna always tried to get me involved in those dating sites. I told her I didn't have time for such nonsense."

"Humph. Whatever. So now I have to come up with a clever username."

I grimaced. "Really? You're going to put that much thought into it?"

He shrugged as he tapped the keyboard. "There. Now I'm GorgeousGeorgia."

"You're weird. Just sign up and type In-Demand into the search bar, and Cliff's profile should pop up."

Tony chuckled from his desk two away from mine. "You do seem to know more than you ought to about that dating site."

I scowled. "Go to hell." I tried to sign up under a female name and was immediately locked out.

Frank groused. "What's going on? I can't conduct a search."

"Me neither," Tony said.

I looked at Kip, and he frowned. "Same here."

"Shit. It's probably because we all share the same external IP address. The dating site thinks something suspicious is going on."

"Then I'll search by myself. You guys log out," Frank said.

I nodded. "Let's give that a try."

Frank typed Cliff's username into the search bar again. "Damn it. Not happening."

I covered my face with my hands and groaned. "Lutz is going to be pissed. Now we'll have to wait for that warrant."

With Liza's description about Cliff being full of himself, I wondered if he had joined other dating sites besides singlechicagoprofessionals.com. I had accounts with a half dozen of them already under various female usernames, and it was worth a shot to log on, type "In-Demand" into the search bar, and see if he had joined any others under that username. I glanced at the guys, and on Lutz's orders, they had settled back into weeding through the hundreds of phone leads after I'd explained our snag from earlier. Lutz had already requested the warrant for singlechicagoprofessionals.com so we could access In-Demand's application, and now we had to wait.

I logged on to my personal email using my phone to see what accounts I had set up in the over-fifty age group sites. With each log-in on my computer, I typed "In-Demand" into the search bar and got zero results. Either Cliff had never joined multiple sites, or he had been clever enough to choose a different username for each one.

Moments later, Henry and Shawn walked in. "We may have something," Henry said.

I minimized my computer's screen and directed my focus to him. "Yeah, like what, because we're striking out here in the bull pen."

"Like a woman who recognized victim number three from the news coverage and coincidentally had an altercation with him just last week."

I raised my hand to stop Henry. "Hang on a second. I think Lutz ought to sit in on this." I called our boss, and he said he would join us in five, which gave me just enough time to make a pot of coffee.

Minutes later, with fresh coffee on our desks, Lutz walked in and let out an involuntary grunt as he took a seat in Henry's guest chair. He jerked his chin—his way of saying "go ahead"—and Henry began.

"This woman, a Jasmine Ortega, had just left the home in Old Town where she works as a nanny. She said she was at a stoplight behind a bright-orange Jeep, and the light had gone from red to green, but the Jeep didn't move, so she honked at him."

I huffed. "The jerk was probably checking his dating messages."

Henry and Shawn frowned.

"I'll explain that part later."

Lutz shushed me and told Henry to continue.

"Anyway, she said the man jumped out of his vehicle and stormed toward her car. She cranked the wheel, got past him, and then stopped just long enough to snap off a picture of his license plate before taking off again. To her surprise, he chased her, ran her off the road with his Jeep, and continued on. She called the cops but never heard anything after that."

Lutz cursed. "What district did it happen in?"

"The eighteenth, sir, still in Old Town."

"I'll talk to the district commander and Abrams. So she doesn't know his last name?"

"No, or his first. Did we miss something while we were gone?"

Lutz jerked his head at Frank. "Update them." He turned to Henry. "I need that Jeep's license plate number."

"I have it right here, Boss." Henry stood and pulled his notepad from his pocket. He flipped to the last page, folded it over, and handed the notepad to Lutz.

"I'll get back to this later. Right now, I need a word with the commanders."

I returned to my online search of Robert Smith's apartment in hopes of finding a manager's phone number so I wouldn't have to drive there. From the photos of Sunnyview Apartments and the fact that the website itself looked to be from 1990, I wasn't surprised that no manager's number was listed. The complex probably changed managers every year.

I looked at Frank. "Want to take a drive to Robert Smith's apartment complex after lunch? Maybe the manager will know more than Beth Riley did, and there's always the chance that he'll let us into Robert's apartment."

"Yep, but I'm not holding my breath. The majority of people don't go out of their way to make things easy on cops."

Chapter 36

Frank and I arrived at the steel-and-tinted-glass apartment complex on West Fifteenth Place and Halstead just after twelve thirty. The apartments looked better in person than they did on the dated website with its underexposed pictures. Robert's building was one of four that appeared to be in the same complex, with two on one side of the street and two on the other.

I shrugged as I stepped out of the cruiser and onto the sidewalk. "See any signs that say office?"

Frank did a three sixty and said no. I didn't see any signs either.

"May as well check this side first, then." I walked to the nearest building on our side of the street and pulled open the glass door. Inside the vestibule was the tenant directory showing the apartment number, the tenant's name, and a button for the intercom. A wall of built-in mailboxes was next to the panel. Looking through the door that opened to the hallway, we saw an elevator, an exit sign at the back of the building, and an arrow pointing left to the exercise room and pool. I imagined each building was the same.

I scanned the directory of forty-eight names—none were Robert's, and none had Manager written next to them.

"Let's move on," Frank said.

We checked the building next door and had the same results.

"The manager has to be in one of those buildings across the street." I tipped my head that way.

"Are you sure there's an on-site manager at all?" Frank asked.

I didn't know that to be a fact, but I assumed there was—most apartments had managers. I jerked my chin toward the other side of the street. "There's only one way to find out." I looked both ways before stepping off the curb.

We entered the third building and scanned the directory.

"Here's Robert's name." Frank tapped the ninth name on the panel. His apartment was on the first floor—number 1-9. "No manager listed, though, and we have one more building to check."

We walked out then entered the last building. The first name on the directory for apartment 1-1 showed T. Sorensen-Manager.

"Thank God." I pressed the buzzer, and we waited. Thirty seconds passed, and I pressed it again. "Damn it, he isn't home."

The glass door opened, and a woman and her dog walked out. She gave us a smile as she passed to the outer door.

"Excuse us, ma'am, but do you know where the manager is?" Frank exposed his badge so she wouldn't think we were solicitors.

A surprised expression crossed her face before she answered. "You're the police? Did Ted do something wrong?"

"Is Ted the manager?" I ignored her question.

"Yes, but he works during the day. If someone calls with an emergency during his work hours, he has an assistant who helps out."

"Do you know where Ted works or what time he gets back home?"

"No and yes."

I stared.

"No, I don't know where he works, and yes, I know when he gets home because I live next door to him in apartment number two. He's usually home by five thirty."

"Do you know Robert Smith from the building next door?" I asked.

She shrugged. "Most everyone does their own thing. We don't really get together unless there's a community event going on, but no, I don't recognize his name."

We thanked her, and I pushed open the door, allowing her and her pup through. "So it's safe to say that Ted should be here between five thirty and six?"

"Yes, I always hear him open his door around then."

We had no reason to stick around, so we headed to the precinct, where we exchanged updates with Lutz. We explained that the manager of the apartment where Robert lived would be home later, and we would try again then. Lutz told us that Cliff was Cliff Howard, and officers from the Eighteenth District had gone to his residence and asked him about the incident with Jasmine Ortega. He'd denied running her off the road and said she was driving erratically, so he got past her as quickly as he could. When he glanced at her car, she was texting on her phone. The officers pulled his driving record and saw that it was clean and he'd never been arrested. He lived in a nice home in a nice neighborhood, so they gave him a warning and left.

Lutz raised his palms. "That's all I know about the incident, but now we have his full name and know where he lived. I'll get a warrant to search his home and Robert's too. Maybe we'll find a common thread that connects those two men with someone else."

Little by little, our case was advancing. We knew two out of the three victims' names and where they lived. Now to get inside their homes and find some shred of evidence that would tell us what they were doing, and with whom, on the last nights of their lives.

Chapter 37

Anxiety was getting the best of her, and Janet paced as she watched the clock. Gail only worked until three p.m. that day, and she had Cliff's Jeep. They were foolish not to have thought that through. With Cliff's face aired on the news last night, it was just a matter of time before somebody would call the police tip line, give Cliff's name, and the cops would realize that the blue Sienna wasn't his vehicle.

Later that night, they would have to drop off the Jeep at Cliff's home—unseen—then rent another van.

Janet began searching the free sites that gave possible matches, phone numbers, and addresses of any name typed into the website's search bar. She found two Cliff Howards listed in Chicago—one in a shitty neighborhood and one in Old Town. She assumed the second address belonged to Cliff. They would rent a different vehicle, drive by to check the home's layout, and return that night.

The creak of the door made Janet turn—Gail was home. Janet breathed in relief.

Gail's eyes locked with her mother's as she closed the door behind her. "What's with the look?" She hung her purse on the chairback and took a seat.

"I'm just relieved you're home. What if the police are searching for that Jeep? It isn't like it blends in with other vehicles."

"How would they connect Cliff to the Jeep?"

"He was a dog, honey. Remember, that's why he was left with other dogs. Do you think you were the only woman who went out with him? Somebody probably called the tip line already."

"Mmm… you might be right. So now we have to ditch the Jeep just as I was starting to like it."

Janet shook her head. "I know, but it's too risky. We'll take it to Cliff's house late tonight and leave it in the driveway."

"Okay, then I better get another rental set up that can be delivered here. We'll use your fake ID again since that works like a charm."

"Sorry." Janet stared at the table.

"For what, Mom?"

"For needing to do this."

Gail patted Janet's arm. "We both needed to do it. For our sanity."

Chapter 38

The warrants for the residences had arrived, but the one for the website would take longer to get. We still had an hour before Ted Sorensen would be home to allow us entry into Robert Smith's apartment. Lutz sent Frank, Henry, Shawn, and me out to serve the warrants on both residences. Since both men were dead and nobody knew who their next of kin were, serving the papers was just a formality and something we legally had to do. We would enter Cliff's home ourselves since there wasn't a landlord to let us in. We hoped to find evidence of a will, insurance policies, an address book, or something similar to help us track down a family member who would handle his property and belongings. After that, we planned to secure the home until somebody took it over. Robert's situation would be less complicated, and all we hoped to find—besides the common thread between both men and the killers—was the name of his next of kin.

We grabbed two cruisers and headed out, planning to go through Cliff Howard's home first. When it was time for Ted Sorensen to arrive home from work, Frank and I would leave for Robert's apartment and begin searching it.

We arrived at what appeared to be a recently refurbished brick two-story, now with a white contemporary look. Situated on a tree-lined street, it resembled several of the others in the well-to-do neighborhood. The style, somewhat like my own home, had the garage tucked under the living quarters. A row of narrow windows spread across the overhead garage door. They looked to be just above my eye level, but since Frank was several inches taller than the rest of us, he'd be able to see inside. He parked along the curb, and we climbed out. Henry snugged the nose of his cruiser against our rear bumper, then we walked up the driveway together.

Standing on his tiptoes, Frank peered into the garage. "There's a Corvette inside but no Jeep."

"Meaning the killers definitely have it," Shawn said.

We continued to the front door. Frank turned the knob—it was locked as we'd assumed it would be.

"Check the usual places for a key before we pick the lock." I began by looking under decorative stones strategically placed in the flower beds along the stoop.

Henry and Shawn scoured through the shrubbery, and Frank ran his hand along the top of the doorframe then patted the top of the porch light. "Got it."

I shook my head. "At least it wasn't under the welcome rug."

We entered into a long hallway that doubled as a foyer. It opened up to an expansive living room with a huge eat-in kitchen to the right. From all appearances, Cliff had it pretty cushy—modern furniture, an expensive home in a well-off neighborhood, and possibly a housekeeper who kept the place immaculate. It was the quintessential bachelor pad.

"Let's do a quick walk-through and then put our focus on the kitchen area and wherever the office space is located. Those two places are where we'll find his computer, tablets, possibly a phone, and paperwork."

We walked the main floor first. The living room, kitchen, dining area, a half bath, and laundry room were on that level. Below that were the stairs that went to the garage and a partial basement. We took the staircase to the second floor, where we found the en suite master bedroom with an attached office, two other bedrooms, and a full hallway bath.

"Okay, let's go through the master bedroom first, and then when we have to leave, you guys can finish off the rest of the house. I'd like to clear the entire upper floor before we go if that's possible."

We immediately spotted the laptop sitting on the desk, and I powered it up. I was disappointed to find it would open only by facial recognition or the PIN, meaning we couldn't access the contents. We would take the computer back to the tech department and let them try their hand at it. Cliff probably stored his passwords in a file on that computer, which could give us valuable information.

I took a seat at the desk and began going through the drawers, looking for whatever we could use. Finding Cliff's log-in information for the dating site would likely tell us who his killer was. That would be the second thing on my list of to-dos after feeding Bandit when I got home. With a different IP address, I could look through singlechicagoprofessionals.com to see if Cliff Howard, or In-

Demand, had something worthwhile to tell us.

After finding nothing in his desk that would lead us to his killer, I resigned myself to focusing solely on the dating site. If I could find messages between Cliff and the last person he dated, we could follow the bread crumbs and apprehend the people responsible for his death and probably seven others.

With the laptop cradled under my arm, I left the office. Frank had just finished going through every dresser drawer. He'd already checked between the mattresses, under the bed, and behind the artwork on the walls.

Shawn called out from the walk-in closet. "I found a safe!"

We crossed the room, not sure why that wouldn't have been the first thing he noticed when he entered the closet.

I looked around, as did Henry and Frank. "Where?"

Shawn grinned. "Check this out."

What appeared to be rows of drawers was actually a false front with a safe behind it. I wondered why Cliff Howard had gone to the trouble of having that built. What was he hiding?

"Let's leave everything as is and give the kitchen a quick look. I think the tech department and Forensics need to be on scene. Somebody has to get that safe open and see what Cliff felt needed to be hidden so well."

Henry piped in. "He could have rented a safe-deposit box unless—"

Frank furrowed his brows. "Unless what?"

"Unless it was something he wanted to access whenever the urge or need arose."

"Interesting theory, Henry, and I tend to agree. I'll give

Lutz a call and see what he thinks. Meanwhile, start going through the kitchen. I remember seeing a built-in planning desk in there. If luck is on our side, you'll find an address book with names we can follow up on or a calendar with important dates circled." Once we were downstairs, I excused myself, stepped out onto the small deck off the back of the house, and called Lutz. "Boss, we've found something interesting at Cliff Howard's house." I pressed Speakerphone and placed my phone on the wooden railing.

"Go ahead."

"Other than his laptop, which is locked, but we'll bring it back to the district, we found a safe."

"Interesting."

"I'd say it's a little more than interesting." I scanned the horizon as I talked, and in the distance was the top of the Willis Tower.

"Sure, you have my attention."

"The safe is located behind a false row of drawers in the master closet. If there's something inside that's so valuable, then why wouldn't he just rent a safe-deposit box?"

"True. So that means he needed to keep whatever it was well-hidden but wanted instant access to it any time day or night."

"Exactly."

"Does it look like something a locksmith could open?"

I sighed. "I'm not an authority on safes, but I'd like to have Forensics and Tech give the house and safe the once-over before we call in outside help. Cliff may have gotten himself killed because of what's inside."

"Okay, I'll have them head out."

I checked the time. "Frank and I are going to head out, too, so we can have that talk with Robert Smith's landlord, but Henry and Shawn are going to keep searching the house for anything that might help." I hung up and went indoors. "Lutz is sending Forensics and Tech out, and Frank and I need to get going." I tipped my head at Henry and Shawn. "Be thorough, guys."

Chapter 39

With the curtain pulled aside, Janet watched out the window for the rental van to arrive. "I think that's them," she said when a cranberry-colored Sedona and a car driving slowly behind it finally pulled to the curb in front of their apartment complex.

Gail peeked out. "You know you're going to have to go out and deal with them."

"Yeah, yeah, I've done this shit before, but I don't have to like it." Janet slipped on a pair of oversized sunglasses and snugged a wide-brimmed hat on her head. "Come on. You have to sign the papers for me." Janet handed her wallet to Gail, who pulled out the fake driver's license and credit card that had been created using the name of Janet St. James. They stepped outside and walked to the driver's side of the van. The representative—who wore a name tag that read C. Noble—exited the van and introduced himself.

"Afternoon, ladies. I'm Carl. Right this way." He escorted the women to the car parked behind them. "We have a mobile computer system set up in this unit so we can collect your information. We'll email you a receipt when the paperwork is complete." He pointed at the driver. "This is Chuck McBride."

With a nod, Janet passed her driver's license and credit card to him.

"Will you be the only driver, Ms. St. James?"

"That's correct," Janet said.

"Do you need additional insurance for incidentals, and do you want us to fill up the vehicle when you return it?"

"No to both questions. We've got it covered."

"Very well." Chuck gave the cards back to Janet. "I just need your signature in the three spots I've circled." He handed the clipboard to Janet, who passed it to Gail. "Um... ma'am."

Janet cut him off. "She's my power of attorney and has legal rights to sign documents on my behalf." She jerked her chin at Gail. "Go ahead, honey."

Carl pointed at the van. "Let's do a check of the vehicle and note if there's any damage before you take possession of it." He walked around the vehicle with Janet and Gail at his side.

"That looks like a door dinger." Gail pointed at the front passenger-side door just below the handle.

"Good eye." Carl put an *X* in that location on the diagram of the van. "See anything else?"

Janet took her time. She wasn't about to be held responsible for someone else's damage to the vehicle. "Looks okay."

"Good, then we just need one more signature that the vehicle is satisfactory and we'll be on our way." He passed the clipboard to Gail, and she signed as illegibly as always then handed it back. "Any questions, ladies?"

"Nope."

"All right. Have a nice day."

They watched as he opened the passenger-side door of the car and climbed in. As soon as the men were out of sight, Janet locked the apartment, and they climbed into the van, with Gail behind the wheel.

Janet pulled up Cliff's address and let the phone lead the way. They'd have a half-hour drive to Old Town.

"What are we going to do about the other van?" Gail asked.

"Who cares? Your name wasn't on the paperwork, so they can't hold you responsible. We'll be long gone and in another state in a few months, and as far as my name and signature on it goes? It isn't really me, anyway. I wouldn't sweat it, honey, and that's why they have insurance."

Janet stared out the passenger window as Gail took State Street north all the way to Old Town. She turned left on East Division then made a right on North Sedgewick and then a final left on West Blackhawk. The house was a white brick two-story on the even-numbered side of the street.

"We're looking for house number two twenty-four," Janet said. "I'll watch for it since the even numbers are on my side."

"Mom?"

"Yeah, honey?"

"There's a police cruiser parked along the curb up there on your side."

"Where!"

"Four houses up. It has the spotlights on the sides and the big antenna. I can spot a police cruiser anywhere."

"Stay calm and drive by slowly. I want to see if it's Cliff's house they're at or if we're worrying about nothing."

Gail continued on as Janet watched the house numbers.

"Shit. The house coming up is two twenty-two. That means the next one is Cliff's."

Gail punched the dash. "And the one the cops are at, damn them all."

Chapter 40

The drive to Robert's apartment was almost six miles away, a half hour with traffic. We left Cliff's house at five fifteen with that in mind. When we arrived, I pressed the buzzer for the manager, Ted Sorensen, and waited.

Seconds later, a gruff voice answered. "This is a no-solicitation apartment complex."

"Good to know," Frank said. "It's the Chicago police, and we need to speak to you face-to-face."

We waited a few seconds, then the door buzzer sounded. I grabbed the handle and pulled. Twenty steps in was apartment 1-1, the manager's. Frank gave the door two hard knocks, and we heard steps heading our way. The sound stopped, and I expected the knob to turn. Instead, we continued to wait. I figured he was sizing us up from his side of the peephole. I lifted my badge and held it out so he could see it and also to cause a little embarrassment on his end. The door immediately opened.

"You can never be too careful, you know." He gave us another once-over.

"Ted Sorensen?" Frank used a no-nonsense tone.

"Yeah, that's me. What did someone accuse me of now?"

We ignored his question. "May we come in?" I asked. "It's about one of your tenants."

He turned and looked at the mess behind him then huffed. "I guess. Wasn't expecting company, and I just got home from work."

"Not a problem. We need to know everything you can tell us about Robert Smith from apartment 1-9 in the building next door."

"Robert?" Ted shrugged. "He's a non-issue kind of guy, and I barely know him. I don't interact much with the tenants unless there's a complaint against them or they're late on the rent. He doesn't gripe about the apartment, but there's really nothing to complain about. All of the apartments in that building were remodeled last year." Ted chuckled. "I take him as a loner, but I wouldn't know that for a fact. It's just my assumption. I'm at work Monday through Friday, nine to five, and unless there's a community event, I never see him."

I took notes as Frank continued on.

"When was the last time you did see him?"

Ted rubbed his chin. "Probably at our Labor Day party on the rooftop of this building. Is he in some kind of trouble?"

"You could say that. How about guests? Did he have anyone with him at that party, or did you see him talking mainly to one person?"

Ted swatted the air. "Nah. With a few hundred people up there—besides the catering crew—you barely notice anyone in particular. I just happened to be grabbing a beer at the same time he was and said hi, that's all."

"We'll need to see Robert's rental application," I said.

Ted crinkled his nose. "Yeah, you'd probably want to get his okay first. I don't think I can legally do that without his permission."

Frank got right to the point. "We're giving you permission."

Ted shook his head and smiled. "I don't know—"

"Ted, Robert is dead. Do you want to cooperate with our investigation into his death or not?"

Ted's eyes bulged. "Investigation? That could only mean foul play. I know that since I watch a lot of crime shows on ID."

I held up my hand. "Then as someone who's an expert in the field, you know we can't discuss the case with you. Now if we can have a look at his application."

"Oh, sure, give me a minute to pull it from my file cabinet." Ted jerked his head toward a couch that had blankets strewn across it. "Have a seat."

He left, and we remained standing. I spoke in a low voice while Ted was gone. "What's your take? I doubt if anyone here at the apartment was responsible."

Frank nodded. "If he *was* a loner, maybe he was looking online for companionship too."

"Yeah, maybe."

Ted was back in a matter of minutes. "I printed out a copy for you. Want to do my part to help the PD, you know."

"Appreciate it." I gave it a quick look before we left. The paperwork showed Robert had moved in only two months prior. "Looks like he was a new resident."

"Yep, hadn't lived here long."

I continued down the application. "Ever say why he moved to Chicago?"

"Not that I recall."

"The previous address section shows he lived in Oakland, California, from 2009 until 2016. Where has he been since then?"

Ted shrugged. "He said he'd been traveling."

"Uh-huh. And no references listed? That didn't raise a flag with you?"

"Nope. I pulled a background check, it came up good, and he paid the first month in advance. That was all I needed. He said he had a lifelong pension from the shipyards that would easily cover his rent."

"Sure." I handed my card to Ted, and we thanked him and left. I called Henry as Frank drove. "How's it going on your end? Any progress with the safe?"

"Nope. Tech says we should contact a safe company that's familiar with that brand. They'd probably be able to drill it open."

"Find anything more at the house? An address book, calendar, that sort of thing?"

"Nah. He must have kept everything on his phone, computer, or in that safe. Forensics didn't see anything that would lead them to think a crime had taken place here. They even sprayed Luminol in the usual places. Nothing lit up."

"Okay, so Tech will take the laptop back to the precinct, and then we're waiting on somebody that'll pop the safe?"

"That's about it, and the safe company won't be out until tomorrow. It's already after hours."

"Damn it. Okay, we're heading back in."

"We're wrapping it up too. See you there."

I couldn't wait to get home, where I could research both Robert and Cliff on my own computer. Although it was probably a long shot, Robert might be a member of singlechicagoprofessionals.com too. Either way, I would go through every male profile on that site, starting with In-Demand.

Chapter 41

They were back at the apartment by six o'clock, and Janet was fuming. Inside, she paced as she thought.

Is it better to return Cliff's Jeep to his house or leave it in some random place?

"Mom, stop pacing already. You're making me dizzy. So, what should we do with the Jeep?"

Janet poured a shot of vodka and gulped it. "They already know who he is and where he lives. Damn it, we should have smashed his face in. He would have deserved it, anyway."

"Then the best place to leave the Jeep is right in his own driveway. Why give the cops anything else to work with? We'll stick to the plan and drop it off later tonight. Right now, let's find another lonely man who's looking for a date."

Janet smirked. "And he won't get off as easy as Cliff and Robert did. When we're done with him, there won't be anything left above his shoulders that's recognizable."

Chapter 42

Another twelve-hour day had come and gone. Hour by hour and inch by inch, we were getting closer to the killers, but we still weren't there. We needed that warrant to access Cliff's dating-site messages, then we would be home free—I hoped. Tomorrow we should have answers about the messages and about what Cliff had in his safe that he'd wanted so well hidden.

I didn't know if we would ever identify our second victim due to his head injuries, but when the killers were behind bars, and if they wanted a deal, perhaps they'd give up his name and the names of all the other victims in North Carolina and California.

It was after eight o'clock by the time I pulled into my garage and dragged my body up the stairs. Bandit greeted me the same way he always did—enthusiastically. After he got a good head pet, a run around the backyard, and food in his belly, he was content.

I ordered takeout since I wanted to spend the rest of my waking hours searching the dating sites for Cliff Howard and Robert Smith. For that night, a calzone would suffice.

Even though I couldn't access Cliff's messages, or log in as a female since I'd already opened my own account with my home IP address, I could search female profiles to see if any looked like the type who would have interested Cliff. In light of Liza Wakefield's description of him as a full-of-himself, arrogant man, he had probably gone after younger, beautiful, and cosmetically altered females.

In the search bar, I typed in the age parameters—twenty-five through forty—since chances were slim that anyone younger would be a well-established professional. I doubted that Cliff had wanted anybody older than forty on his arm either. I wasn't sure whether their occupation had mattered to him or even their salary, unless it was solely for bragging rights. He seemed well-off on his own. I also typed in that the match would have to live within twenty-five miles of Chicago. Cliff didn't seem like the kind of guy who would have traveled far for a date, and he would likely have expected women to be drawn to him instead. With those parameters set, I began my search, starting with the youngest group of women who insinuated they were interested in older men to serve as "sugar daddies" in exchange for companionship. I understood what that meant—they were both using each other. Cliff would have a hot babe on his arm, and the woman would benefit financially with gifts and vacations. I set the first group search for those between the ages of twenty-five and twenty-nine. After that, I would move to thirty through thirty-five, and I'd end with thirty-six through forty. The first group consisted of eighty-seven women.

You've got to be kidding me!

I'd had no idea how daunting that task would be, and waiting until tomorrow for that warrant would probably save me hours of searching for a needle in a haystack. I was about to log off when I noticed I had three new messages. Curiosity got the best of me, and I began reading what they wrote. The first woman, CallingMyOwnShots, was a work-from-home sales administrator for a large cosmetic firm. I had no idea what that meant. She said she was thirty-seven—my own age, which was fine—divorced, and had two kids under ten. I would pass on that one. If I ever did get married, I'd want my own kids. Being the stepdad that kids didn't listen to wasn't in the cards for me.

The next woman, NinetoFiveChick, was twenty-four—a bit young for my taste—the assistant manager for a high-fashion boutique downtown, and lived in the northern burbs. That was a hike from my home. Although both women were extremely pretty, I didn't feel we'd find the connection I was hoping for. I was about to close my computer and forget the whole dating scene since I knew deep down I'd never find that compatible woman. I told myself she didn't exist, but I knew I was really looking for an excuse to give up on the marriage-and-kids chapter of life. Although I was already dozing off, I forced myself to check out the third message. At least then I could delete all three and probably my account too. I clicked on the third message, from TravelingBabe90.

Interesting username. Maybe she's a photographer for National Geographic and travels the world for that once-in-a-lifetime shot, my own dream that never came to fruition.

I imagined the ninety stood for her birth year.

What else could it be? That would put her in my age group.

Her profile sounded nice. She traveled for work, like I'd thought, although she didn't say what her job was. She was twenty-nine, never married, and had no children. She grew up in Bismarck, North Dakota, and even though she was an only child, she'd spent a lot of time with her extended family. Her parents, unfortunately, had parted ways just over a year ago. She'd recently moved to Chicago and wanted to meet new people and experience big-city living. Even though Bismarck was a nice size, it was still under one hundred thousand people. She said she enjoyed reading my profile because we shared similar interests, like football games, running, hiking, sightseeing, dining out, and the fact that I had a dog was definitely a plus. I sounded like a well-rounded person, she'd said, with family values, much like herself.

Hmm... she sounds compatible.

Before I responded—if I did—I felt the need to check out her pictures. With that wannabe photographer's eye, I would notice if something looked staged, copy and pasted, or if stock photography had been used. I pressed the photos tab and opened her gallery. Inside, I found eight pictures—ten was the limit for free. I'd posted three on mine. Two of hers looked to be from family gatherings years earlier, but the others looked current. One was of her standing in front of what appeared to be a capital building, and several more seemed to be travel-related photos, including candid shots at restaurants and several shots of hiking trails. She *did* mention she liked hiking. She was a pretty blonde, and her hair color appeared natural. She looked fit, as if she could be a runner, and her profile stated she was five foot six and weighed one hundred and twenty pounds.

So far, so good, and none of the pictures appear to be doctored.

I didn't know—I wasn't sure. Could I be opening up a can of worms by typing in my credit card number and posting a response? My life was busy, even too busy to justify having a pet, although Bandit and I made it work, especially with my neighbor Dean's help. I sucked in a deep breath, weighed the pros and cons, pulled my credit card from my wallet, and tapped the computer keys.

Chapter 43

"It's done." Gail closed the laptop, reached for two wineglasses in the kitchen's top cabinet, and filled both.

Janet smiled while shaking her head. "You've got guts. I'll give you that. Don't you think you're inviting trouble?"

"Maybe, but no guts, no glory. We *are* that good, Mom."

Janet returned her comment with a wagging finger. "I wouldn't get overconfident. It'll be our downfall if you do."

Gail waved her off. "Nah, it's all for fun. I know he's nothing like Dad, but I'm daring myself to do it just to see if he's the same as the rest—stupider than shit."

They both laughed.

"Don't worry. I won't do anything to jeopardize our mission, but it'll be fun to mix it up a bit and then kill him like the others. What a shock wave that'll create in the Chicago Police Department, and it'll serve them right for snooping so much. Just leave us the hell alone and let us do what we're meant to do."

"That's right." Janet took a seat at the table, licked her index finger, and lightly ran it around the rim of the wineglass. It rang out a deep tone. "I'm impressed. Real crystal."

Chapter 44

I stopped by Lutz's office and gave the door two raps. He called out for me to come in.

"What's up, Jesse?"

"Just wondering if that warrant for Cliff's dating-site messages has come in yet."

Bob chuckled. "You're chomping at the bit, aren't you? You do realize the courthouse doesn't open until eight, right?"

I glanced at the clock on the opposite wall—7:49.

"Damn it, my mind is preoccupied with getting those killers behind bars as soon as possible."

"Understood, but I can't do anything until they open for business. I'll give the judge a call before our morning updates. That way, I can let the entire team know when to expect the warrant."

I patted his doorframe. "Fair enough. And the guy about the safe?"

"He'll meet with the person I put on that detail at Cliff's house at nine thirty."

"I'll volunteer."

"Okay, that'll work. See you at roll call in a half hour."

My head was filled with too many thoughts. I'd entered my credit card information on the dating site last night but hadn't responded to TravelingBabe90. I needed a minute to think about the consequences of beginning a relationship with someone. I pictured the loving parents I had, and the happy home I grew up in came to mind. I doubted that many people had that kind of relationship in today's world. Thirty years ago, life was simpler, and love was stronger. At least it seemed that way in my home.

As I sat at my desk, I worried that I had become jaded, and I didn't want to be that person. I pulled my phone from my jacket pocket and logged on to singlechicagoprofessionals.com and responded to TravelingBabe90's message. I kept it short and simple. "I'm interested. Tell me more about yourself." That was a safe start—baby steps. It gave me a chance to learn more without committing to a meetup right out of the gate. I needed to know if there was a spark before I wasted her time or my own. I hit Send and logged off, then I put my phone away. It was time for our morning roll call and updates. I grabbed a coffee and headed down the hallway with Frank.

Just like every other day, Lutz put his fist to his mouth and cleared his throat before beginning. The room went silent. He took roll call first then moved on to the updates.

"Confirmation has just come in from Judge Banks that the warrant has gone through. I should have it on my desk by nine o'clock, and it'll be forwarded to the administrator at singlechicagoprofessionals.com to give us access to the messages received and sent by Cliff Howard. They've been given until the end of tomorrow's workday to provide us access to Cliff's communication logs, or they'll be held in contempt. Those messages should contain valuable information and hopefully enough to crack this case wide open. I'm cautiously optimistic that by tomorrow, we'll have our killers in custody."

The room erupted with hoots and hollers. It was time to put an end to the mutilating and killing of innocent Chicago men. If it was proven that the killers had also committed the crimes in Charlotte and Sacramento, then the police departments in both cities could close the books on those open cases too.

We returned to the bull pen, and like me, everyone appeared to have had a fifty-pound weight lifted from their shoulders. Smiles lit up faces for the first time that week. Our detectives and officers could get back to a normal life, go home at a reasonable hour, and spend long-overdue time with their families.

My desk phone rang at a quarter till nine. It was Lutz calling.

"Go ahead and leave for Old Town. It's going to take a while to get there with the morning traffic. Maybe by the time you and Frank return, we'll have news from the dating site."

"And maybe we'll have news about what was so secret that Cliff needed to have a faux dresser built into his closet to hide his safe."

Lutz sighed into the phone. "It might turn out to be a good day after all."

Frank fired up the cruiser and we pulled out of the parking lot. I was curious to find out what was inside that safe and couldn't wait until the technician opened it. It could be nothing more than common documents or even old photos he wanted to preserve, but to go to that extreme to protect something was odd. We reached Cliff's street at 9:22—traffic had been reasonable.

"What the hell!" My head snapped forward.

As Frank approached the home, we saw the bright-orange Jeep sitting in the driveway.

"You better call Lutz and get Forensics back out here. That vehicle absolutely wasn't here yesterday."

We turned in time to see a van with an advertising logo that read UnLockIt on the side panel, and he parked at the curb behind our cruiser. The safecracker had arrived.

I jerked my head toward the man and walked to the porch. "You deal with him while I call Lutz."

Frank approached the locksmith, who had pulled his tool bag from the rear of the van and was headed our way.

I waited as the phone rang on Lutz's end.

"Come on, already. Answer it." I didn't have time to leave a message since it looked like a storm was brewing over the lake, and valuable evidence could be washed away with rain. I hung up and called the forensic office. I was relieved when Mike answered on the second ring.

"Forensics, Mike Nordgren speaking."

"Thank God you answered, buddy. It's Jesse."

"Sure, what can I do for you?"

"Frank and I just arrived at Cliff Howard's house to meet with the safecracker. The damn orange Jeep is sitting in the driveway!"

"No shit?"

"No shit. I tried Lutz's office phone, but it just goes to voicemail. Time is of the essence, Mike. It looks like a storm is heading toward us."

"Roger that. I'll get the flatbed on its way so we can bring it back to the garage. I'll be right behind it, but first, I'll track down Lutz and let him know what's going on."

"Okay, but have Lutz call Abrams to get the closest officers from Patrol over here to canvass the neighborhood. These are decent homes, so maybe something got captured on a security camera. Meanwhile, we're going to take the safecracker inside so he can get started. Have Bobby call me when he gets here with the truck."

"Will do."

I hung up and gave Frank a nod. "Mike is coming out, and the flatbed is on its way. Mike said he'd let Lutz know that we need guys out here to look for home security systems on this block."

I apologized for the holdup and introduced myself to the man whose shirt had Zack P. embroidered on the chest pocket.

"So there's a safe you need to access, huh?" he asked.

"Yep. The homeowner is deceased, and we're trying to find his next of kin. Hopefully, there's information in the safe that can help us."

"Weird. That type of information is usually kept in a file cabinet or a simple address book."

Frank took his turn. "Well, we weren't able to find either, so the safe is all we have left. Hope you can open it."

"Let's take a look."

Zack followed us up the stairs and into the master bedroom.

"Right this way," I said as I entered the enormous walk-in closet. "For some reason, the homeowner felt the need to hide the safe even though it's too heavy for anyone to walk off with, plus it's mounted to the floorboards."

Zack looked around. "Where is it?"

I smirked. "Watch this." I pulled the handle on what looked to be the bottom drawer. A click sounded, then I pressed the façade, and the false dresser front popped open.

"What the hell?"

Frank chuckled. "That's what we said."

Zack scratched his forehead as he knelt down and took a closer look. "That's a first. Let me see what I can do. Looks like a midlevel safe, nothing too complicated. It has a combination dial and a key lock, so I can try to jimmy it open first, and if that doesn't work, I'll drill it out. It'll have a simple direct-drive cam mechanism, so it shouldn't take more than a half hour."

I tipped my head toward the door. "Okay, just let us know when you get it open, and don't touch anything inside."

"Will do."

Frank and I wandered downstairs and out the front door. I pushed back my sleeve and checked the time—the flatbed should arrive in about twenty minutes. I shielded my eyes and looked in the direction of the lake. The clouds had become darker and closer.

"Let's glove up and take a quick look at the Jeep," I said.

"I just hope they get it back to the garage before the storm hits."

Frank opened the cruiser's trunk and pulled two sets of gloves out of the box. We stretched them over our hands and approached the Jeep. I grabbed the door handle, gave it a jerk, and was surprised to see that it opened.

"Nice of the killers to make getting inside an easy task."

We weren't going to disturb anything, just observe. I snapped a few pictures of the dash, door pockets, floor mats, and console then moved to the back seat and did the same. Frank went to the rear of the Rubicon, opened the gate, and looked inside.

"Not seeing anything suspicious."

"Yeah, me neither, but take pictures, anyway."

Minutes later, the flatbed arrived. Bobby pulled to the curb, parked, and climbed out. "Mike said to wait for him before I load the Jeep."

"Yep, good plan." I glanced down the street, and two patrol cars were coming our way. The troops were arriving. "Frank, tell them what we need. I'm going to check on Zack."

"On it."

Chapter 45

I found Zack in the master bedroom closet with his drill in hand. He glanced at me as I walked in and squatted at his side.

"How's it going?" I asked.

"Almost done. A few more screws and a couple of hammer taps and I should be able to pop out the locking mechanism. It ought to pull right open then."

"Good. I'll hang out here. There are plenty of people taking care of business downstairs, and they don't need me in the way."

"Okay, this should do it." Zack drilled out the last screw, tapped the mechanism several times, then pulled it out with pliers. He nodded. "Go ahead, Detective McCord. It's all yours."

"It's open?"

"Yep."

I stopped Zack as he reached for the handle. "Okay, I'll walk you out, and the Chicago PD sure appreciates your help."

"Not a problem. It's my job to UnLockIt." He chuckled at his play on words.

I grinned. "How many times a week do you say that?"

"Plenty."

I escorted him to his van, shook his hand, and told him to send the invoice to our accounting department. I watched as Zack drove away, then jerked my head at Frank and Mike.

"Mike, can you join us upstairs while Bobby loads the Jeep?"

"Sure, but hang on a sec." Mike opened the back doors of the forensic van and pulled out a large tarp and a half dozen bungie cords. "That storm will hit before I get this Jeep under our garage roof. Better safe than sorry." He yelled out to Bobby. "Wrap that thing good and tight with the tarp. We'll give it a thorough inspection at the precinct." Mike turned to me. "Okay, I'm all yours."

Back in the master bedroom, we entered the closet.

"Have you checked inside yet?" Frank asked.

"Nope. I figured we should do it together." I pulled the gloves I had on earlier out of my back pocket and slipped them on. Mike was already gloved, and Frank was putting his on too. I looked at each man. "Okay, let's see what was worth hiding so well." I opened the safe's door and peered inside to see three shelves. A 9mm Sig Sauer handgun sat on the top shelf. The second one down held stacks of banded paper money lined up side by side. "What the hell? Those bills are wrapped in thousand-dollar bands."

Frank rubbed his brow. "It seems that Cliff was up to something, but what?"

Mike snapped a half dozen pictures. "Go ahead and open that box on the bottom shelf."

I reached in and pulled out a box that couldn't have been more than five inches by five inches square. I carefully lifted the flaps and looked inside.

"Well?" Frank asked.

"It's full of thumb drives, at least a dozen of them." I pulled out several, and they were dated by month and year.

"I wonder what's on them," Frank said.

Mike nodded at us. "I'll be right back. I have a video player in the van."

"Whatever Cliff was involved in was likely illegal and possibly what got him killed," Frank said.

I frowned with doubt. "I don't know. If the killers are targeting certain types of men, then that would mean all of them were involved in similar activities. Maybe Cliff had some sort of shady side hustle going on that had nothing to do with his murder."

Mike was back minutes later. "Okay, ready to check them out?"

I nodded. "I'm more than ready." I handed one of the drives to Mike, and he inserted it into the port and hit Play.

The scene that unfolded before us had clearly taken place right there in Cliff's bedroom. I groaned.

"You've got to be shitting me. Not only was he an arrogant son of a bitch, he was a slimeball too." I jerked my head at Frank. "Grab some more of those thumb drives. We need to make sure these are all the same thing. That asshat was probably videotaping women without their knowledge."

"And maybe all those hundreds were blackmail money."

Mike glanced around the room. "It looks like the camera

should be somewhere over there." He pointed toward a built-in bookcase across the room that had a direct view of the bed. "Go ahead and enjoy those X-rated movies while I look for the camera."

Frank pulled out the thumb drive and inserted another. The results were the same for the next four, so we assumed they all had a similar theme.

"All of this has to go back to the district with us. Finding anything, Mike?"

"Give me a few minutes. Better yet, you guys can lend a hand as long as you have them gloved."

It took another ten minutes for Mike to find the hidden camera among the books and knickknacks on the shelves. The lens protruded slightly through a hole cut into the spine of a novel. Between the front and back covers, the book was empty, and that was where the compact camera was positioned. Mike took a few pictures before disturbing it then carefully lifted the entire book and camera and slipped them into an evidence bag. Everything that was removed from the safe was also taken into evidence. Our findings that day wouldn't change anything—Cliff was dead, and our only purpose was to find his killers—but there could be a connection, and having that evidence at our disposal was crucial.

Mike packed up everything we needed to take to the precinct, and we left. Bobby was likely back at the district by now, and hopefully, the Jeep was unloaded and dry in the evidence garage. The storm had begun, and the rain pelted us as we drove south to District Two.

Chapter 46

As Frank drove, I pulled my phone from my pocket out of habit more than anything else. I wanted to see if a text or call had come in from Lutz about the dating-site warrant, but nothing had. Out of curiosity, I logged on to my emails and saw a notification for unread messages from singlechicagoprofessionals.com. I clicked on the email, which contained a link to the site. I glanced at Frank—he was paying attention to the road. I would read the message quickly, possibly respond, then log out. By then, we should be near the precinct.

The message was from TravelingBabe90, and she asked if we could meet for a drink later that evening. She said she might have an out-of-town work gig that could last for several weeks and would like to meet before leaving.

What's the harm? If she's gone for a few weeks, I can reevaluate if going forward is the right move or not, but I won't know unless we meet face-to-face.

I fired off a quick reply with my personal phone number. I cringed since we hadn't met yet. Giving somebody my number was a big step, but I could always block her calls if it became a problem. I told her to text me the time and place to meet, but it would have to be after seven o'clock that night. I took a deep breath and pressed the green arrow.

Frank turned in to the parking lot behind Mike. We entered the building through the lower level, where the evidence garage was located. Inside, the Jeep sat uncovered and waiting to be gone through. We approached the vehicle, and Danny was already setting up their forensic equipment on a roller table.

"Okay, guys, give this vehicle a double check. The killers had it for more than twenty-four hours. Their fingerprints or some sort of evidence had to have been left behind. Print every square inch, Luminol it, give it the works."

"You got it, Jesse," Mike said as he and Danny dug in.

I pulled my ringing phone from my pocket as Frank and I took the stairs to our level. It was Lutz with an update on what the officers combing the neighborhood around Cliff's house had found on residential cameras.

"We're back and heading upstairs," I said. "We'll come to your office."

"Good. I'll queue up the footage that was emailed to me and have it ready to view."

I jerked my chin at Frank. "Apparently, Patrol found something on a home surveillance system during their knock and talks."

"What about the warrant?"

I shrugged. "He didn't say."

Seconds later, we arrived at the commander's office and walked in—the door was open.

"Boss."

"Pull those guest chairs around to my side so you can watch the footage with me."

We did.

"Okay, here goes. This footage is from a home camera at a residence two houses away from Cliff's. It's the closest camera the officers found. There were others farther down the street, but their footage didn't show anything."

"So the footage is from across the street?" Frank asked.

"No, and that's unfortunate. Same side of the street, but the Jeep passes that house, and then you can see the beams of the headlights as they turn in to Cliff's driveway." He pointed as he started the video. "Here we go. There's the Jeep passing."

"Nighttime and tinted windows. No help there." I checked the time stamp on the footage—1:47 a.m.

Lutz sighed. "Correct, but keep watching."

It couldn't have been more than a minute later when we saw two shadowy figures pass the camera again and disappear down a side street.

"Son of a bitch, it's the same MO as always. They don't drive the secondary car to the scene but instead walk off into the darkness on foot." I frowned at Lutz and Frank. "Whatever happened to the comparison Tech was making of the perps' height against the height of the Sienna?"

They both shrugged.

I dialed Todd's phone in our tech department. "Hey, buddy, it's Jesse. What did you come up with as far as perp height compared to the height of the Sienna? You did? Sorry, my mind is on overload. So in short, what did you say? Okay, got it, thanks." I hung up. "Damn it, he left a voice message on my desk phone yesterday."

"Don't beat yourself up, partner. We're all busy," Frank said.

I repeated to Lutz and Frank what Todd had told me. Either both figures were female, or one was a shorter-than-average male. I was sure his first assessment was right—we were dealing with women.

"Okay, so there's two women who have a vendetta against certain types of men."

Lutz joined in. "Yeah. Older, possibly new to the area, and possibly looking for companionship."

I sneered. "And they ended up with Cliff, who was looking for a round in the hay with blackmail as a chaser."

Lutz scratched his neck. "So you found a gun, cash, and sex tapes in that safe?"

"Yep, and the sex tapes could be motive, but then why kill Robert and victim number two?"

We didn't know.

"What's going on with the warrant?" I asked.

"We hit another snag."

I swore under my breath. "Now what?"

"We need warrants for every woman who responded to Cliff's messages too. Something about violating their rights to privacy otherwise. It'll take a day or so for the administrators of that site to cough up the real names of those women before we can serve individual warrants on their messages."

Frank piped in. "More damn red tape. Another man could be killed by then."

"Or already has been," I added.

"I don't get why they brought the Jeep back to Cliff's house at all. It almost feels like they're challenging us. They could have easily left it somewhere with the keys in the ignition, and it would have been stolen in seconds."

"You could be right, Frank," Lutz said. "Maybe they're looking to play a game of cat and mouse with us."

I leaned back in the chair and stared at the ceiling while I thought. Those women were good at their craft and slippery as hell. Maybe it was a game after all—a challenge tossed out to the police force to try to catch them or be left in the dust as they moved on to another city and began again.

Chapter 47

Gail rubbed her hands together enthusiastically. "He bought my story about taking a job out of town, so we're going to meet up tonight. My message must have left a good impression on him."

Janet grinned. "Make sure to introduce yourself as Lynn Waters, like always, especially since he's a cop."

"Yep, not a problem. I told him I was from Bismarck, North Dakota."

They both laughed.

Janet lit a cigarette and took a deep drag. "That's one city and state we've never been to."

Gail continued. "I'll invite him back here just like the others, and then you can deal with him."

"Nope, a cop is someone special, so we have to consider him a bonus that we'll both enjoy. We'll deal with him together—and do it slowly."

Chapter 48

Lutz barked out orders for the first shifters to go home and let the night crew do their job. I wasn't about to argue, and I had to shower and change, anyway, to go out for that drink I'd agreed to. Lynn had texted me an hour earlier saying to meet her at seven at Woodland Tap, a bar not too far from my home. It was already five forty-five, and I was just leaving the precinct.

I gave the meetup a lot of thought as I drove the twenty minutes to my house. If I ever truly wanted a wife and family like some of my friends, I had to put myself out there, but doing nothing was also doing something. It was my safety net. I didn't want to fall in love and have it all come crashing down because of my commitment to the police department. I had happily single and happily married friends, but even at my age, I was still on the fence. I sucked in a deep breath and told myself to enjoy the hour with Lynn and possibly look forward to a second date or parting ways—no harm no foul.

I arrived home shortly after six, grabbed the mail, and closed the overhead door at the wall switch. Inside the house, I tended to Bandit then headed for the shower. I wasn't sure if I should eat something quick and easy or have appetizers at the bar. I was familiar with the place but had never been inside, so I had no idea whether they served appetizers, bar food, or actual meals, but I would be fine with any of those options.

Showered and dressed, I stared at my reflection in the mirror after changing my shirt three times. I was done and would wear what I had on. The shirt and dark jeans looked fine, yet I'd rather be ordering a pizza, sitting on the couch with my pup, and slugging down a beer over a TV murder mystery.

Jesus, no wonder I don't date. I'm neurotic and overthink everything. It's just a drink, for God's sake. Maybe I'll end up with a new friend. Who knows? But I need to relax, and chances are, I'll enjoy myself.

At six forty-five, I set the alarm and walked down to the garage. I'd be at Woodland Tap in ten minutes. I didn't want to get there too early or make a late appearance—that was rude.

There I go, overthinking things again. Take a breath and calm down. I'll be right on time.

I found a parking spot along the curb just around the block from the bar. I wasn't entirely comfortable leaving my car where I couldn't see it, but I'd likely be able to hear the alarm wail if somebody tried breaking in. In that particular area, it could go either way. It was safe enough most times, but on occasion, riffraff slipped through the cracks.

Clicking the fob, I looked over my shoulder to make sure the lights blinked, then I pocketed my keys and rounded the corner. My heart began thumping in my chest at the possibility of this meetup becoming something real.

Jesus, I need to take it down a notch. I know how people exaggerate their profiles so I need to hope for the best but expect the worst.

I entered Woodland Tap, but because I didn't know the layout, I remained by the door and scanned the area for a beautiful blonde sitting alone. Chances were, I'd arrived before her. Since I didn't see anyone, I took a seat at the bar, facing the door. When she walked through, if she actually showed up, I would see her immediately.

The bartender approached me. "What can I get you, pal?"

"I'll have an amber ale."

"Tap or can?"

"Can and a glass, please."

"Coming right up."

The bartender went to the refrigerator and pulled out one of my favorite ambers from Idaho and held it up. I nodded— it was one of the best. He pulled the tab, set it on a coaster, and placed a glass next to it. "Waiting for someone?"

"Actually, I am."

He reached for the rag that was draped over his shoulder and used it to wipe wet rings off the bar. "Shall I open a tab for you?"

"Sure, that's fine." I pulled my credit card from my wallet and handed it to him.

"New to the area? I've never seen you in here before."

"Nah, I've lived nearby my whole life, but I've never been in here. My date suggested it, so I guess she knows the place."

"Okay, I'll be back when she shows up."

"Appreciate it."

I sipped my beer and tried to make it last. Chances were Lynn was a wine drinker, and I would switch over to wine, too, if that was what she ordered.

Moments later, and after checking the time—7:07—I glanced up to see the door open. A couple walked in, and right behind them was a gorgeous blonde entering alone. It had to be Lynn. I smiled and waved, and she nodded and walked toward me.

"Jesse?" She extended her hand, and I squeezed it.

"Please, have a seat. I saved this stool for you unless you'd like to sit at a bar table."

She waved off my comment. "This is fine, thanks. Sorry about being late, but finding a parking spot was tough."

"Completely understand, but that's typical of Chicago."

I held up my hand to get the bartender's attention, and as he walked toward us, he frowned at Lynn then locked eyes with me. I had no idea what that was about, but I planned to ask when the opportunity arose.

"What can I get you to drink, miss?"

"I'll have a glass of Malbec."

I nodded at the bartender. "Make that two. So have you been here before, Lynn?"

"No, but I pass by now and then, and it's close to my apartment. The little neighborhood paper shows they have live music on occasion."

"Cool. I'll have to check that out sometime."

The bartender came back with two glasses of Malbec and set them on coasters then took my beer glass away.

"So, you're from Bismarck, huh?"

She chuckled. "Is it my accent that gives it away?"

"No, you don't have an accent at all, but you did state that in your profile. Actually, most Midwest people are accused of having heavy German accents. I try to be mindful of that. So, how long have you been in Chicago?"

"A few months."

She took a sip of wine then slowly licked her lips. I wondered if she was coming on to me or if she was just licking her lips.

"And you said you may be leaving town again soon?"

"Well, that's my job. I'm in sales, so I travel a lot, hence the user ID."

"Right. Have you eaten yet?"

"Um, no, since I wasn't quite sure what we were doing. Sorry."

I laughed. "No apology needed. I'm hungry too. Let's see if they have a menu."

"They do."

"But I thought—"

She cut me off. "It's by the door."

"Ah, I must have missed it." I called the bartender over. "Can we look at the menu?"

"Sure thing. It's just bar food and appetizers, though. We aren't a full-service restaurant."

"That's fine."

He handed two menus to us and walked away and waited on another patron. He looked back. "Holler when you're ready."

I leaned a little closer to Lynn. "See anything that interests you?"

She smiled and brushed her hand against my leg. "The cheese-and-sausage platter looks good."

"I agree. Let's have that. Anything else?"

"Not yet."

It seemed like she was throwing out innuendos, but I didn't know why.

"So, Jesse, your profile says you work at the Chicago Police Department."

I nodded.

"In what capacity?"

"I'm a homicide detective."

"Are you serious? That's fascinating. So what crimes have you solved lately?"

I laughed openly. "Chicago has its fair share of murders, so I never run out of work."

"So you aren't going to tell me anything juicy?"

"Nothing specific, sorry. Ongoing cases, that sort of thing."

"Humph." She pointed. "Looks like our cheese platter is headed this way. Excuse me for a minute. I'm going to use the ladies' room."

After she left, the bartender set the platter in front of me. "I'll grab some napkins for you."

I glanced toward the restroom. "Hang on a second."

He turned back. "Yep?"

"You gave my date a strange look earlier. What was that about?"

"Sorry. I was just surprised to see her again so soon. That's all."

"Meaning? Do you know each other?" I glanced at the restroom door again. It was still safe to talk.

"No, but she was in here a few nights ago with a different guy."

"You sure?"

"Yep. She ordered a Malbec then too."

I saw Lynn approaching. "Thanks, pal."

He nodded.

She took her seat. "Mmm… that looks good."

"Sure does. Go ahead and dig in."

Chapter 49

We sat at the bar for the better part of two hours. The appetizers were good, and the conversation got better over time. Maybe it was the three glasses of wine we each had that loosened us up. Thinking about the bartender's comment on Lynn's earlier visit, I chalked it up as an innocent date Lynn had, not unlike our own. The chances of meeting that perfect person on the first date weren't realistic, yet I wondered why Lynn had told me she'd never been at Woodland Tap before. I assumed it was because meeting someone at the same bar she had just been at a few nights earlier might have been embarrassing. I wasn't sure, but I wasn't going to dwell on it either.

It was after nine o'clock, and I had a full day ahead of me tomorrow. The wine was kicking in, and I needed to get home before I ordered another glass. I told myself to end the night on a good note so there would be a chance of another date.

"I really ought to get going. I have a busy day tomorrow."

She smiled. "A current case?"

"Yep, you can say that."

She looked at the time on her cell phone. "Really? It's only a few minutes after nine. Why not come to my place for a nightcap, and then I promise to let you leave. I only live a few blocks from here."

I chuckled. In my half-drunken mind, it sounded like a great idea, but as with most great ideas, I had to put on my cop hat and decline. "Sorry. Even though it sounds like fun, I really can't."

"Come on, please? You won't regret it."

I glanced at her hand caressing my leg and knew it would be trouble if I left with her. Things were moving too fast for my comfort level, and although I wasn't positive about what she was insinuating, I had a pretty good idea. I needed to rethink her intentions. I wasn't a prude in any sense of the word, but I also wasn't looking for a one-night stand. The way she'd presented herself on her profile and her actions in person didn't match up.

"Sorry, but that isn't in the cards tonight." I waved to the bartender to get his attention. "I need to settle my tab."

"Sure thing." He brought back my credit card and the slip for me to sign. "Thanks, folks, and have a nice evening."

I tossed a ten on the bar, thanked the bartender, and turned to Lynn. "Can I walk you to your car?" I could tell by her change in attitude that she had grown cold, but she agreed to let me walk her out.

"I'm around the block over there." She pointed in the same direction where I had parked.

"Good. I'm parked over there too." We walked in silence for a minute. "That's my car."

"The yellow one?"

"Uh-huh. So, was tonight a deal breaker?" I asked.

"No. I'd like to see you again. I can't help it if I find you attractive, and I'm sorry if I came on too strong."

I laughed. "Usually, that's the guy's line. When are you leaving town?"

"Sunday."

"Then you'll be busy Saturday getting ready to leave. Want to shoot for tomorrow night? Hopefully, I won't have to work Saturday."

She smiled. "I'd like that, and I'll text you."

"Good." I held the driver's-side door open for her. "Dinner, then?"

"Dinner would be nice."

I gave her a hug and closed the door of her van once she was settled in. Then I walked to my car with a strange feeling about the night. I liked Lynn and she was beautiful, but something about her seemed off.

Chapter 50

Gail texted Janet before she drove away. "No dice. The son of a bitch wouldn't take the bait. I'm on my way home, and I'll explain everything when I get there."

Five minutes later, Gail parked in her designated spot and stormed into the apartment. She tossed her purse onto the table and plopped down in a chair.

Janet leaned against the kitchen counter. "So what went wrong?"

"Hell if I know." Gail stood up, grabbed two glasses and the wine bottle, then took her seat again.

"Let me do it." Janet uncorked the bottle and poured. "Tell me everything."

"There isn't much to tell, Mom. We had drinks and appetizers and made small talk. I accidentally on purpose brushed against his leg and made a few subtle innuendos. I figured I'd let his imagination run with that before I pushed harder. Whatever. Plain and simple, he didn't bite."

"Maybe he wasn't desperate like the old guys were."

"Thanks a lot."

"Sorry, honey, I didn't mean it like it sounded. So now what?"

"Now I have one more chance to get him here tomorrow night."

"He asked you for another date?"

"Yes, but probably because I said I was going out of town."

"Then all is not lost. Dress sexier and be irresistible. Play it up for all it's worth. We don't have a notch on our belt for a cop yet, but I damn well want one now."

Chapter 51

I assessed the evening as I drove home. I was stumped. Lynn was gorgeous and, according to her profile, just the kind of woman who would be compatible with me, yet something felt strange. Getting her to open up about her life—past, present, and future, as well as stories about her travels and interests—had been like pulling teeth. She was more than vague with her answers. I felt as though she had more to say but nothing she wanted to discuss with me yet as a friend or possibly with me as a cop. I wasn't sure which it was and figured she just needed to get to know me before opening up.

I would have liked an opinion about the date from a friend, but I couldn't ask anybody from the police department. I would be heckled for sure, especially by Frank.

It was nearly ten o'clock by the time I climbed the stairs to the main level of my house. Bandit—already out for the night—didn't stir. I grabbed my laptop and a beer and headed for my bedroom. As I lay in bed, I logged on to the dating site and pulled up Lynn's profile. I read it for probably the tenth time since I had gotten the first message from her. I shook my head with doubt. She was unusual, yet I couldn't put my finger on why she struck me that way. As I was about to log off and call it a night, a message alert popped up—it was from her. I wasn't savvy enough about the site to know whether she'd seen I was on it or if it was nothing more than a coincidence that she'd logged on too. A simple message from her said she was glad she met me and that she enjoyed our time together. She was looking forward to a do-over tomorrow night. I powered off my computer, and with a smile, I realized I was looking forward to it too.

That was the first night in ages that I drifted off to sleep without work on my mind.

The next morning, I woke with a sense of optimism. Hopefully, that was the day we would get the warrants for the messages that had been sent to Cliff's dating profile. We'd interview each woman who had communicated with him and weed out the killer. Searching for Robert on the site might prove too time consuming, but I planned to look at his rent application, locate the shipyard he'd worked for in Oakland years ago, and see if there was a next of kin listed on his job application.

As I passed the break room on my way to the bull pen, I saw Lutz peering into the vending machine. I turned back and walked in. "Boss."

"Jesse. Get any sleep last night?"

"Actually, I slept really well."

Bob rubbed his chin. "Feeling okay?"

I laughed. "I'm optimistic. We're going to find those killers real soon. I don't even want to think about another man's life being at risk."

Lutz dropped a handful of quarters into the machine as he mulled over his breakfast choices. He hit F-3, and a banana-cranberry-nut muffin fell to the door below.

I raised my brows. "That looks pretty good." I pulled out my change and bought the same thing.

We walked to the bull pen, where Lutz conducted roll call and gave our updates. Without new leads, he had only a few things to report.

Lutz took a seat in Frank's guest chair and began. "Forensics has confirmed that the blood droplets they found in the back of the Sienna did indeed match our prior victims. There's no shadow of a doubt that the killers are one and the same for all three murders, and the Sienna rented by a fictitious Janet St. James was the vehicle that transported them to the dump sites. Also, we've issued a blanket warrant that'll cover every incoming and outgoing message to Cliff Howard's dating profile. Like before, the site's administrators have twenty-four hours to give us all those women's names, or they'll be held in contempt. Meanwhile, what do you have?" He looked from face to face.

"Still following leads," Henry said, "but they're getting cold, and fewer are coming in."

Lutz folded his arms over his expanding belly. "What about Robert Smith?"

I spoke up. "I think our best bet, since we don't actually know if he was on a dating site, is to follow the information from his last known job at the Oakland shipyards. I'll use whatever I can from his rental application to find out more."

Lutz pointed at me. "Okay, you take care of that." He

slapped his hands together and headed for the door. "Get busy, guys. Let's make this a productive day."

I hunkered down at my desk and stared at the rental application I'd received from Ted Sorensen, the manager at Robert's apartment complex. Robert had lived in Oakland for seven years, so he'd left a trail behind. His penmanship could have been better, so reading the name of the shipyard he had worked at was difficult. I would have to look online to find out more.

With a half dozen shipyards written down for Oakland, I began making calls to the human resources department of each. On the third call, to Troy Shipyards, I struck gold. A Robert Smith had worked there between 2012 and 2016. It had to be the same Robert I was asking about. Companies had to keep prior employees' records for five years before they could shred them, so I was in luck. They still had Robert's file.

"I'll need everything sent to me in a zipped file right away."

I gave the department head my contact information, thanked her, and said I'd be waiting for the attachment to show up in my in-box. Meanwhile, I walked to the back of the room and started a fresh pot of coffee. I wasn't about to pour one more cup of the burnt-tasting swill that had probably been sitting there since our night shift crew had made it. With a fresh cup in hand, I returned to my desk and checked my email. The file from Troy Shipyards had arrived. After clicking on the attachment, I opened it and saw the job application for Robert Smith. I immediately printed out three copies—one for the legal records file, one for the PD file, and one to take notes on. I ran my finger down the sheet, searching for an emergency contact name, and found it—a Mrs. Gladys Smith of Santa Rosa, California.

Who the hell is Gladys? That's an old-fashioned name. I wonder if she's his mother.

I pulled up the DMV database and typed in her name and the state of California. There wasn't a driver's license shown for her, but there was an ID with her name and an address in Santa Rosa. It had to be the right Gladys. I typed that address into the search bar, and a nursing home's name popped up.

Loving Care of Santa Rosa? Shit, she's an old woman who lives in a nursing home. Who knows if Robert even visited her?

I made the call and asked to speak to the person in charge of patient admissions. Smooth jazz played in my ear while I waited. It couldn't have been more than a minute before a different woman came on the line.

"This is Fay Brooks speaking. How may I help you?"

"Mrs. Brooks, I'm Detective Jesse McCord with the Chicago Police Department. I need to ask about a patient who resides at Loving Care."

"I hope I can help you without violating patient privacy laws, Detective McCord."

I groaned silently and felt the red tape tightening around my neck. "Ma'am, I just need to know if Gladys Smith is still a resident there and when the last time was that she saw her son, Robert. Can you please tell me that much?"

"I would if I could, but Gladys passed away in 2016, and we haven't seen Robert since her funeral. Of course, there wouldn't be a reason for us to anymore."

That time, I groaned audibly. "Were there other family members who visited Gladys or were listed as contacts besides Robert?"

"I'm sorry, but her residency file is in our archives department. I'd have to go find it and call you back."

"That's fine, and I need that information as soon as possible."

"Detective McCord, may I ask why?"

"Unfortunately, Robert has also passed away, and we don't have a contact person to handle funeral arrangements or dispose of his belongings. At this point, I'd say any next of kin would do."

"I understand, and I'll call you back as soon as I locate Gladys's file."

I thanked Mrs. Brooks, hung up, and called the forensic lab. Mike answered before the second ring. "Hey, buddy, it's Jesse. Anything on the Jeep?"

"Yeah, we're entering all the viable prints into the database. There were a good number of them but none that have come up as a match for anything besides Cliff's own prints we collected from his house."

"Anything else?"

"Just the usual items in the glove box and console. Registration, insurance card, owner's manual, tire gauge, that sort of thing. Nothing so far that would raise a red flag and nothing that would appear to be from our killers."

"Okay, thanks." I was about to hang up when a thought came to mind. "The keys were found under the floor mat, correct?"

"Yep, why?"

"Have you actually started the Jeep?"

"Yes, we have, but I thought searching it took top priority."

"Sorry, and it was. Not trying to jump down your throat, but you need to start it again since Cliff may have synced his phone to the Jeep. All of his contact numbers would have transferred, plus the navigation should tell us where the vehicle has been."

"Only if it was used, but I'll get back to you as soon as we know something either way."

We were making progress, and with several irons in the fire, I was feeling good. Lutz wanted it to be a productive day, and maybe we could give him that.

Chapter 52

I grabbed the ringing phone from its base. "Detective McCord speaking."

"Detective, it's Fay Brooks again."

"Thanks for getting back to me so quickly, Mrs. Brooks. What have you found?"

"There was a different name listed on Gladys's DNR orders as well as her advanced directive. It's actually another son, but I don't believe I've ever met him and don't remember him visiting her."

"Okay, and what do you have on him?"

"His name is Philip Smith, and the advanced directive shows that when it was filled out, he lived in Walnut Creek."

"That's in California too?"

"Yes. Sorry, I assumed—"

"No worries. I'm a Chicago guy, born and raised. I'll still need Gladys's file emailed to me, though."

"I'll zip it and send it now."

I thanked her, hung up, and began my search for Philip Smith of Walnut Creek, California. Hopefully, I would get lucky, and Robert's body and belongings would be taken care of by a family member. I'd found three Philip Smiths within a hundred miles of Santa Rosa. None showed up in Walnut Creek, but I found one in San Mateo, one in Stockton, and one in Hayward. I would call them all and hope that one was Robert's brother.

Hitting my computer's refresh icon before making the call, I saw that an email had come in from Fay, and Gladys Smith's complete file was attached.

Good, that's taken care of. Now to track down Philip.

I was surprised to find that many people still had landlines. I dialed the first number, and a man answered. I asked if he was related to a Robert Smith, and he said no. After thanking him for his time, I hung up and dialed the Stockton number. That number picked up with a voicemail, and I left a message and my contact number. I had one more chance before hitting the proverbial brick wall, and I held my breath as I called the Hayward number. A woman answered. I introduced myself then told her why I was calling and who I was hoping to speak to. She put her husband—Philip Smith—on the phone.

I listened to his explanation for being estranged from Robert ever since their mother had died. Something about the will and the fact that she had chosen Philip—the eldest of the brothers—to be her power of attorney. Philip admitted there was bad blood between him and Robert and said they hadn't spoken in years. I gave him as much information as I could about Robert's death, and he said he'd catch a flight to Chicago tomorrow. We planned to talk more when he arrived to identify his brother's remains.

With that chapter closed, I could focus on Cliff. At that point, I had my doubts that we'd ever identify victim number two. I called Lutz's office to tell him what I'd found out about Robert, and he said he was on his way—he had news of his own.

Moments later, I looked over my shoulder, and Lutz entered the bull pen. He stood against the doorframe and addressed all of us. The warrants had been issued, and singlechicagoprofessionals.com had acknowledged that they'd received them. They were gathering the names for us, yet each woman would have to be notified before the site would send us the names.

"We're getting there, guys, and by the day's end, we should have the names of the women who messaged Cliff, or at least a partial list. It's a good start."

"How will the process be handled?" Tony asked.

"We'll make unannounced visits to each residence after we perform background checks to see if any have police records. Regardless of whether they have a record or not, each woman will be questioned thoroughly. I'll let you know when the names start rolling in." Lutz tipped his head at me. "You have news on Robert?"

"Yep, that part of the investigation is coming to a close. I found his long-lost brother who lives in California, and he's going to catch a flight here tomorrow to handle Robert's affairs."

"Did you go into detail about his death?"

"I didn't tell him everything, but I said I'd explain what I could once he arrives."

Kip rubbed his chin as if something was on his mind, then he spoke up.

"Several of the murders took place in California. Do you think it's a coincidence that Robert lived there, too, or do you think the killer followed him to Chicago?"

I offered my opinion. "According to what Ted Sorensen—Robert's landlord—told us, Robert left California in 2016. Apparently, he'd been traveling the country since then."

Frank piped in. "That's what he said, but now I'm wondering about that. Do you think he was really traveling, or was he running away from someone?"

That was a theory we hadn't checked into yet, but it did raise some questions. "Wasn't one of those traveling nurses from California?" I asked.

Henry flipped through his stack of notes. "Here it is, a Gail Fremont."

I couldn't recall what city she was from. "What area? California's a big state."

"Um, Petaluma, wherever that is."

My mind went into overdrive. "Let me think about that for a second. Robert lived in Oakland, the politician was from Sacramento, and what about the other two men who were too decomposed to identify? Where were they found?"

Lutz had those answers. "One was found in Concord and the other out in the Delta near Martinez."

I raised my brows as I had an epiphany. "And Gail Fremont just happens to be from California too. Maybe that's where everything began." I looked at Kip. "Print out a map of California. I want to see how close those cities are to each other."

Ten minutes later, we gathered at the back table with the map in front of us. We had already missed our lunch break, but since this revelation could prove helpful, nobody seemed to mind.

"Okay, let's figure this out. Put a red dot on Sacramento, one on Oakland, and the other three on Petaluma, Martinez, and Concord."

We stared at the cluster in front of us. The cities were close together, with Sacramento being the farthest away, and that victim was the only one ever identified. We had a clear connection for those cases—opportunity and proximity.

"Did you ever get the tox reports from California?" I asked.

"Only from the politician, and he had ingested liquid ammonia. The other two couldn't be tested because they were too decomposed."

"Jeez. What about North Carolina?"

"Still waiting."

Frank spoke up. "I think we should pick up Gail Fremont for questioning."

Lutz shook his head. "Not until we have confirmation that she was one of the women who communicated with Cliff. We have no evidence whatsoever to say she was involved in a crime. Living in the same state as several murder victims is far from proof of wrongdoing. If that were the case, then everyone in Chicago would be a person of interest, so we have to wait it out. Until we have that information, start digging into the backgrounds of Robert and the politician to see if there was ever a reason for them to cross paths."

A few hours passed without significant leads. We couldn't find any connection between Robert and the politician. At three o'clock, Lutz stormed into the bull pen and waved a sheet of paper.

"We have a few names. Let's get started."

I pushed back my chair with excitement. I was raring to go and needed to get out of the bull pen. Lutz jerked his head at Frank and me. "Hold your horses. We need information first on a Debbie Bachman and a Patricia Moore, both from Chicago. Pull up their names to see if they have police records, get their most current addresses from the DMV database, and then head out."

"You got it, Boss," Frank said.

"Nothing on Gail Fremont yet?"

"Nope, still waiting on her and six other women's information."

"I'll take Debbie Bachman," I said as I dug in. I pulled up her name, got her current address—which matched the one on her credit card payment method for the dating site—then did a nationwide criminal background search on her. She was clean—no arrests ever, not even a speeding ticket. Lutz said we had to interview everyone, so I programmed her address into my cell phone's navigation system. "How does it look for Patricia Moore?"

"Hmm… she had one arrest for solicitation in 2013. Misdemeanor charges, paid a fine, and did community service for six months. Clean ever since."

"Has she always lived in Illinois?"

Frank tapped a few more keys and pulled up her address

history. "Looks like she lived in Virginia for a year, and that was in 2011."

"Okay, let's head out. Got a workplace for her in case she isn't home?"

"Yep, I've got it all."

Chapter 53

My phone vibrated in my jacket's inner chest pocket. I reached in, pulled it out, and saw that a text had come in from Lynn. She wanted to meet at Harry's Steak House in Hyde Park that night. The location was convenient enough and possibly a halfway point between our homes. She asked if seven o'clock would work. Even though I had no idea how long our interviews would take, I sent a short reply saying it was fine. I'd worry about the time once it was closer.

"Something important?" Frank gave a side-eyed glance in my direction.

"Nah, just my cell phone's bill reminder, and it looks like the cost went down a bit. Maybe it's finally paid off."

He nodded. "Less money spent is always a plus."

We arrived at Debbie Bachman's address fifteen minutes later. Frank parked along the curb in front of a small white house, and although it looked clean and the yard was maintained, the house could still use a fresh coat of paint. When we reached the porch, Frank folded his hand and knocked twice on the steel door. We heard footsteps approaching, meaning somebody was home.

The door opened with a chain lock separating us from a woman who appeared to be in her early forties.

"May I help you?" She kept most of her face behind the door.

I showed her my badge. "We're from the Chicago PD, ma'am, and have a few questions for you."

She pulled back. "Me? Why?"

"May we come in?"

Her eyes looked beyond us and at the cruiser before she responded. She looked at Frank. "Can I see your badge too?"

"Sure thing." Frank unclipped his badge from his belt loop and held it out on our side of the door but in plain view for her to see.

"Okay, I guess." She closed the door, and we heard the chain go through the slide. A second later, she pulled the door wide open. "May I ask what this is about?"

"Sure, we'll explain why we're here once we're inside if you don't mind."

She led the way to the room nearest the front door—a family room. She offered us seats on the couch then faced us from a side chair.

"We're here about a dating site you're a member of."

"What? You can't be serious."

"We're very serious, ma'am. Do you know a Cliff Howard?"

"I've exchanged messages with a man named Cliff, but I don't know his last name. He went by the username In-Demand, which in itself rubs me the wrong way. Our communication fizzled quickly. He was too full of himself."

"So you never met him in person?" Frank asked.

"No."

"Where were you two nights ago between eleven p.m. and three in the morning?"

"At work. I'm employed at Strategic Communication Corporation, and I work third shift. That's easy enough to verify with the personnel department. They have my time sheet."

"Have you communicated with Cliff since then?"

"No, and he hasn't messaged me either, which makes me more than happy. He was just creepy." She shook her head. "I'll probably cancel my membership and try to meet people through friends, which seems much safer."

As cops, we had heard horror stories about online dating, and now, without anyone's knowledge, I had put myself in that very pool. We thanked her for her time and left. I discreetly glanced at my wristwatch as we headed to the cruiser.

"Busted." Frank chuckled. "Where do you need to be, and why?"

I groaned and wondered if I would regret telling Frank about Lynn and the dating site. Frank was a tough codger, a lifelong bachelor like myself but far more cynical about marriage—likely because both his parents had been married and divorced three times. He was my partner, though, and closest work friend. If I couldn't spill the beans to him, I couldn't spill them to anyone.

We climbed into the cruiser, and he sat behind the wheel, staring at me. "If you don't start talking, I'm going to light up a cigarette and lock all the doors and windows."

"You wouldn't."

"Try me, because I'm not kidding." He pulled a cigarette out of the pack he had stashed in his pocket and pressed it between his lips. The lighter came out a second later.

"Okay, fine. I'll tell you everything." Since I didn't want to be asphyxiated by second-hand smoke, I caved in. "I need a sincere promise from you first." I pointed at the window locks. Frank pushed the lever to disengage the locks, and I opened my window several inches. "I'll talk as you drive."

"Because you have somewhere to be."

"I need you to promise not to laugh at me."

Frank smiled. "Now you have me wanting to laugh."

I ignored his comment and began. "I've been thinking about this for months and finally joined a dating site."

A wide grin spread across Frank's face. He was definitely doing his best to hold back his laughter.

I gave him a stern frown. "I'm done."

"Come on. I'll control myself."

"Whatever. Anyway, I was browsing the site a few nights back and saw I had three messages. I eliminated the first two women right away simply because they wouldn't have been a good match."

"And the third?" Frank seemed genuinely interested now.

"Her profile matched up pretty well with my core values and desires in life. Plus, she's a beautiful blonde."

Frank snickered. "Probably a picture purchased from stock photos."

"You said—"

"Sorry, go ahead. I'll zip it."

"They weren't stock photos because I met her last night for drinks."

"No shit? Where?"

"At Woodland Tap."

"And?"

"And she's nice enough, but she seemed to be glossing over her life when I asked questions."

"Dude, it was the first date. Nobody normal would cough up their life story to a perfect stranger."

I rubbed my furrowed forehead. "I suppose, but then she came on to me."

"Hell, I'd be on board with that. What happened?"

"She started rubbing my leg and suggested we go to her place for a nightcap."

"Tell me you did."

I rolled my eyes at my overly enthusiastic partner. "Really? Would you jump in the sack with someone you just met?"

"Depends on how she looks. If she was hot, hell yeah."

"You're disgraceful."

"And you're a prude." Frank chuckled. "Okay, get back to the story."

"There isn't a story to tell. I didn't go to her place, but I did walk her to her van, and then I asked her out for tonight, this time for dinner."

"And then after dinner, you'll go home with her for a nightcap because you aren't strangers anymore, right?"

"I'm not sure. We'll see how it goes." I looked down at my phone. "We're almost to Patricia Moore's place. Should be a half mile up on my side of the street."

"I'll try to keep the interview under an hour," Frank joked as we took the sidewalk to the front door.

I pressed the doorbell. "Thanks, buddy. I know how you can get long-winded." We waited for a minute, then I pressed the bell again and listened at the door. I didn't hear anything. "Think she's at work?"

"Maybe. She works at a daycare center, and they usually have to stick around until all the parents have picked up their kids. The daycare my sister uses opens at six a.m. and closes at six p.m. Monday through Friday."

"Well, we better get over there and have a word with her before we cross paths on the highway."

Now it was Frank who pushed up his sleeve and he said it was five fourteen. "With a twenty-minute drive there and another thirty minutes back to the district, you'll be late for your date, and that doesn't even include the interview itself. You won't have time to go home and clean up. Where are you meeting her, anyway?"

"At Harry's Steak House in Hyde Park."

"Yeah, you'll never make it. Drop me off at the daycare, go back to the precinct, and tell Henry to come out here to pick me up. By then, I'll probably be done with the interview. You'll have to deal with Lutz in your own way."

"You sure?"

Frank swatted the air. "Yeah, no sweat, but I want to hear all the juicy details tomorrow."

"Thanks, pal, but let's make sure Patricia Moore is actually there first."

Chapter 54

Janet watched out the window for her daughter to arrive home from work. She had spent the last hour plotting the detective's demise. Gail would bring him home, make sure he was comfortable, then retreat to the kitchen. She would make two drinks, one laced with crushed sleeping pills. She would begin a lengthy description of her life—all made up—while the drug began working its magic. By the second round, the detective would be unable to stand, and his words would be slurred. He'd be putty in their hands, completely at their mercy. Janet was sure a homicide detective had seen plenty of tortured victims during his years behind the badge, and soon, he would learn firsthand what slow torture really felt like.

Something flashed past the window. It was the van, and Gail was home. She had just over an hour to shower, dress to impress, and get to the steak joint. That night, she planned to work her magic like never before.

Seconds later, the door opened, and Gail passed through into the kitchen.

"Tonight's the night, honey. Are you excited?"

"Hell yeah, but I'm going up against big time moral resistance. It'll be a test to see who wins."

"You have to win. You told him you were leaving town on Sunday."

"I got this, Mom, so have some faith. I'll bring him home, and between you and me, we'll work our own kind of magic on Detective Jesse McCord."

Chapter 55

It was pushing 5:40 p.m. by the time I had parked the cruiser and entered the back door of the precinct. That was the most direct and shortest route to the bull pen. I would call Lutz after telling Henry to head out and pick up Frank, who was interviewing Patricia Moore. With the address of the day-care facility in hand, Henry walked out and said he'd see me tomorrow.

I took a seat at my desk and grabbed the receiver off the base. Keeping the conversation with Lutz short and to the point, I simply said Debbie Bachman had never met Cliff Howard and Patricia Moore was being interviewed by Frank. I told him I had to leave on a personal matter, but Henry had gone to pick up Frank. Lutz seemed okay with that and signed off, making it easier than I'd thought it would be. I said good night to Kip, Shawn, and Tony and clocked out for the day. I had exactly one hour before I was supposed to meet Lynn for dinner. I calculated my travel and prep time, and I estimated arriving at Harry's at approximately 7:20. I texted Lynn to let her know. As I fired up my Camaro, a return message came in.

"Not a problem. I'll see you then, and I'm looking forward to it."

I smiled. Lynn Waters might be a very good fit for me after all.

It was five after seven by the time I backed out of my driveway. At Dean's insistence, I took Bandit to his house. Jackson and Bandit were way overdue for a play date. I thanked Dean, told him I'd pick up my pup before midnight, and left. If I could find a parking spot in Harry's lot, I was sure to arrive on time.

For the first time in as long as I could remember, I looked forward to a relaxing night that didn't involve my couch and a can of beer. I was done with the excuses for why I shouldn't date. Now to get Lynn to open up about her dreams for the future so I could see if we were truly compatible. If not, I'd move on and continue my search for the right woman.

I was lucky enough to find a parking spot in Harry's lot just as a vehicle pulled out. I thought I noticed Lynn's van in the distance about six spaces down, but I wasn't sure— darkness was creeping in. Checking the time on my phone, I saw that it was 7:22. I was right on time, and she was probably waiting inside.

The hostess stand was just beyond the entrance with bench seating in the waiting area to its right. I glanced that way but didn't see Lynn, so I approached the hostess.

"Table for—"

"I think we have reservations." I smiled as I realized that sounded stupid. Either we had reservations or we didn't, and I had no idea.

"Well, let me take a look. What name is it under?"

I chuckled. "Try Lynn Waters." I watched as she went down the sheet of names.

"Nothing for a Lynn Waters, sir."

"Okay, then try Jesse McCord."

She grinned. "Here we go. It looks like your date has arrived and is waiting in the bar for you. Your table is ready whenever you are, so just let the bartender know." She turned and pointed. "The bar is right around that corner to the left."

I thanked her and continued on. As I made my way back, I saw Lynn across the bar. She faced my way and waved as soon as she spotted me. I waved back. Once again, she was stunning, and her dress left little to the imagination. I was going to find it difficult to focus on anything other than how she looked.

When I reached her side, I leaned in and kissed her cheek. The scent of her perfume added to the desire I felt. She was mesmerizing. I took a seat on the barstool next to her and sucked in a silent, slow breath. "I hope you haven't been waiting long."

Her smile lit up the room, and her perfect teeth gleamed. "Not long. Just enough time to order two glasses of Malbec. I hope you don't mind that I ordered for you."

"Not at all. How was your day?"

"Same as always. Sales calls and a lot of driving from place to place. How was yours?"

She had diverted to questioning me pretty quickly without me learning anything.

"Chasing bad guys and gals."

She propped her fist under her cheek. "Really? There are women criminals too?"

I laughed. "Not as many as men, but yeah, they're definitely out there."

"And you're after some now?"

"Possibly, but we haven't confirmed it yet." She seemed very interested in my work, but a homicide detective's job was interesting most of the time, except when it came to paperwork.

"So what do women usually do wrong, shoplift?"

"Well, sure, but that wouldn't involve my department."

Her eyes lit up, and she moved in closer to my ear. Her warm breath lingered on my skin as she whispered. "You mean they actually kill people too?"

I smiled. "Sometimes they do, but it doesn't matter to us if they're men or women. A murderer is a murderer."

The bartender interrupted our conversation. "Would you folks like to see the menu?"

"Sure." I turned toward her. "How about we continue our conversation at the table?"

"Uh-huh, and more Malbec please."

We were ushered to a private corner table with little foot traffic passing by. It was just right. I asked the bartender to bring a bottle of Malbec and to tell the waiter we'd be ready in ten minutes.

"What kind of sales are you involved in?" I knew I would have to be direct with my questions to learn more about Lynn.

"Medical supply sales. Everything from hearing aids to

gauze, medical tape, blood pressure cuffs, and syringes."

I nodded. "Got it. I've heard medical sales is a pretty lucrative career."

"It is if you have a regional route like I do. I can't complain since it's served me well."

"But you still have time to enjoy life, right?"

"I enjoy every second I'm off the clock. I love my hobbies."

We paused our conversation when the bartender brought a new bottle of Malbec to the table. He corked it, poured, waited for my approval, then walked away.

I picked up a menu and opened it. "Let's see what looks good."

Chapter 56

I hadn't realized two hours had passed until Lynn excused herself to the ladies' room and I checked the time. It was after nine thirty. Our conversation had flowed effortlessly, and the steaks were delicious. All in all, it was a successful date, much better than the night before, but was I ready to end the evening or continue it elsewhere? I had to decide what to do with the next few hours. Frank's description of me came to mind—prude. I chuckled to myself. Lynn was fun and very sexy, and the thought of spending another hour together in a private setting like her home sounded appealing. I would follow her lead and see where it went.

"Care for dessert and coffee?" I asked as she returned to the table and the waiter took our plates.

"I'd rather have it at my place if you'd like to join me." A blush covered her face. "I don't want to sound presumptuous, and I realize I was much too forward last night, but I bought a chocolate cake and ice cream just in case you wanted to stop over. I have wine, beer, and cocktails too."

I smiled at her attempt at being demure, but I saw her point. There was no harm in continuing our date at her place for another hour or so. Bandit was in good hands, the night had been going well, and I wouldn't see her again for a few weeks.

"That sounds like a great idea." I pulled my credit card from my wallet and caught the waiter's attention. "We're ready for the check."

"How about I drive us to my place and then I'll bring you back here before eleven when the restaurant closes?"

"That's way too much bother. I can follow you."

"You aren't going to find a parking spot close to my apartment. The parking is terrible in my neighborhood, but thankfully, each tenant in my building has a designated space."

I signed the dinner receipt and handed it to the waiter. "Okay, if you really don't mind."

"I don't, and it isn't far."

We exited the restaurant and crossed the parking lot, where she clicked the fob for the van I'd thought was hers when I had parked earlier.

I chuckled. "Why does a beautiful young woman like you have a van? I'd picture you driving a bright-red sports car."

"It's what works best for my job. During the week, the back end is full of boxes loaded with medical supplies."

"Makes sense." I watched out the window as she drove. "How far is your apartment?"

"An easy ten minutes north. No big deal."

Before long, Gail clicked the blinker and pulled into a driveway that circled around to the back of an apartment building. She parked in the first spot.

I thought about the apartment complex name after we passed the sign. "Parkview Arms?"

"Uh-huh."

"I wonder why that sounds familiar." I shrugged it off, knowing I had never been there before.

She parked and killed the ignition. "This is it, my humble abode." She climbed out and waited for me to exit the van and join her. "It's the first door, right there on the side of the building."

"That's pretty convenient. A first-floor unit and the closest apartment to the parking lot."

She nodded. "I got lucky. Come on in."

We entered her modest apartment, which threw me off for a minute. She clearly made a good living, yet the apartment was sparsely furnished, and I didn't see anything that looked personal. It felt like I'd just walked into a staged unit.

"So make yourself comfortable. Would you like cake and ice cream?"

"How about a glass of wine first? I'll admit, I'm still stuffed."

"Sure. Malbec again or white?"

"Why switch? Malbec is fine."

"Coming right up. Would you like to listen to music?"

"That'd be great." I looked around for a radio or a record player. It seemed that vinyl was back in vogue. I heard glasses being pulled from the cabinet and the wine being corked. "Need any help?"

"Nope, I'm almost finished. What kind of music do you like, Jesse?"

"Classic rock, blues, and some country. How about you?"

She appeared from the kitchen, carrying two wineglasses. "Pretty much the same. We have more in common than I originally thought. How about some blues?"

"Sure." I looked around the tiny living room. "From where?"

"My phone's playlist." She picked up her phone and chose a sultry blues song. "How's this?"

"I like it, and the company is good too."

She smiled and took a sip of wine. I did the same.

"So where are you traveling to on Sunday?"

"Albany, with several stops along the way. I have the Northeast and the Midwest states."

The conversation and wine continued with a few light kisses in between. Within a matter of minutes, I was starting to feel groggy. I chalked it up to too much wine—I was more of a beer guy. Although tomorrow was Saturday and I normally wouldn't be working, we had hoped to pay Gail Fremont a visit. I put my hand to my mouth and yawned.

"Sorry, it must be my long work hours mixing with the wine. I can barely keep my eyes open."

"You can spend the night."

I laughed. "That's really sweet, but I think I ought to go home. My neighbor is watching my dog for me, and I said I'd come and get him tonight."

Lynn leaned in and gave me a passionate kiss. "A few minutes more won't hurt. One more glass of wine and I'll take you back to your car."

I gave in and agreed, but as usual, my job was always on

my mind. Even now, when my thoughts weren't very clear, I knew I should leave and try to get home without falling asleep behind the wheel. I tried to focus as I watched her walk away with our glasses. Her body was nothing but a cloudy silhouette, and I couldn't clear my vision. Rubbing my eyes, I looked again, but she had already disappeared into the kitchen.

Can I really be that tired? I may need to call Frank and have him take me home from Harry's.

Squinting, I saw Lynn heading my way—or was it Lynn? The person coming toward me wasn't wearing a dress. Did Lynn change clothes?

What the hell is going on, and why is that person raising something over their head?

I tried to stand up, but a sharp crack above my ear stopped me in my tracks, and I felt myself fall. Then everything went black.

Chapter 57

"For chrissakes, Mom, you probably killed him."

Janet huffed. "At the rate you were going, it would take all night to get anything accomplished. I was sick of sitting in the bedroom and staying still. I couldn't even watch TV."

Gail leaned over the unconscious detective, whose scalp wore a bloody gash. He lay sprawled out—a combination of getting clubbed with a full wine bottle and passing out from the sleeping pills. Gail retreated to the hallway linen closet and got a towel so the floor wouldn't become stained. She looked at Janet with raised brows. "What's the plan?"

"We secure him to the radiator like we did with Mr. Hennessey."

Gail interrupted. "We both know how that turned out."

"Only because we didn't realize he woke up." Janet cocked her head toward Jesse. "We're going to have fun with him, and we're not about to let him play us for fools. Cops are smart, so we have to stay one step ahead of him. Let's get started."

Together, they dragged Jesse to the radiator. They placed several blankets under him to muffle noise, and plastic sheeting lay on top. That would come in handy when the torture began. They duct taped his hands around the cast-iron coils—he was lucky it wasn't winter when the radiator was scalding hot to the touch. They removed his shoes and socks to prevent sounds if he were to kick, then they taped his feet together. The socks went into his mouth, and Gail watched with interest as Janet cut a small hole in the tape and placed it over his mouth.

"What's that for?"

Janet snickered. "A straw. Then we never have to remove the tape."

Gail chuckled "What's the beverage of choice?"

"What mixes well with green energy drinks?" Janet winked at her daughter. "And you're going to the hardware store tomorrow to pick it up."

"I better go through his phone before we call it a night. The pig told me he'd mentioned to his partner, Frank, that he had a date tonight."

"Shit!"

"Don't worry, Mom. I'll text Frank now and tell him how awesome the date was. That'll satisfy him for the time being"—she kicked Jesse in the stomach—"while we have fun with the cop."

Plopping down on the couch with Jesse's phone in hand, Gail scrolled through his contact list until she found Frank's name. She giggled. "Here we go." With the text completed and sent, she turned off the locations and powered down the phone then tossed it on the kitchen counter. "Tomorrow, the cop is in for a world of hurt. We'll have to see how creative we can get."

"As long as you're going to the hardware store in the morning, pick up a few more tools."

A smile crossed Gail's face. "I think I will, but right now, I'm going to bed. Tomorrow is going to be an interesting day."

Chapter 58

Frank laughed as he crossed the parking lot and pulled open the precinct's main door. He looked back and shielded his eyes as he scanned the lot. Jesse's car wasn't there yet. He chuckled again with thoughts of the ribbing he looked forward to giving his best friend and partner when he finally got to work.

He grabbed a coffee from the cafeteria's vending machine and continued on then entered the bull pen a minute later. Frank checked the time—7:53. Jesse, a creature of habit, always had his back end planted in his chair by seven forty-five. Frank frowned.

Maybe there was a car accident somewhere, or because it's Saturday, he's taking his time.

He looked at Shawn and Henry, the only other daytime detectives at their desks. "Either of you talk to Jesse on your way in?"

They both shrugged. Frank chalked it up to Jesse getting a slow start that morning—too much alcohol and a late date last night, but roll call was going to begin in ten minutes.

With the updates between the detectives covered, the night

shift crew headed home, leaving Frank, Henry, and Shawn alone.

"Was everyone scheduled to work today?"

"Yep, until the killers are apprehended. I'm sure Lutz will let us know if the rest of the dating-site names have come in," Shawn said.

The bull pen door opened, and Frank turned in his chair. It was Tony with Kip right behind him.

"Morning, guys," Henry said.

They grunted their responses.

"Where's McCord?" Kip asked as he passed Jesse's desk.

Frank spoke up. "Sleeping in, I guess."

Tony laughed. "Yeah, right. Like that ever happens. He has a dog, remember? I've taken care of Bandit before, and he doesn't let anyone sleep in."

Frank pushed back his chair and headed for the door. "Let's go. Roll call is about to start."

Once everyone was seated, the chair next to Frank remained glaringly empty. Lutz entered the room and walked to the podium. He scanned the crowd before beginning the morning's roll call and updates.

"Where's McCord?"

"No idea, Boss," Henry said, "but Jesse's never late."

Lutz raised a brow. "Anyone call him?"

The group shrugged.

"He texted me at eleven o'clock last night. Everything seemed normal," Frank said without going into detail that Jesse had been on a date.

"Call him now. It isn't like Jesse to be a no-show for work even if it is a Saturday."

Frank pulled his phone from his pocket and tapped Jesse's number as everyone silently watched. Frank shook his head. "Voicemail."

"Okay, Frank and I are heading to his house. There are two more names on my desk that came in from the dating site. Shawn and Henry, go find those women and interview them. We'll be back in an hour." Lutz jerked his head at Frank. "You're driving, and I hoped to hell nothing is wrong."

They raced out the door and grabbed the first cruiser in the lot.

Frank cranked the wheel and pinned the pedal to the floor. "It'll take twenty minutes to get to his house."

"Do it in fifteen," Lutz said, "and I'll keep trying his phone."

Frank tapped the steering wheel as he drove. Lutz gave him a side-eyed glance.

"Is there something you aren't telling me? You seem nervous."

"I'm just worried."

"About what? If you know something, I need to hear it now."

Frank groaned. "Jesse tried keeping it to himself simply because he expected us to rib him. He had a date last night."

"Then maybe he stayed out later than he planned and didn't hear his alarm."

Frank glanced at the dash. "It's nine o'clock. He'd be awake by now. Bandit would make sure of it."

"You said he texted you last night. What did he say?"

"Only that the date went well. I imagine he was going to

tell me more today, and like I said earlier, that was around eleven o'clock. He'd have no reason to oversleep."

Frank jerked the steering wheel and pulled into Jesse's driveway—it had taken all of twelve minutes to get there. Both men bolted from the cruiser and ran up the sidewalk. Lutz folded his hand and pounded on the door. Nobody answered, and the absence of a barking dog raised even more concern.

"Where the hell is Bandit?" Frank asked.

"Hit the neighbor's house while I check the backyard."

Frank ran across the lawn to Dean's house and banged on the door. He heard the distinct sound of two dogs barking.

"Shit."

The door opened only slightly, and half of Dean's face peeked out. "Detective Mills? I thought it was Jesse. Sorry, but these two will bolt if I open the door all the way."

"Dean, have you talked to Jesse this morning?"

"No. He said he was going to pick up Bandit last night, but he never came by. I figured he got home later than he expected to and was sleeping in. Isn't he home?"

"He didn't show up at the precinct, and he doesn't answer his phone. Where does he keep his spare key?"

"Hang on. I'll get mine." Dean closed the door but was back within seconds. "It's the gold one."

"Got it, thanks. You guys stay put." Frank raced to Jesse's house just as Lutz was exiting the backyard. "See anything?"

"Only closed blinds."

"I have the key."

Back at the front door, Frank slid the key into the knob

and turned. Other than the foyer light, the house was dark. He turned off the alarm and with his hand cupped to his mouth, yelled out Jesse's name. There was no response.

"I'll search this floor. You run downstairs and check the rec room and garage," Lutz said.

They met on the main level several minutes later.

"His car is gone," Frank said.

"And the living quarters are empty. His bed is made. He was either here and we just missed him, or he never came home last night."

Frank shook his head as he paced. "He would have picked up Bandit. The only explanation is he spent the night with that woman, but his text didn't come off that way. I'll call the bull pen and see if he's shown up yet." Frank dialed, spoke to Kip, then hung up. "He's not there."

"Okay, we need to head back and figure this out. Run next door and tell Dean to keep the dog. Give him your card and tell him to call you if he hears from Jesse."

"Will do." For the second time, Frank ran across the lawn. He relayed the message to Dean then jumped in behind the cruiser's steering wheel.

"Tell me everything you know about the woman he went out with."

Frank rubbed his brow as he thought. "Um, they were meeting at Harry's Steak House. That in itself is a good start. I think they were supposed to meet at seven, but Jesse thought he might be late."

"So he wasn't picking her up?"

"Nope. They were definitely meeting there."

"Okay, and how about her name?"

Frank punched the dash. "Damn it, I can't remember. I was too busy thinking of ways to stick it to him. I think it began with an *L*, though."

"Lisa, Lori, Lily, Lorraine?"

"No, but I'll remember if I stop trying so hard." Frank barreled through the yellow light.

"What dating site did he use?"

"He didn't say. He did express a concern that when they met the night before, she seemed different from her profile."

Lutz snapped his head toward Frank. "Last night was his second date with her?"

"The night before was just for a drink. He made the second date to give it another try. Maybe it was nerves or something when they first met. He said she seemed off or aloof, something like that."

"And where did they meet?"

"At Woodland Tap."

Lutz looked at the clock. "Shit, we aren't far from that place, but a small corner bar like that wouldn't be open at nine thirty in the morning." He waved Frank on. "Keep going. Anything else about that night that he mentioned?"

"Only that he walked her to her van when they left."

"Okay, so she has a van. That's something."

They arrived at the district at 9:55 and entered through the back. As they passed the crime lab, Lutz stopped.

"Hang on. I need to ask Mike a quick question."

They entered through the glass door of the lab and headed toward Mike.

Mike gave them a head tip when he saw them. "Commander, Frank."

Lutz spoke up. "Jesse said he wanted you to check on whether that Jeep had any locations or phone numbers programmed into its infotainment system."

"Right. I gave all that information to Todd in Tech. He's better equipped to handle that stuff."

"And he has the data?"

"He should be done with it by now, sir."

Lutz headed for the door. "Thanks, Mike." He turned to Frank. "You can follow up with Todd on that. It could give us valuable information."

They reached the bull pen several minutes later, and both scanned the room as they entered—no Jesse.

Lutz barked out orders to Kip and Tony. "Jesse had a date last night, and now he's unaccounted for. That isn't going to fly with me, so find out when Harry's Steak House and the Woodland Tap open and get the managers' numbers. We need to speak to someone yesterday."

"On it," Kip said.

"Frank, call Todd and have him email you that info on the Jeep right away. There's a chance we can get something useful from the data that'll help find Jesse."

Frank grabbed his desk phone and dialed Todd.

Lutz paced the bull pen and rubbed his balding head. "Maybe he was run off the road on his way home last night. Who the hell knows?" The commander's cell phone rang in his pocket, and he jerked it out and answered. "Lutz speaking. Yep, Abrams, what can I do for you? What! Are you sure it's Jesse's? Son of a bitch! Have it brought to our garage immediately." Lutz's face went pale as he pocketed his phone. "That was Commander Abrams. He said Patrol towed a car that was left overnight at Harry's Steak House to their impound lot this morning. It's Jesse's Camaro." Lutz jerked his head at Kip. "Do you have the steak joint's number yet?"

"Got it, Boss."

"Call it now!"

Kip dialed the number then shook his head. "It's a recording that gives the restaurant's hours. Says they don't open until four."

"Well, somebody called it in. Find out who did, and who from Patrol responded to the call. We need to know if anyone is actually there right now."

Lutz rifled through the sticky notes on Jesse's desk, looking for anything that could be a clue. "What's going on with Woodland Tap?"

Tony spoke up. "I found the manager's name, sir, but it just takes me back to the bar's number."

"Find his home number and address. Get him on the line now!"

"Yes, Boss."

Kip yelled out, "Patrol sent Beecham out with their tow truck. He said the restaurant's cleaning crew called it in."

"Get a name of somebody who worked there last night after seven. I want to speak to them, and preferably, it's the hostess who seated them, a bartender who served them, or the waiter who brought them their food."

Frank slammed his open hand on his desk. "I have it, Boss!"

He pointed at his computer monitor. "Her name was Lynn, and it was programmed into the Jeep's infotainment system."

Lutz spun Jesse's desk chair toward Frank. His brows furrowed as he stared at his detective. "So you're saying Cliff knew Lynn too?"

"That's not all. The nav shows the route from Cliff's house to Woodland Tap programmed four nights ago."

"The same night Cliff died. Son of a bitch! This Lynn woman is likely the killer. You said Jesse was there with her the night before last?"

"That's what he said."

"Then they should have him and Cliff on camera with the same woman two nights apart."

Tony waved his hand toward Lutz. "I got the manager, Kyle Link, from Woodland Tap on the phone, Boss."

Lutz crossed the room in three strides and grabbed the receiver. "Mr. Link, this is Commander Bob Lutz from the Chicago PD. We need to see Woodland Tap's camera footage for Tuesday and Thursday nights immediately. Yep, we're on our way." Lutz pointed at Tony and Kip. "Good work, Detectives. Stay on Harry's Steak House. We'll need to see their footage too. Meanwhile, find out what Henry and Shawn have learned from the women they've talked to and check to see if any other names have come in. We still need to know if Gail Fremont is one of the women who messaged Cliff. That California connection could be relevant."

"But her name wasn't programmed into the Jeep, Boss," Frank said as they headed to the door.

"I don't care. We're going to check her out, anyway."

Chapter 59

Gail had already made the early-morning run to the hardware store to pick up the antifreeze, a needle-nose pliers, a box cutter, a weeding knife, and a small pruning clipper. Along with those supplies, she brought home a box of doughnuts.

Janet elbowed Gail as they sat on the couch drinking coffee and enjoying the doughnut selection. "Look, he's starting to move."

"Good. We want to make sure he's fully awake so he can appreciate what real pain feels like." Gail squeezed her mother's arm. "One cop or one hundred, we don't need them messing with our mission. Right, Mom?"

"That's right, honey, and we have all the time in the world to enjoy Detective McCord's company, so go ahead and have another doughnut."

Chapter 60

I woke with a staggering headache and tried to open my eyes but couldn't. It took only a second to realize they were taped closed, and so was my mouth. My arms and legs wouldn't budge. I thought back to the night before. Lynn and I had had a great dinner at Harry's, then we went back to her place for a nightcap. I couldn't remember anything beyond that.

Where am I? Did I leave her place and something happened on the way home? No—she drove. What the hell is going on?

A female voice caught my attention, and I heard the sound of footsteps coming my way. A hard kick to my gut knocked the breath out of me, and I doubled over in pain.

"It's about time you woke up, Detective McCord. Now the real fun can begin."

I didn't recognize the voice, but I knew I was in serious trouble. Lynn had to be involved in whatever this was, but why? I forced myself to stay calm and breathe through my nose. If I panicked, I'd pass out from lack of oxygen. My head spun with a million questions.

How do I get out of this predicament, and why am I in it? The only person who knew my plans last night was Frank, but how the hell is he going to find me? I don't even know where I am.

Another voice spoke up. I recognized it, and a sick feeling washed over me. It was Lynn, and she had been part of the scheme all along. She approached me and knelt at my side. I felt her presence within inches of my face, and her hot breath blew against my skin. She kissed my cheek, whispered her intentions, then clubbed me in the head with what was likely her fist.

My thoughts bounced around in my brain like the pulse setting on a blender. Could Frank find me before my fate was sealed? I didn't have the answer to that. I remembered seeing a sign when Lynn pulled into the driveway last night—Parkview Arms—but without telepathy, I couldn't forward that apartment name to Frank.

I heard the first woman's voice again. "Finish your coffee, honey, and then we'll make that cocktail for the detective."

Two women with intentions of killing me. The one whose voice I don't recognize called Lynn "Honey." Mother and daughter, maybe? Son of a bitch! They have to be the killing team we're searching for.

The dating site I was on was the very one Cliff had used. That was how she drew both of us in. She had initiated the conversation, not me, and I didn't fit the profile they went after—older men, all similar in appearance, and apparent loners, new to the area, or someone who wanted a beautiful woman on his arm. I didn't understand why she'd targeted me, a cop, and I couldn't believe my own stupidity that had allowed her to lure me into her trap.

I knew one thing for sure—there was no way in hell I was going to drink the cocktail they were preparing for me.

Chapter 61

Frank jerked the steering wheel to the right and slid into a parking spot along the curb. He and Lutz leapt from the cruiser and walked the half block to the front door of Woodland Tap. Frank pulled the handle—the door was open.

Inside, a man waited on a barstool. When they entered, he stood and extended his hand. "I'm the manager, Kyle."

"Good to meet you, sir." Lutz introduced himself and Frank. "It's urgent that we see those videos immediately. It could be a matter of life and death."

"Right this way. I already have Tuesday queued up."

They followed Kyle down a short dark hallway to the only door on the right—the bar's office.

"Have a seat, gentlemen."

They did while Kyle tapped a few computer keys. He looked up and across the desk. "Any particular time on Tuesday night?"

Lutz frowned and looked at Frank. "What do you think? After six?"

"Yeah, that sounds about right."

Kyle tapped the keys again and spun the monitor to face

the men. He rounded the desk and stood against the wall behind the commander and Frank. "Our only cameras are at the bar till and front door, which captures everyone who comes in. The door camera is the one we're watching."

"Can you speed through the footage until someone enters or exits?"

"You can by sliding the scrubber bar to the right. Speed up, stop, or go back by holding the cursor on the plus or minus sign."

"Got it." Frank took the reins while Lutz stared at the screen.

Minutes passed, and Frank was getting the hang of it. He sped up the footage considerably without missing anyone entering or leaving.

"Wait! Back up a few seconds and pause it."

Frank did as instructed. "What did you see?"

"I'm positive that was Cliff Howard entering alone a minute ago, alive and in the flesh. Slow, slow, there! That's definitely him."

Frank leaned in closer to the screen. "Yep, I'd have to agree, that's Cliff Howard. Either Lynn is already there, or she's on her way."

Lutz cocked his head toward Kyle. "How much can you see on the bar camera?"

"About ten feet to either side of the till. I can click over to that camera and see where he goes."

Lutz nodded for Kyle to make the adjustments. "We're going to need that since we don't know what Lynn looks like."

"I do remember Jesse saying she was a beautiful blonde."

"Good. That definitely helps."

Kyle switched over to the bar camera, but we didn't see Cliff anywhere.

"Where the hell did he go?"

Kyle frowned. "Tuesdays, we have live music. He may be sitting closer to the band and out of camera view."

"Shit. Okay, go back to the front-door camera."

They continued watching for ten minutes, then the door opened, and a very attractive blonde wearing a snug-fitting black dress walked through alone.

"That has to be her. Is there any way to see where she went?" Frank asked.

"Maybe we can catch her pass by the bar camera if that man sat near the band."

"Let's try it," Lutz said.

Kyle went to the bar camera and forwarded the footage to the same time as on the door camera. He pointed. "That had to be her. I saw blond hair and the edge of a black dress as she passed."

"Okay, can you give us a screen grab of her as she came through the door? We need to see if that same woman was here Thursday night with one of our detectives."

"You bet. Let's go back to the door camera."

Seconds later, the still shot was forwarded to Lutz's cell phone.

"Okay, we need to do the same for Thursday. Did Jesse say what time he met her here?"

"Nope, but they were supposed to meet last night at

Harry's at seven, so let's shoot for the same time."

"Go ahead with a few minutes before seven," Lutz said.

Kyle set the time at 6:55 and started the footage. Within minutes, we saw Jesse walk in.

"Shit." Frank looked away and rubbed his forehead. "Why can't we go back in time?"

"Yeah, that's tough, but we need to stay focused, Mills." At 7:07, the door opened, and a couple entered. Right behind them was the woman from Tuesday night.

"There she is!" Frank said. "Same damn woman."

Lutz squeezed his temples. "I've got to think. We have proof that Jesse was with the same woman that Cliff was, but how does that help us?"

"I've got it," Frank said. "I need to call the bull pen and see how many profiles we can access now with the warrant. Each woman who messaged Cliff will have a profile picture."

"Still, how does that matter? Her name is Lynn, we already know that, but it's all we know." Lutz groaned. "What about those temp nurses who lived near Bixler Park?"

"Right. There were fourteen within the proximity of the park but only three within a few blocks. One was a guy, the other two were Leah Standish and Gail Fremont. Gail's record came in clean, so we only interviewed Leah Standish, but the woman in the footage definitely isn't Leah."

"Do we have a photograph of Gail Fremont?"

"Tony did all the background and DMV checks. I didn't look at any of the IDs."

"Pull up the database on your phone and type in her name and California. See what pops up."

Frank ripped his phone from his pocket and logged in to the DMV database. He typed in the name Gail Fremont and California. Her ID came up. "Son of a bitch, it's her!" Frank turned his phone toward Lutz.

"Shit! Call the bull pen, Frank, and tell whoever answers to pull up her temporary address. We need patrol units there now!" Lutz thanked Kyle for his help, and they bolted out the door.

Chapter 62

The women delivered a few more rounds of kicks and punches to Jesse for refusing to let them put a straw in his mouth. Janet ripped the tape off his face and tried to force his mouth open but couldn't.

"Knock him out. I'll get this shit down his throat one way or another!"

"Wait, Mom, listen! The police scanner is dispatching patrol units to this address. We have to get out of here!"

"Damn cops! Grab all the supplies you bought this morning and back up the van. We'll make short work of this piece of shit detective once we get out of the area. Nobody will ever be able to identify Jesse McCord when we get done with him."

Janet grabbed another wine bottle and swung. With his eyes taped and hands and feet bound, Jesse couldn't block the blow. He fell unconscious while blood dripped from his drooping head.

After grabbing a knife from the block, Janet sliced through the tape that secured him to the radiator, then she ran down the hall and got a blanket to put around him. With

Jesse flat on the floor, she waited for Gail to reappear.

"Hurry! We need to cover him up and toss him in the back of the van. We don't have much time."

The two women rolled him in the blanket and dragged him to the door. Gail jumped inside the van and pulled while Janet pushed from the doorway. With the cop safely tucked inside, Gail yelled to her mother to grab their purses, phones, and laptop. She dove in behind the wheel as soon as Janet reappeared.

"Climb in the back and keep your eyes on him. Club him with the tire iron if he starts coming to." Gail shifted into Drive and peeled out of the parking lot.

Two squad cars with lights flashing and sirens blaring passed them a block away.

Janet yelled out from the back of the van. "That was close! Head northwest out of the city. We'll find a remote location where we'll finish him off."

Chapter 63

"Buckle up, Boss. I'm not letting off the gas until we're there."

With two more cruisers on his rear bumper, Frank cranked the wheel and hit the lights.

Lutz locked his arms and braced himself against the dash while the car spun around the corner. He pinned the phone against his ear and spoke to Abrams. "How far from the apartment is Patrol? Okay, we're on our way too." He pocketed his phone and cursed. "If anything happens to Jesse, I swear I'll—"

Frank stopped Lutz from jumping to the worst-case scenario. They had seen firsthand what those two women were capable of. "Nothing is going to happen to him, Boss. Jesse is as tough as they come, and look at everything he's been through in the past. He'll come out of this okay. He has to."

Lutz's phone rang just as the police radio chirped to life. "What? Son of a bitch!" He abruptly hung up and yelled out a round of colorful adjectives. "Patrol said the apartment is empty, but there's plenty of blood evidence near the heat radiator." Lutz dialed the district's forensic lab. "Mike, write down this address and get out there now. Patrol found where Jesse was being held, and they said the living room is full of blood. I want that apartment torn apart."

"Now what?" Frank asked.

Lutz pointed out the windshield. "Keep going. I want to see it for myself."

Chapter 64

My head was wet and sticky—it had to be blood—but I was conscious. My restraints were gone, and that was a good thing. I lay as still as possible while I evaluated my situation. I felt movement near me along with the vibration of being in a vehicle. They were transporting me somewhere else, likely to a spot where they planned to kill me and hope I would never be found. I had one chance at survival, and I had to make my move.

From beneath the blanket, I couldn't see who was near me—or the actual position they were in—but the back of a van had only so much space. If I took them by surprise, tossed off the blanket, and began kicking and punching, I was bound to connect with someone.

My guess was that Lynn, or whatever her real name was, was behind the wheel. That left the woman whose voice I didn't recognize sitting within a foot or two of me and likely holding a weapon, ready to strike. I prayed that it wasn't a gun, but I had to do something—and fast.

With the slightest movement possible, I grasped the blanket's end so I could toss it off and not become tangled in it. I sucked in a deep but quiet breath and lunged at the unknown.

I connected with the other woman and slammed her against the side of the van. Her head bounced off the interior wall, then she scrambled for what I soon learned was a tire iron, but I was able to beat her to it and swung. I heard the sickening crack as it connected with her skull. She slumped over and wasn't an issue anymore. The van swerved wildly as Lynn tried to see what was happening in the back. I clawed my way to the driver's seat and grabbed a handful of her hair. I ripped her head back as the van bounced across three lanes of traffic. Cars honked and hit curbs while trying to avoid colliding with us.

Lynn fought me tooth and nail as she gunned the gas pedal. The van jerked this way and that and nearly flipped as we hit cars on our right and left. I had to stop the moving missile before somebody got killed. Wrapping my forearm around her neck, I tried to choke her into unconsciousness while grasping for the steering wheel. Using her fingernails and flailing wildly, she tried to gouge my eyes. I had to end her rampage—the van had become a speeding weapon and was hitting everything in its path. I nailed her with a hard punch to the head, and it bounced off the driver's-side window. She went limp. I wedged my body over the console as I tried to steer out of traffic. At the last second, I realized we had jumped the median, and I was in the oncoming lane. I wedged my foot alongside hers and found the brake pedal just as a school bus swerved out of our way. The hard tap to the rear driver's-side quarter panel told me I was being pitted.

The flashing blue lights behind me caught my attention for a second, then I felt the van spin and a hard crash that knocked me senseless.

Chapter 65

"Look out!"

Lutz braced for the collision. A van had just jumped the median and was heading directly at them. Frank cranked the wheel, hit the car on the cruiser's right, and sent it careening over the sidewalk and into a front yard. A school bus nearly tipped on its side as it swerved to avoid a head-on collision.

Hand over hand, Frank turned the wheel the opposite way, spun the cruiser to the left, and jumped the median.

"What the hell are you doing?"

"That's a van and the apartment is empty. Put two and two together, Boss. Jesse is inside that runaway vehicle."

The van bounced off cars on its high-speed collision course four vehicles ahead of them.

"Shit!" Lutz got on the radio and yelled out to stop the out-of-control red van that was heading north in the southbound lanes of South Dr. Martin Luther King Jr. Drive. "Get Patrol to lay spike strips, block the road, and divert traffic before somebody gets killed!"

Frank gunned the cruiser until he was right behind the van. "I have to pit it. It's the only way to stop it!"

Lutz yelled out. "Just do it!"

Frank inched up on the van's left side then smacked the rear quarter panel with the cruiser's front passenger-side bumper. He immediately backed off so they wouldn't get tangled in the spinning van. Cars crashed, and pedestrians scrambled to safety. The van smashed into a utility pole and finally stopped in the middle of the median.

Lutz and Frank bolted from the cruiser, guns drawn, and screamed out orders. Henry and Kip surrounded the van with their cruisers and leapt out too. With a half dozen guns pointing at the van, officers and detectives yelled commands. The passenger door finally opened, and Jesse fell to the ground.

"Secure that van! Get paramedics here immediately," Lutz yelled when they realized who the blood-soaked person was.

With the van surrounded, the unconscious driver in cuffs, and the dead woman in the back secured, the detectives and Lutz knelt at Jesse's side.

Frank leaned in. "Partner, can you hear me?"

Jesse moaned as he did his best to respond. "Is it over?"

"You bet, buddy. It's definitely over, and the paramedics are on their way. You'll be okay. Just hang tight."

In a whisper, Jesse asked if the women were dead.

"Only the one in the back," Lutz said. "The other hit the driver's-side window and has a gash on the head, but she's alive."

Jesse coughed. "That's Lynn."

Frank patted Jesse's shoulder. "We know, pal, but she's really Gail Fremont. Now, lay still. We've got this. The paramedics are a few minutes out."

Lutz pushed off his knee and stood, then he yelled out to the officers on-site to direct traffic to neighboring streets. He turned to his detectives. "You guys know what to do. Get Don out here, check to see if people in those crashed cars are injured, the whole nine yards. Henry, you're in charge."

"Yes, sir."

Minutes later, two ambulances arrived at the scene. Lutz flagged the first one down.

"This is my lead detective. Get him the best care possible. Definite head injuries and who knows what else. The other injured person with a head contusion is in that van. My officers will escort you. She's a criminal and needs to be cuffed at all times."

"Yes, Commander, and they'll both be transported to Chicago Mercy Hospital."

Lutz nodded and turned to Jesse. "They're taking you to the hospital, buddy, and we won't be far behind."

The coroner's van arrived within five minutes of the ambulances. Don climbed out and approached Lutz. "What have we got, Bob?"

"Dead female in the back of the van. We'll find out the details later when Jesse is stable. From the looks of it, she got cracked in the head with the tire iron."

Don grimaced. "I'll check it out."

Lutz shielded his eyes and scanned the scene. Crashed cars, mangled signs, and torn-up curbing and grass were strewn everywhere. He waved Henry down. "Frank and I are heading to the hospital. Keep me posted and call more ambulances if they're needed."

Chapter 66

The officers had been waiting for several hours before the doctor finally headed in their direction. Lutz had just gotten off the phone with Henry and Abrams. Between the detectives and patrol officers, the scene was somewhat under control. He pocketed his phone and stood.

"What's the word on my detective, Doc?"

"You can go in now. Jesse has had X-rays, and he's stitched up. Nothing is broken, just scrambled, but he's been given pain medication, so he may become groggy. All in all, he should be okay by tomorrow."

"We sure appreciate it, and how about Gail Fremont?"

"The same. One hard blow to the right side, which gave her a contusion on the left when she hit the car window. She'll recover, and she's downstairs in our secured wing in room 107 with police guarding her door."

"Thanks, Doc." Lutz turned to Frank. "Come on. We need to talk to Jesse."

They entered Jesse's private room. A table lamp on the dimmest setting cast shadows throughout the space. Bandages covered Jesse's wounds, and his eyes were swollen from the injuries.

"Who's there?" he asked.

Lutz stepped closer to the light and pulled the guest chair next to Jesse's bed. "It's me and Frank. How ya doing, pal?"

Jesse groaned. "I've had better days, but I made it out alive and still have all my fingers and teeth."

Frank huffed. "And you're damn lucky. Henry found their bag of torture tools in the van along with a bottle of antifreeze. Needless to say, most of the tools were cutting and clipping instruments."

Jesse nodded. "And the antifreeze was likely the cocktail they were trying to force me to drink. How'd you figure out Lynn was Gail?"

"Cliff's Jeep had Lynn's name and the address of Woodland Tap programmed into the infotainment system. We went from there, watched the camera feed from the bar on Tuesday and Thursday nights, and saw her with both of you."

Jesse coughed out his response. "The bartender told me she was there with someone a few nights earlier. I should have figured it out. Her dating username was TravelingBabe90, but she said she worked in medical sales."

Lutz swatted the air. "Don't beat yourself up. After connecting the dots, we realized Gail Fremont was the last person on our list of traveling nurses who hadn't been interviewed or seen, except by Tony, who checked her file." Lutz grinned at Frank. "Mills pulled her DMV photo, and sure as shit, it was the same woman you, Cliff, and I imagine everyone else knew as Lynn."

"So who was the other woman?"

Frank rubbed his forehead. "Not sure how she plays into the whole scenario yet, but she had that fake Janet St. James driver's license in her purse, plus that disturbing connection."

Jesse frowned. "Yeah, what was that?"

"You didn't notice?"

"Notice something with the woman I smacked with the tire iron? Guess I was busy trying to save my own life. What did I miss?"

"The left side of her face was severely scarred, and according to Don, her jawbone on that side was pinned together." Lutz sighed. "Not only that, but all her fingers had been removed at the last knuckle."

"Jesus Christ!"

Lutz continued. "We'll find out everything tomorrow when Gail is discharged and we interrogate her at the station."

"I'll do it."

Lutz shook his head. "Not the best idea, Jesse. There's no way you can be objective."

"I'm doing it, and I'll be fine. She owes me an explanation. Those bitches tried to kill me, and I didn't know them from Adam."

Frank patted Jesse's shoulder. "Don't get riled up, partner. You need your rest. We'll be back tomorrow to pick you up and have Patrol transport Gail to the station. After that, she's all yours."

Lutz and Frank walked to the door.

"Hold up. Does Dean have Bandit, and does he know what's going on?"

Frank nodded. "Bandit is in good hands, and Dean's happy to care for him. You've got a damn good neighbor, buddy."

"Yep, I sure as hell do."

Chapter 67

The next day, I stared at her from our jail's observation room. Other than the black eye and bandaged head, she still looked beautiful.

Maybe I should swear off women altogether. It's obvious that I'm no good at reading the opposite sex.

Gail was the perfect example of why I would likely remain a lifelong bachelor.

Frank entered the observation room. "Ready, Jesse? I can take over if you're feeling uncomfortable about it."

"Nope, I'm good." I sucked in a breath to calm my anger just as Lutz entered the observation room.

"You going for it?"

"Yep, right now." I walked out, took two steps, and entered the interrogation room.

She turned her head to the right, clearly trying to see who had entered, then looked away when she realized it was me.

"Can't face me, Gail?"

She shrugged. "Just surprised to see you're back at it already. You damn cops just don't let up, do you?"

I laughed as I took a seat facing her. "Was that a serious

question? You and that other woman killed a half dozen men that we know of and probably more that we don't."

She leaned across the table and snarled. "That woman was my mother, and she spent most of her life being abused by my piece of shit father!"

Her comment took me by surprise. "So that's what all of this was about? Killing men because your father was an abuser?"

"Yes, and he abused me, too, but in a different way."

"I'm sorry to hear that, but those men you killed weren't your father. They had nothing to do with the shitty life you and your mom lived. Why didn't the two of you just pack up and leave?"

She stared at me with hate-filled eyes. "What do you know? I bet life was easy for you, wasn't it, pig? Now my mom is dead and you're the one who killed her, you piece of shit!"

"I didn't have a choice."

"There's always a choice, and we chose to stay until—"

"Until you found a permanent solution?"

She spewed her reply. "I caught the bastard torturing my mom. He was going to kill her and had already cut off her fingers and smashed her jaw and teeth. He wanted to make sure she would never be identified once he disposed of her. I thank God she was unconscious at the time. I lunged and stabbed him in the back with a butcher knife. He needed to be put down, and *that* was my permanent solution. I cut him into manageable pieces and tossed the wrapped body parts into the freezer. Every week, a freezer bag was added to the trash bag and placed at the curb with the rest of the garbage. Nobody noticed his absence because he didn't have any friends, anyway, and that's when I began the traveling gigs. He was retired, and we still collect and cash his Social Security checks."

I looked over my shoulder at the one-way mirror behind me. I knew Frank and Bob were listening to her every word.

"How many men have you and your mother killed, Gail?"

"Fourteen, and you would have been next."

"Why me?"

She laughed. "Now and then, I deserve a break from those old codgers. I wanted to go out with a good-looking guy, and you being a cop was a bonus. Nothing personal."

"Why Robert and Cliff? Was it because Robert lived near you in California and Cliff was a porno-taping pig?"

She laughed again. "You cops overthink everything. I didn't know shit about either of them. Mom chose them because of their hair. It was just like my father's. No other reason."

I shook my head and walked out. Gail was definitely certifiable. Back in the observation room, I looked at Lutz and Mills. "I think you have all you need, Boss. I can't stand to be in that room with her for another second."

"You did good in there, Jesse, and she'll be locked up for life. Thanks, pal. Now go on home and get some rest."

The thought of lying on the couch with a beverage and my pup sounded pretty good. At that moment, it was all I needed. I hadn't picked up Bandit yet, but I knew he'd be happy to see me and spend the day sleeping on the couch.

Twenty minutes later, I pulled into my driveway. Glancing to my right, I saw a car that I didn't recognize at Dean's house.

Shit. He has company, and yet he's still watching Bandit for me.

I felt like a jerk as I climbed out of my Camaro. I went directly to his front door and knocked, and seconds later, Dean answered.

"Jesse!" He gave me a relieved but careful embrace. "Frank told me everything. Come on in. I want to introduce you to my cousin, Lee Bradley, and her daughter, Hanna. They're moving to Chicago from New York to be closer to family."

"No, no, I don't want to intrude. I'll just scoop up Bandit and be on my way."

"Not on your life. I just started the grill, and we're having brats, burgers, and beans. You're staying for dinner and I won't take no for an answer, so come on in."

I reluctantly followed Dean to the patio, where Bandit charged across the yard and nearly knocked me to the ground.

I laughed. "Settle down, boy. It's okay."

Dean smiled and turned to his cousin. "Lee, this is my neighbor and a Chicago police detective, Jesse McCord."

I reached out and shook her hand. "Nice to meet you, Lee, and I must say you have quite the cousin. I don't know what I'd do without Dean. He's a godsend." I looked to my right and saw a beautiful thirtysomething woman laughing happily.

"I just love your dog! Bandit and I are already best friends."

Dean continued proudly. "And this is Lee's beautiful daughter, Hanna, who happens to be a veterinarian."

Hanna gave me an oversized smile, and her eyes twinkled playfully while she knelt and petted Bandit.

I reached out, shook her hand, and smiled back at her. "It's nice to meet you, Hanna." In an instant I was smitten, and at that moment I knew my life was about to change.

THE END

Thank you!

Thanks for reading *Deadly Pursuit*, the third book in the Detective Jesse McCord Police Thriller Series. I hope you enjoyed it!

Find all my books in the Detective Jesse McCord Police Thriller Series at http://cmsutter.com

Stay abreast of my new releases by signing up for my VIP email list at: http://cmsutter.com/newsletter/

You'll be one of the first to get a glimpse of the cover reveals and release dates, and you'll have a chance at exciting raffles and freebies offered throughout the series.

Posting a review will help other readers find my books. I appreciate every review, whether positive or negative, and if you have a second to spare, a review is truly appreciated.

Find me on Facebook at
https://www.facebook.com/cmsutterauthor/

Made in the USA
Middletown, DE
26 October 2023